THE FORGER'S DAUGHTER

Bradford Morrow

Grove Press UK

First published in the United States of America in 2020
by Grove Atlantic
First published in Great Britain in 2020 by Grove Press UK,
an imprint of Grove Atlantic
This paperback edition first published in Great Britain in 2021 by
Grove Press UK, an imprint of Grove Atlantic

1 3 5 7 9 8 6 4 2

A CIP record for this book is available from the British Library.

Paperback ISBN 978 1 61185 459 6
E-book ISBN 978 1 61185 896 9
Printed in Great Britain

Grove Press UK
Ormond House
26–27 Boswell Street
London
WC1N 3JZ

www.groveatlantic.com

For Cara Schlesinger & Susan Jaffe Tane

I am not more certain that I breathe, than that the assurance of the wrong or error of any action is often the one unconquerable *force* which impels us, and alone impels us to its prosecution. Nor will this overwhelming tendency to do wrong for the wrong's sake, admit of analysis, or resolution into ulterior elements.

—Edgar Allan Poe,
"The Imp of the Perverse"

The original is unfaithful to the translation.

—Jorge Luis Borges,
"On William Beckford's *Vathek*"

THE
FORGER'S
DAUGHTER

A scream shattered the night. At first it sounded feral, inhuman, even unworldly. I leaped up from my wingback reading chair in the study, dropping my book on the wide-plank floor, and heard my husband's studio door jolt open at the back of the house. When he found me waiting in the front hall, he was gripping his letterpress composing stick, still wearing his stained apron with its rich scent of printer's ink. We said nothing, just waited in shaken silence. Our sash windows were raised both upstairs and down to let in the evening air, and outside noises, we both knew, often seemed closer in the dark. Still, the scream was so sharp it seemed to have emanated from nearby, maybe even from the unmowed yard out front. I wondered—hoped, really—if coyotes were about to chorus, as the local pack sometimes did upon being prodded by the single wailing cry of an alpha individual. But no other voices joined in. By the time we opened the door of the farmhouse surrounded by enveloping black maples, the world was calm again aside from moths and name-less insects thudding against the porch light, and, from indoors, the faint continuation of a piano concerto by Saint-Saëns on the radio.

"Maisie?" I shouted, peering into the near darkness past the overgrown hedge of lilacs that bordered the yard as I called our daughter's name.

Moths and Saint-Saëns were joined by the drone of crickets from every quarter of the woods and fields around the house. Nothing else. Often, I reminded my-self, the lone coyote who isn't answered simply moves along. Or perhaps what we'd heard was the death screech of a rabbit being killed by one of those same neigh-borhood coyotes. In Ireland once, I heard a hare being snatched from life, probably by a hungry fox, and the bloodcurdling scream that ripped the night in half was one I'd never forgotten.

My husband called her name again, louder. "Maisie!"

Our older daughter, Nicole, who still lived in our East Village apartment, wouldn't join us upstate until the weekend, several days hence. But young Maisie was spending her August here as she had done for half a dozen years running, at the restored farmhouse in the Hudson Valley where we'd made it our annual custom to take off work the last month of summer and flee the city for greener terrain. Earlier that afternoon, she had biked, as she often did, the couple of miles to town—if a church, gas station with deli, antiques barn, and road-side bar can be so designated—to hang around with friends, play video games, stream movies, maybe cook out. Her girlfriends sometimes came here too, even though we couldn't provide them with a decent Internet connection, and the joys of bird-watching, picking wild blueberries, and swimming in the nearby water hole only went so far. She should be heading home at any moment.

Whereas the scream unsettled us before, now it was the throbbing quiet. At half past eight this time of year there was still light, if faint and swift-fading. Without exchanging a word—Will and I had been married some two decades and often intuited each other's thoughts— we hastened down the steps, across the uneven bluestone path, and out to the country road, where we headed in the direction of town. Whether consciously or not, he still brandished his metal composing stick, a classic tool used by centuries of letterpress printers and one, I expect, rarely if ever used to fend off a possible assailant.

We hadn't gone fifty paces before we caught sight of her coming toward us, dully luminescent against the murky backdrop. Not racing on her bicycle, as that shriek—now I knew it had been human—might have led me to expect, she was walking it along with an oddly deliberate, slow, rigid gait, her head tilted forward. When we reached her, I saw the determination set on her tear-streaked face, ashen as pumice in the waning light. My words tumbled over Will's as we stood together in the unpaved road, hugging the girl, stiff with fear, between us.

"Maisie, what happened? Was that you? Are you hurt?"

"Your brother," was all she said in response, her voice reedy and breathless, gripping the handles of her old Schwinn Black Bomber, which she had spotted at a yard sale several summers before and lovingly restored with her father.

Looking over at my husband, I saw that he was as bewildered as I.

"You mean Uncle Adam?" I asked, as gently as I could, glancing around in the growing darkness, feeling at once alarmed and a little foolish.

"He was just there," she insisted, voice tight, and pointed back down the road in the direction she had been coming from.

"But, Maisie. My brother's been gone since before you were even born. He's not with us anymore. You know that."

She shook her head violently, like a much younger girl. "He was, though. I know he's dead. But he looked just like in the photos."

"Stay here," Will said, and walked back into the gloaming—beyond where we could see him—less to confirm whether my dead brother was inexplicably, impossibly, lurking there than to convince Maisie that the road was deserted.

When he returned to us, striding with a bit of fatherly exaggeration, he assured her, "Nobody's down there, honey. No ghosts, no nothing. Even the birds have gone to bed."

"Please, I want to go inside," was all she said in response.

Without another word, my hand on Maisie's shoulder, I marched next to her toward the house. Will, wheeling the bicycle on her other side, kept glancing back into the dark, apparently pantomiming his concern, as if to reassure her no one was following. Ahead, the familiar windows of the house were illuminated with an amber glow that on any other evening would have filled me with a sense of peace. Tonight, the long ribbons of shadow and light they cast across the lawn had instead an intimidating noir effect.

As my husband leaned the bicycle against the porch rail, Maisie retrieved something from the basket. It wasn't until we were up the steps and into the entrance hall, with the door closed behind us, that she spoke again, her dark eyes averted. Choking back tears, she managed, "He said to give this to you," and held out a thin, rectangular package wrapped in butcher's paper and tied with bakery twine.

Will scowled as he took the package from her hands. "Who said?" he asked, before slipping it into the wide front pocket of his apron.

Now in the warm light of the hallway, it was plain that Maisie had taken a nasty fall. Her right forearm and elbow were abraded and caked with bloodied dirt, and her thin, tanned right leg and both knees were scraped. I interrupted, "My God, what's this? Maisie, you're bleeding all over."

She looked down at herself with reddened eyes, examining her knees as if they were someone else's. "I guess I must've fallen off my bike harder than I thought." At that, I saw both palms were also chafed.

"You guess? Let's get you cleaned up," I said, again hugging her to me, not only to comfort the girl but to steady myself as well. "That looks like it hurts."

"A little," was her benumbed response as we walked, Maisie limping a bit, down the foyer into the kitchen, where I washed her wounds with warm, soapy water. To my relief, her lacerations appeared to be superficial, but I fought to hide the anger welling in me, crowding out my earlier fear. I applied antiseptic ointment and bandages, crushing their wrappers in my fist.

Distracted and looking pale himself, my husband set his composing stick on the counter, removed his apron and draped it over the back of a chair, then sat down with us.

"Do you want some cold water, Maze?" I asked, noticing that Will was staring at me instead of at our daughter, his breathing a bit labored. "Or, I think we have some apple juice?"

"Water's fine," she said.

Tossing the crumpled bandage wrappers into the wastebasket under the sink, I poured a glass from the tap, dropped in ice cubes, and sat next to Maisie at the round oak pedestal table that centered our kitchen. "You're safe now, all right?"

She nodded and took a drink.

"I'm confused," I said, placing one of my hands on her uninjured arm. "It couldn't have been my brother who gave you this. Your scream, it sounded like—can you say who did this to you?"

"He said you'll know."

Will and I looked at each other with even greater alarm, as part of what had happened suddenly became as clear as a shard of broken crystal. Slowly, quietly, I asked her to tell us once more what she saw, in whatever detail she could manage.

Maisie shifted in her seat, wincing, looking embarrassed. "He just, this man came out of nowhere. I was riding, saw the house lights up ahead. Then he was there, like that. I had to turn really hard to miss him, and I skidded and fell. I thought he was going to kill me."

"Did he have a weapon?"

"No, I don't know," she said. "He just surprised me. Like in a nightmare. He had this weird white smiling face. I'm sorry I screamed."

"Don't be silly," I consoled her, hiding my own horror as I smoothed aside a stray strand of hair that had fallen across her forehead and caught on her eyelashes. "Believe me, I would've screamed bloody murder too."

Will was sitting rigid in his chair. Now he asked, "Did this man say anything to you, Maze? Was anybody with him?"

Gingerly wrapping her hands around the ice-chilled glass, Maisie answered, "Not that I could see. He warned me that if I knew what was good for me, I'd get it to you safely."

"That was all he said?"

"He was kind of in a hurry to get away."

I noticed the Saint-Saëns concerto had ended and a string quartet had taken its place, probably by Haydn, though many of that era's string quartets sounded much the same to me. It had the disconcerting effect of briefly becoming a kind of soundtrack, one that made everything in our otherwise very real, very lived-in kitchen, with my collection of copper pans, vintage Amish baskets, and homegrown dried herbs hanging from the rafters, seem like a scene from a movie, a scene I didn't want us to be actors in.

Will, clearly stricken by Maisie's description of the man's threat, reached behind him to remove the package from his apron pocket and place it on the table. "Can't you tell us more what he looked like? I mean, beyond any resemblance to your uncle Adam?"

"It was too dark, happened too fast," she explained, brushing tears from her eyes and glancing from the glass

of water over at the parcel. For a moment we all studied
it in silence. A thin dun mailer, the kind you would send
a sheaf of photographs in, or perhaps a children's book,
with a cream-colored envelope secured beneath the
knot. Will's name was written on it with a calligraphic
flourish. On either side of his name were skilled pen-
and-ink drawings of what appeared to be black flowers.
Black tulips. I saw a fleeting look of curiosity pass across
Maisie's face as she regarded the decorations on the envelope, rendered in an elegant art nouveau manner that
belied, it seemed to me, the meanness of this act of terrifying a young girl.

Maisie reached over to touch the tulips on the mailer,
then snatched her hand back as if to avoid being bitten.
Glancing at Will, she continued, "He came at me from
behind a tree, or bushes along the road, I'm not sure."

"How old do you think he was?"

"I don't know. My headlamp wasn't working."

"That we'll fix in the morning, but about this man.
Was he thin? Short-cropped hair, maybe bald?" he
pressed. I shot him a glance meant to suggest he needed
to ease up, but, intent on Maisie, he appeared not to
notice. "Could you see what he was wearing?"

She shrugged her shoulders, jutted her delicately cleft
chin. "He came out so fast, and then I was on the ground
and he was standing over me with his smile. Then he just
shoved that package at me, told me to give it to Will—"

"Wait, so he specifically said your father?"

Maisie nodded; I felt awful for the poor girl. Her
cheeks were blushing crimson with confusion and guilt
at not being able to answer Will's salvo of questions.

My husband, who was seated on her left with his arm
on the back of her chair, stood up as if to go somewhere,

breathed in and out, then sat down again. I waited for
him to speak, but he had fallen mute, agitated, preoccupied. For a moment it seemed he wasn't fully with us
in the room, while the wall clock continued indifferently
to tick, the refrigerator hummed away, and the faucet
softly went on dripping into the sink, as in my haste I
hadn't completely closed the spigot.

"Do we call the police?" I asked him, gently squeezing
Maisie's slender forearm.

Abruptly alert again, he said, "And tell them what?
That a man, possibly a ghost, who didn't at any rate identify himself, gave our daughter—who has no idea what
he looks like other than your dead brother—a package
on her way home from her friends' house?"

"Will," I warned.

Hearing me, and all of a sudden self-aware, he turned
to Maisie with a concerned frown, and quietly asked,
"Look, I know he frightened you. But did he touch you
in any way?" He leaned forward and clasped his hands
tightly, prayerlike, on the table.

In that moment, I was forced to admit to myself that
my husband, three years shy of sixty, seemed even more
unnerved by the incident than eleven-year-old Maisie.
This was not a criticism but a fathomable truth.

"No," she said, shaking her head. "At least, I don't
think so."

"Would it make you feel better if we reported this to
the police?" briefly overcoming his stubborn reluctance—
the result of a serious encounter years ago—to have anything to do with the authorities.

"No," she repeated, surely to Will's relief, and took
another swallow of water. She rubbed her eyes with the
back of her wrist and forced a smile meant to let us know

that she'd answered every question as best she could. "I'll be fine. Can I go upstairs now?"

"I'll go with you."

"Meg, honestly. I'm all right."

Sometimes I still wished Maisie felt comfortable calling me *Mom* instead of by my name—though I wished far more that her biological mother had lived to raise the girl herself. My best friend, Mary Chandler, was the only person for whom that appellation would ever make a natural fit. Maisie wasn't bothered when we referred to ourselves as her parents. But just as she rarely called Will *Dad*, I would always be *Meghan*, her loving, stand-in mom, even though I mothered her as naturally as I did our natural-born Nicole.

"There's an analgesic in that ointment that should help with the pain," I said, aware that I needed to let her retreat to her room. Unlike Nicole, Maisie, for all her friends, was a private soul, and I'd learned there were times, like now, when I could minister to her afflictions only so far.

"You'll let us know if you need anything," Will added, his supplicating expression revealing to me, if not to Maisie, that he was displeased with how he'd handled her disturbing experience. Her eyes still red, she gave him an oddly wise and forgiving smile—the kind only the young can offer to the old, the innocent to the informed—pushed her chair back, and rose.

"Everything's good. Don't worry about me." And with that, she left us sitting at the table looking at each other.

My thoughts were addled as I tried to make sense of what was going on. Why the man had chosen Maisie to be his messenger, the blameless handmaiden of a convicted criminal, I could only imagine. But if he was who Will and I both tacitly assumed he was, I knew he'd have no qualms about terrorizing anybody associated with my husband. Given the thick woods surrounding the front and sides of our house, as well as our isolation here, it wouldn't have been much of a challenge to spy on us for a time and mark our young daughter as his target. I got up, poured each of us a glass of Scotch, and set them on the table, thinking it was likely cowardice behind the assailant's decision to make Maisie deliver the parcel on his behalf. Or at least a disinclination to confront Will face-to-face, unannounced, after such a long time and given the bad blood between them.

When I'd heard Maisie close her bedroom door and knew she was out of earshot, I asked Will, my voice lowered, "Henry Slader?"

"Who else could it possibly be," he said, sipping his drink.

"Is he even out of prison?"

"So it would seem. I've spent as little time thinking about him as humanly possible."

He was right. Slader's wretched name had rarely come up since his trial and conviction for his brazen assault on my husband years ago.

"But Adam didn't look anything like Slader," I said.

"Who knows what he was up to. The question is why he's doing any of this now."

We sat at the kitchen table for a time, as the music faintly continued and the clock calmly ticked. I broke our silence.

"Aren't you going to open the package? Or at least read what's in the envelope?"

Will hesitated, swirled the contents of his glass, intent upon its golden hue. "You know, it's entirely possible he's out there in the yard looking at us."

An owl, a great horned that nested nearby, hooted. It reminded us both that while, yes, we were sitting in the relative privacy of the house, the world just outside the windows was very much with us. In the distance, a lower-pitched female owl faintly answered our neighbor's call.

"Maybe we should pull the shades," I said, eyeing a kitchen window through which I could see nothing other than inky darkness.

He shook his head. "And give him the pleasure? No, I'm sure nothing he's written or sent needs immediate attention. Damn his eyes anyway. Attacking Maisie, even if he never laid a finger on her, tells me more than I need to know at the moment. I'll open it in my own good time, when I'm sure he won't be able to watch."

I felt bad for both of these people I loved, even as I was petrified about what was to come. More than anything, I hoped Maisie would not retreat back into her defensive shell as a result of this incident. In the first years after she was orphaned she'd been a bit of a loner, withdrawn and diffident, so any circumstances that helped her to blossom and reenter life were ones we encouraged. We'd all worked so hard to get her this far, to where she truly felt she was a member of our family, appellations aside. As for my husband, I worried that he too might withdraw into paranoia from days long gone, paranoia he'd struggled with considerable success to bury. I knew he would share with me what Henry Slader—if indeed it was Slader who'd accosted Maisie—had delivered in this coercive, cryptic way, once he'd had time to digest the tectonic shift that had just unsettled our placid lives.

I rose, put my hand on his shoulder, told him I'd shut the first-floor windows and lock up, then left him alone as the string quartet flowed on, a whisper of empty encouragement from a distant century.

When I went to secure the screen door on the front porch, I saw someone stirring on the far side of the road, just beyond the perimeter of light. No body was visible to my eyes, just the vaguest nimbus of a face afloat out there like an illusionist's trick in a blackened theater. I was reminded of lonely No-Face in Miyazaki's *Spirited Away*, or those enigmatic flat-faced Cycladic sculptures I loved to see whenever we visited the Met. But this wasn't some anime film figure staring at me or an ancient visage carved from limestone. It was palpably real, gradually withdrawing into the woods, never looking away.

My natural impulse was to call out, demand an explanation. But I didn't dare. For one, my family had been through enough tonight. What was more, I wasn't sure I wanted to know the answer. As the gaze that was fixed between me and the mystifying face continued for a troubling minute, maybe longer, I realized Maisie was right. The face's features, however ambiguous and shadowy in what postdusk light remained, resembled those of my brother, Adam, dead these twenty-two years. Murdered and laid to rest without his killer's ever having been brought to justice.

Impossible. Ghosts were for children and dime novelists. But this apparition was real, and my mind was not playing ghoulish tricks on me. Was the face, so rigid, slightly smiling as Maisie had said? Did I hear soft laughter, or was it the whispering breeze that ruffled the maple leaves and pine needles? I glanced behind me to see if the sound might have come from the hallway. No one was there. And when I turned back again to look across the yard, the face had vanished. Ignoring any fears I felt, I ventured outside and down the steps, where I hesitated by Maisie's bicycle, clutching the newel post at the foot of the railing. Blinking hard, hoping to see something further, I realized the visitation, or whatever had just happened, was over. I looked up toward the stars, but none were visible. The overcast sky promised rain by dawn.

After lingering another moment, I returned inside, locked the doors, extinguished the porch light, and went upstairs to bed. It wasn't until the following afternoon, when curiosity drove me out across the front yard in my slicker and into the wooded thicket on the far side of the lane, that I discovered evidence I'd not been hallucinating. An oversize black-and-white headshot of Adam lay propped against the trunk of an ash tree, its eyes neatly and nightmarishly cut out and an elastic string fixed on either side so it could be worn as a mask. Unthinking, I wrapped my arms around myself as if taken by a sudden, fierce chill. This image was one I'd never seen before. My brother looked relaxed, carefree, happier than in most photos of him as an adult. It seemed to have been taken in the last year of his life, given the pronounced crow's-feet at the corners of his eyes and the deep wrinkles on his forehead. I was afraid to touch the photo mask—it looked like a freakish religious talisman out here among the tiny wildflowers, club moss, and orchard grasses beneath the shimmering canopy of damp leaves.

Strange, I thought. The glossy photograph hadn't been damaged by the rain that had fallen off and on, a fitful deluge, most of the day. The way the mask had been placed, protected from the elements against the fissured bole of the old tree, seemed, however morbid, almost like a shrine. Not wanting to handle it, distressed that anybody would have been cruel enough to use it to torment us, I left it where I'd found it. As I hurried back through the woodland toward the house, the world before me began rivering, wavering, growing more and more indistinct. No sooner had I brushed away my tears than they welled up again. I hoped against hope that neither Maisie nor Will, nor anybody else, was watching as I made my hasty, unsteady way home.

O nce a forger, always a forger. For twenty long years I had been an exception to that truism, never practicing the dark art I had once loved so well, the mystical crafting of a new reality with ink and a steel-nibbed wand. Until I was arrested for injecting countless beautiful faked literary manuscripts and inscriptions into the bloodstream of the rare book trade, I had quietly earned my living as a master mimic, an impersonator on paper of some of the most revered writers in the canon. So fully had I escaped my past, I'd almost forgotten that I myself was my own best forgery. But now my nemesis had returned, angrier, it seemed, crazier than before. If my wife and daughters were the foundation of my life, and the leafy lushness of our upstate house was meant to be free of strife, free of cares, then his message to me tonight was that I was living in a fool's fortress. One in which barely perceptible fissures could easily open, zigzag from the roof of the building to its base, causing everything to collapse and swallow me whole. We all have demons. Some imaginary, others flesh and blood. Mine had resided for years as an ugly memory, one so suppressed it seemed unreal. Would that it had stayed in the realm of nightmares.

I lowered the wooden blinds, despite my reluctance to convey fear to the man I imagined might be lingering outside in the pitch-dark field, and slowly opened the envelope string-tied to the package Maisie had delivered. Though my wife and daughter were surprised I hadn't opened it immediately, I couldn't possibly have risked revealing its contents in front of them, given that I had no idea what Slader had secreted inside. Alone in the letterpress printing studio I shared with Nicole, set up in an extension at the rear of our house, I unfolded the letter.

Dear Will-o'-the-Wisp, it began, *We both knew this day or, better yet, night, would eventually come, did we not?* Before reading another word I folded it back up and returned it to its envelope. The handwriting, I immediately recognized, was impeccably that of Edgar Allan Poe. My gut went hollow.

I hadn't bothered to track this man, the true author of the letter, after he had been arrested, tried, and imprisoned back in the late 1990s for his attack on me while I slept with Meghan in our cottage outside the fairy-tale Irish village of Kenmare, near the Ring of Kerry in the southwestern elbow of the country. After I'd made my barest minimum of statements to the authorities, I did my best to cut—sever, slash, cleave—the assailant Henry Slader from mind and memory. Meg and I had moved to Ireland in order to live quietly, simply, above reproach and outside the turbulent, churning stream of life, of which he was a small if virulent part. Pipe dream, I suppose. But then, most dreams are. Still, I never imagined my past would catch up with me in the hinterlands of Eire in the form of a man attempting to butcher me in bed, hacking at me with my own kitchen cleaver, any more than I imagined it would find me again here, a hundred miles north of New York City on a narrow road in the upstate sticks.

Meghan was seven months along in her pregnancy then, so I had more than my share of reasons to get well, or at least functional, as soon as possible. Our idyllic haven having turned out to be anything but, we were set on returning to New York to have the baby. Before our ship sailed back across the pond, I plodded through weeks of recovery and long hours of rehab each day to learn how to work with a partially severed, if nondominant, right hand. My physical therapist, an amiable young woman named Fiona, who filled our time together with tales of a Galway childhood and her passion for bodhrán and fiddle playing in pubs, was more than skillful at her day job. And I, her patient and pupil, strove to make my work with her proceed apace. A southpaw since youth, I hadn't realized how much I had relied on my right hand to do simple quotidian tasks. Buttoning my shirt, tying my shoes, buttering my bread—these were paltry acts I did unthinkingly before my injury. Now they all became bedeviling problems that needed to be solved. Motor skills had to be learned anew as I healed, methods of compensation practiced and mastered. Many were the frustrating hours when I had to remind myself that going through life with a fleshy crab's claw at the end of my right arm was better than having no hand at all.

Thanks to Fiona's expertise, and that of my doctors both in Ireland and stateside, as well as the support of my devoted wife, I succeeded bit by bit. No doubt, my own vinegary stubbornness played its role as well. And on a wet February morning, as freezing rain blistered the windows of the sublet Meg's friend and former store manager, Mary, had found for us, Meghan, with the help of a midwife, gave birth to a healthy, bouncing, elfin baby girl. At Meg's insistence we named the child Nicole, in honor of my mother, who I knew would have been thrilled by her granddaughter, though not by the events that had led up to the baby's father having to flee a would-be assassin. An amateur assassin, quite literally a hatchet man, whose motivations, I had to admit to myself though not to those who held him behind bars, were not entirely without reason.

After Nicole's birth, I continued my work with a physical therapist on Union Square through the rest of that winter and deep into spring. Meghan and I were bewitched, if run a bit ragged, by the presence of little Nicole in our lives. Insofar as things could settle back to normal after such upheaval, they did, and the fear of Henry Slader that had haunted me slowly began to dissipate, like thinning mist under a strong morning sun. Stretches of time passed now and then without his coming into my waking mind or even visiting me in dreams. His name had surfaced in the local County Kerry papers for a brief period after his crime was made public, but he and his victim soon enough slipped from view. Which was fine by me. Memory is gossamer. Most of us have, I always believed, the attention span of a kitten rushing from one toy to another. Once the food is set down, the string and the tinfoil ball are swiftly forgotten. Whether my theory is true or not, I hold it as close to my heart as a mackintosh in mizzle.

Spring came and went, as did summer, before Meg and I truly adjusted to having left Kenmare. We loved it there, but told ourselves that enchanting as rural Ireland was, young Nicole should have the advantages of the culture and diversity of experience that life in a metropolis would afford her. Besides, it wasn't as if there weren't expanses of bucolic forests, beaches, and mountains just a few hours' drive from Manhattan. One could, to be sure, make a reasonable argument that growing up in such a pastoral, sane, kind-spirited place as rural Ireland was superior to the hardships of urban living. But we figured we could always visit the old country whenever we liked, once she was old enough to travel. What was more, hadn't we gotten a little homesick for the grit and genius of the city?

By autumn's end, I was more or less healed. Functionally, at least. As I'd told Fiona when we said our goodbyes, I would always be scarred, but thanks to her and the surgeon who salvaged much of my hand, my life had been given back to me. What I hadn't anticipated in Kenmare, or even in New York, when the bandages were finally removed for good, was that missing my middle fingers and some of my pinkie would prove less physically than emotionally onerous. Getting through my days without feeling the embarrassment of being maimed was something I hadn't worked on in physical therapy. It was hardly necessary, as my friends and even people I didn't know personally in tight-knit Kenmare had heard about what happened, so there was nothing to explain or feel defensive about. In the big city, it took a while, but eventually I learned there was no need to

keep hiding my hand in my pocket. Manhattan, home
to its fair share of the mutilated, was forgiving that way.
And if I did happen to notice some ignoramus staring
at me, maybe finding sick amusement in my misfortune,
I could always raise my phantom middle finger in their
direction and they'd never be the wiser.

Meghan and I eventually took up more permanent
residence in our old neighborhood, the East Village. Our
fond plans of living off the grid in Ireland having been
upended by the assault, we craved familiarity. These were
the streets, shops, and restaurants we knew so well from
our earliest days together. Not to mention that Meghan's
brainchild used-book shop, which she had sold to Mary
and the other employees around Thanksgiving the year
before our return, was nearby. Its doors were always
open to us, and while the new owners had expanded
to include first editions of literary gems housed in tall
barrister bookcases, the place retained its same homey
feel. Mary even kept Meghan's favorite overstuffed chair
in the office, with its whimsical upholstery depicting
antique handwriting that was meant to look like the
Declaration of Independence or some such. Ugly artifact,
in my eyes, but like a pair of old shoes that have stood
one in good stead over many miles and difficult terrain,
it was comfortable, reliable.

What we sought was just like that, a known quan-
tity, a safe refuge, an embracing asylum. So when the
rental agent showed us a walk-up in a brownstone not
far from Tompkins Square with lots of light and lots of
room, we leapt at it. Squeaking hardwood floors, old-
school kitchen with a commercial six-burner stove and
cupboards that clung like foolhardy mountaineers to the
walls, electric outlets partly shrouded by layers of paint

from generations before us—what was there not to love?
We shared a bottle of champagne to complement the
Cantonese takeout that first night in our new flat, while
the baby cooed in her crib, blessedly oblivious to her
parents' noiseless lovemaking after dinner.

Once Nicole had graduated from bassinet infancy,
Meg was thrilled to be invited to take on a part-time
role at the bookshop, which was doing well enough that
it had opened a second floor with nicely worn Oriental
rugs, built-in shelving for more stock, even a brick-walled
gallery space for antiquarian maps and prints. As a result
of her exposure to the wide-ranging interests of others
on the staff, she began branching out beyond her earlier
specialties in art and culinary books. I couldn't have been
happier for her. Mary Chandler, who'd been closest to my
wife when Meghan had sold the shop, was the primary
force behind the store's growth and widened focus. A
blessedly incurable book addict, Mary, who had tucked
away a substantial nest egg while working in corporate
law, had, after a few years, fled the mercenary grind of
contracts and NDAs to devote herself to her true love,
plowing her money and energy into expanding and deep-
ening the quality of the shop's inventory. Word was that
she had also benefited from the help of a private backer,
which had allowed her to buy out the other co-owners
during a time when the going got rough with the business, but I never knew one way or the other. Mary had
been the first person Meghan hired, a couple of years
before my future wife and I met, and now, roles reversed,
it was Mary who happily asked her friend and former
supervisor to rejoin the family.

Things went well. Meg was back in her element.
While she used to come home from work talking vintage

cookbooks by Julia Child or Marcella Hazan, or works illustrated by Marc Chagall or William Blake, now it was an inscribed copy of an early Ernest Hemingway or Agatha Christie she'd tell me about, or the two-volume first edition of *The Mayor of Casterbridge* in its original cloth bindings, or *The Pickwick Papers* with its printed pale blue wrappers, published in weekly parts. Fortunately for us both, ours was a marriage of unabashed, unrepentant bibliophiles. I reveled in her newfound enthusiasms and did my best to stay out of her way and Mary's, even though my own knowledge of rare books and manuscripts ran deeper than theirs. Despite my flawed background, I was invited to join the staff as an adviser, or cataloger, or in whatever capacity I might have liked, but I wisely kept my distance. If asked about a book, or the authenticity of an autograph, or any other bibliographic point, I was glad to oblige. But they were riding high on their own, I felt, and didn't need me for ballast.

So, what then? For myself—while refurbishing the old Wolf stove, anchoring some better shelves to the kitchen walls I'd stripped and repainted, and generally sprucing up our new place—I proved to be a far better father than I might ever have expected. We had enough savings that I could devote myself to Nicole for the first passel of years back in the Village, and I loved nothing better than to help feed her, teach her vocabulary, join her with her coloring books and, early on, with her astonishing calligraphy. Just as I'd excelled at the latter under my mother's tutelage, so did Nicole under my watchful guidance. Despite my mixed feelings, not to mention Meghan's, about teaching her the very skills that had gotten me into such dire straits—though by then my path was straight and narrow—by the time the girl began elementary school, she was a precocious natural. Her ability to focus, tongue caught in the corner of her mouth, was a sight to behold. Tracing different alphabets in block and cursive letters, along with basic calligraphic patterns, gave her joy. No other word for it—joy. Nothing made me happier than to watch her mature, believing fully and not without reason that she would never use her instincts and gifts for anything nefarious.

With Nicole in school, it became clear I needed to leave behind the self-protective cocoon I'd spun for myself using my daughter to some degree as my excuse. I wished I could reach out to an old bookseller acquaintance up in Providence for advice, but that was out of the question. Where we'd left things two decades earlier was not unlike a happy marriage ending in acrimonious divorce. Atticus Moore and I hadn't needed a restraining order to understand just how strange things might have become if one of us approached the other. An orchard's worth of olive branches wouldn't have sufficed to prevent some inevitable nastiness, unpredictable and damaging, from coming down on one or both of us. He had sent me a sizable cashier's check with no accompanying letter nor any memo of explanation, and we both knew it represented a comprehensive apology and a warning not to question his role in the ugly things that had happened to me, or to ask him for explanations. If money talks, Atticus's check shouted. It fairly howled.

Be that as it may, I found myself one morning, after Meg had left for work, looking him up on my wife's laptop—that electronic anathema I'd always despised but finally capitulated to using—to see if he still had his store in Rhode Island. He did, and even boasted a website—seems Atticus too had merged Gutenberg with Gates—that offered some beautiful first editions of mostly nineteenth- and twentieth-century literature. Scrolling through his online catalog, marveling at this offering and that, I was reminded again, as if I needed reminding, what impeccable taste the man had. After my father, a consummate rare book aficionado whose own tastes weren't limited to books from the past two centuries but went all the way back to the Elizabethan era, Atticus was the only bibliophile who had truly ever been a soul mate to me. At a book fair in San Francisco once, over drinks at the Fairmont Hotel, he had even floated the idea that I become a partner in his rare book firm. Over the years, I sometimes found myself wondering if I'd made a mistake declining his offer. Water under the Golden Gate Bridge at this point. Still, whatever bad blood lay spilt between us, thanks in no small part to Slader, even now I missed our camaraderie. But that was where I supposed I needed to leave it.

Assuring myself that nothing providential awaited me in Providence, I logged off. Later the same day, I set up an appointment with an old colleague at a Manhattan auction house where I'd worked some years earlier as an expert in literary and historical autographs. While before I had labored in their dignified, well-lit rooms under the cloud of being a confessed forger—the Frank Abagnale of literature, as it were—now I presented myself as fully reformed, a responsible father happily married to a woman admired in the industry, and by every measure among the most discriminating and informed experts in my field. As it happened, one of their specialists was winding down toward retirement, so I started soon afterward. To say I was exhilarated to be back in my element—verifying inscriptions, ferreting out fakes, researching provenance,

collating and meticulously cataloging lots that would go
on the block for thousands of dollars—would be a gross
understatement. Nor was I tempted to undermine my
newfound position at the house by making the slightest
false step.

Even when one of my own early forgeries came over
the transom within the first month of my employment,
I flagged the book. It was a first edition set of Henry
James's *The Europeans*, which I had embellished with
an inscription from the master to George Eliot upon
his visiting her country house at Witley, Surrey, in 1878,
two years after she published *Daniel Deronda* and two
years before she died. The quality of the forgery was
every bit as refined as its existence was improbable. For
all I knew at the time I faked the autograph association,
James may well have given Eliot *The Europeans*, which
had been issued right around the time of his social call
in Witley. But I hadn't bothered putting in the research
to find out one way or another. If he had, this was not
that copy. In the interest of continuing my path on the
right side of the law, I expressed my concerns to the
head of the department, telling him—without confessing to my own handiwork—that the inscription seemed
off. I didn't like the formulation of several letters in the
phrase *With the warmest possible regards of*, and even
questioned the phraseology itself. James, who famously
referred to Eliot as a "great horse-faced bluestocking,"
yet one whose intellect and passion he admired, wasn't
much of a *warmest possible* kind of guy.

As it turned out, however, the seller, who'd consigned
a number of distinguished books to the house on this
particular occasion, insisted on its legitimacy. He had
acquired it in England from a seller with impeccable

credentials, who himself evidently purchased the set at auction in London. My ambitious youthful forgery, it seemed, had made quite a journey before arriving back in its fabricator's hands. I was overruled, which was neither here nor there as far as I was concerned. When the lot came up on auction day and surpassed its high estimate by a tidy sum, it was everything I could do not to laugh out loud. I wished I could share the whole absurd story with Meghan that night—how one of my past bastard creations had orbited into my world once more, like a comet looping around the sun, then ricocheted back into the darkness of the universe, its icy tail burning bright, proud, and false.

Instead, I kept my own counsel, privately thinking, *Godspeed, simulacrum!* Nor would George Eliot's copy of *The Europeans* be the last time such a situation arose and a forgery of mine would continue its vibrant life outside the precincts of reality. More often than not, when I threw shade on the genuineness of a manuscript or signature, my colleagues heeded my advice. I must confess, though, that whenever one of my early forgeries was debunked and removed from circulation, the moment was less professionally satisfying than personally bittersweet.

We hadn't seen such ceaseless gray skies and persistent rain since our days in County Kerry, and the morning after Maisie's confrontation and my odd encounter was no different, with fresh showers pelting the eaves and overrunning the rainspouts. She and I both came downstairs later than usual, having slept in, unawakened by even the slightest hint of a sunrise. Will, long since stirring, had brewed a pot of coffee and disappeared into his studio with a cup, no doubt to read the letter and open that mysterious parcel in the light of day, however dim. I considered wandering out to the garden and collecting some fresh zucchini flowers to fry, but it was too soggy to bother. Fried squash blossoms weren't at the forefront of anyone's thoughts anyway. I offered to make a tomato frittata instead, knowing it was one of Maisie's favorites, if she would set the table.

"How are you feeling this morning?" I asked, reaching out for her right hand, then frowning at her arm, where she'd suffered the nastiest of her injuries.

"Much better," she said, crooking it to show me her elbow as well.

I peeled away her bandages and was relieved to see that, aside from constellations of pitted punctures, some of which had begun to scab over, it looked like she was going to heal apace. Wasn't it Picasso who said, "It takes a long time to become young"? While Maisie was in many ways old for her age, her ability to heal was strictly that of a healthy kid. "Were you able to sleep all right?"

"Well, I sort of got my nightmare out of the way before I went to bed."

Not coming up with any good riposte, I told her I was glad she was doing better but we'd still keep a close eye on her wounds over the next few days. With that, she began to set out plates and silverware, as I reached down a cast-iron pan from the hanging rack and prepped eggs, shallots, tomatoes, and prosciutto for breakfast. This morning it was Claude Debussy on the radio, a marathon celebrating his birthday. But for the disturbing memory of what had transpired the night before, a memory that hung over us like the very dampness outside, it would have been a typical start to one of our August days.

When Will joined us, he looked neither shaken nor relieved. Confused was more like it, bewildered.

Maisie wasted no time asking. "What was in the package, anyway? Guess the guy didn't know they have post offices for that sort of thing."

Post offices, I thought, have security cameras and postmarks, both of which he must have wanted to avoid. A twilight country road was far preferable to a post office suffused by fluorescent overheads.

Will said simply, "I could use another cup of coffee."

"Well, who is he?" Maisie continued. "Are we even safe here?"

She had a valid question. When, last night, Will had finally come to bed, later than usual after sequestering himself in his studio with the accursed package, I was still awake thinking about my brother, wondering as I had myriad times over the years if Slader had been behind his homicide. The way Adam's hands had been severed at our bungalow on the beach in Montauk so eerily mirrored Slader's vicious, partly successful attempt to amputate Will's at our cottage in Kenmare that it seemed impossible the assaults were coincidental. Yet while the authorities apprehended Slader for his attack on my husband, they were never able to bring charges against him in my brother's case.

I had whispered, "It's Slader, isn't it?"

"The handwriting is Edgar Allan Poe's, and a damn good forgery of it, I have to admit. Beautiful, in fact."

Surprised by his candid admiration, I'd switched on the bedside lamp. Earlier, I had drawn the curtains, something I rarely bothered to do, given we had no nearby neighbors with prying eyes to hide from at bedtime. "If they gave him pen and paper, he had plenty of time to practice in prison."

"If you offered a thousand inmates pen and paper, and ten years to practice, they'd never attain this level of craftsmanship."

"Am I hearing a note of jealousy?" I asked.

"Maybe a little," he admitted, turning toward me. "Just because forging isn't something I do anymore doesn't mean I can't admire formidable artistry when I see it."

All I could do was sigh. "So what does he want? How bad is it?"

Dressed for bed, Will slipped in beside me. "I couldn't bring myself to read the damn thing beyond his greeting line, which was oozing with self-satisfied bravado, all chuffed up like a perfect imbecile. So much for crime, punishment, and rehabilitation—"

"You want me to read it?"

"It can wait until morning," he said, not hiding his exasperation. "We both know his game anyway. It's just a matter of what the maniac wants now. Either way, he's not getting so much as a penny or a paper clip. He's literally gotten his pound of flesh from me, and that's more than I ever owed him to begin with. By the way, did you move Ripley's food and water bowls?"

"Of course not. She's your spoiled stray, not mine."

"They're missing from the studio doorsteps out back. For that matter, so's Ripley."

"Will. It's night. She's making her catly rounds," I assured him. "Maisie might have brought the bowls in to refill and forgot to put them back."

"When? She was out with her friends."

"You need to sleep. Ripley's fine," and I extinguished the light.

Now, this morning, back at the kitchen table, I saw the worry that clouded Maisie's face and realized we owed her an explanation. Especially given that she, through no fault of her own, was part of the whole loathsome narrative. "You remember what we said when you asked about your father's hand? That he'd lost his fingers in an accident?"

"I remember."

"Ever since you first came to live with us when you were five, we've always tried to be truthful with you, Maisie," I went on, as Will busied himself with cooking our breakfast; this was a confessional moment he had hoped might never come. "After your mother was diagnosed with cancer and asked us if we'd be willing to raise you like you were our own daughter, we made a pact with her and ourselves that we would do our absolute best, and that included always being honest with you. I hope you'll forgive us for eliding on just this one matter."

"What's eliding?"

"Means omitting things," Will spoke from over at the stove. "In this case, fudging."

I may have nodded, I'm not sure. "The truth is, many years ago, your father had some business dealings with a man that didn't go well. This man—"

"Guy last night?"

"That's what we're assuming. We think he's the one who attacked your father, hurt his hand, and ended up in jail. I hope you'll understand that one of the reasons we didn't tell you the whole story is because you'd had enough of your own hardships, and we didn't want to burden you with another that happened before you were even born. We figured he was out of our lives forever, so why torment you with it?"

Maisie stared at Will's hands for a moment, then at her own. "Who was my real father?" she asked, her voice tight, quiet.

That was unexpected. But then, everything seemed bent toward the unforeseen since the night before. I glanced at Will, who shrugged his assent. Seemed the time had come for this as well.

"Your mother always dreamed of having two things, Maisie. One was the bookshop that I started and she developed into the wonderful mecca it's become. The other was to have a child. To have you. Since there wasn't anyone special in her life she could raise a baby with, she found a donor and had you herself."

"In other words, I don't have a flesh-and-blood father. Strictly speaking."

"Strictly speaking," Will said, "you do. But probably not one you'll ever meet."

Maisie pondered this for a moment. Her oval face, prominent tall brow, and silky reddish-chestnut hair reminded me so much of her mother, while her brown eyes, cleft chin, and lanky figure—Mary'd had bottle-green eyes and a medium build, not short but not as tall as Maisie promised to become—were clearly from her bio-dad's genes.

"I'm afraid," Will added, "your paternity may always be a mystery."

Undaunted, she asked, "You think you ever met this donor?"

"Your mom was a very private person, Maisie," I said, wishing I could offer more.

For not quite half a minute, the kitchen clock ticked louder than I'd ever heard it.

"I understand," Maisie said finally, expression unreadable as she reached over to squeeze my hand before getting up, walking around to the stove, and giving Will a sideways hug. "Thanks for explaining. So now what're we going to do about this man?"

That was it? That was all? Mary Chandler, I reminded myself, had been like this. Settle an issue great or small, and move on. No sitting around, Rodin-style, with chin on fist. I always admired her for the trait, even envied her a little. When she fell ill, she transferred ownership of the bookshop to me and, in trust, to Maisie without so much as a second thought. Like Mary, her daughter—now ours—was often tougher, more stoic, than I sometimes credited her with being.

Will carried the platter with the frittata to the table and set it down. "I'm going to make a couple of phone calls today to check on the status of the man who did this to me years ago"—holding up his right hand as he dished a slice onto Maisie's plate with his left—"and who we think accosted you last night. Meantime, if you want to visit your friends after dark, Meg or I ought to drive you until we know what that was all about."

Impatient now myself, I interjected, "So what did the letter say?"

"He wants to meet."

"What? No—no way are you going to do that."

"Not sure." He hesitated. "The situation's exponentially more complicated than I might have guessed. More complicated and, truth to tell, more intriguing. Believe it or not, good could come of it, if I'm understanding correctly."

"Will, the man is treachery incarnate. Look what happened in Kenmare when you agreed to meet him but refused to do the dirty work he wanted," I argued, raising my voice higher than intended. Maisie gently asked if I was all right, but nothing was right. While she was putting on a brave face, I knew she'd been badly shaken. As for my husband, he wasn't making sense. "Will, listen. If Slader's on the up-and-up, why forge the letter in a hand that can't be traced to him?"

"Because that isn't who Slader is," he said. "Be like asking a vampire to spend a day at the shore, sunbathing. Not in his nature."

"But you'll happily go meet this pathological vampire for a drink?"

"Not happily. Just, let's say, unavoidably," sitting down and blowing on his coffee. "Let's eat, please."

"I want to know what was in the package."

"Honestly, I'd rather not show you. But it's in our house now."

Outside, the rain was finally beginning to taper off. Through the back windows I could see skeins of mist lifting off the wide field that led down to a curtain of second-growth trees ranging along the perimeter of our land. Beyond that were tumbledown drystone walls that early farmers, who originally owned sizable swaths of this county, had built after they cleared meadows from rock-strewn forests. Everything was glistening, like diamonds winking in the greenery. On normal days, no matter how distressed I was—whether it was some problem at the bookshop, with one of the girls, even with Will—I found I could look out on this expanse of rolling grassy earth, stretch my eyes, and recenter myself. Even today, fraught as matters were, I gazed down at the meadow in search of calm.

One of our wisest decisions when we reverse-emigrated from America to Ireland, twenty years ago this summer, was really a nondecision. While we'd incrementally divested ourselves of most of our possessions—Will, his many books; me, my bookshop—we hadn't gotten rid of this farmhouse, which had been his late parents' cherished retreat. On a long-term lease to the family of one of his father's closest business associates and friends, the property had brought us a steady monthly income. Besides, Will felt it would have been a betrayal to them, as well as his father's memory, to attempt eviction and list the place. When, about a decade ago, the Cunningham family had begun to disperse and, well, die off, we found ourselves in a position to take it over again. Will, who loved little better than to restore, renovate, and revive, had spent every possible waking hour away from his job in the city working on the house. Other than a few family heirlooms, including several of his mother's watercolors, my Augustus John drawing in a gilt frame, and an ultrarare literary artifact—Sir Arthur Conan Doyle's own fountain pen, inherited from Will's collector father and given to Nicole on her sixteenth birthday—this was pretty much all that remained from earlier days. And, for my part, long after disposing of my own childhood bungalow in Montauk after the murder of my brother, I made this getaway mine too. Yes, we considered ourselves New Yorkers, city folk. But each of us felt most comfortable in our own skin when we were here.

The sun had begun to peek out as we finished breakfast. Time had come to see what was in the parcel. As we walked down a corridor from the kitchen, past the mudroom in back, toward the studio, Will said, "I hope you'll forgive me for stating the obvious, but it's important that none of us mention a word of this to a soul. Nobody, not a hint of it to anyone. Can we agree on that?"

Maisie and I assented, she more readily than her mother. Being asked to enter into a pact of secrecy only raised my suspicions. Some toxic old sentiments fought to rise to the surface, but I tamped them down.

"We'll tell Nicole when she comes," he added. "Goes unsaid."

An addition to the house—once Will's father's lair, outfitted with leather club chairs, antique rolltop desk, stacking mahogany bookcases—had been converted into a small-press printing studio that Will shared with Nicole, who passed many productive hours with him here whenever she was upstate, helping with one of his, or rather their, projects.

Back in Ireland, when apprenticing at Eccles & Sons' stationery and print shop in tiny Kenmare, Will fell in love with letterpress printing, a skill he developed over the years, one that nearly matched his staggering, if troubled, talent as a calligrapher. When we settled into the farmhouse, he rolled up his sleeves, joined by Nicole, who'd learned the gentle art of letterpress printing at the elbow of her craftsman father. Together, they dedicated themselves to hand typesetting and printing limited-edition fine press chapbooks, which they sold under the imprint Stone Circle Editions, named in honor of the Bronze Age stone circle known as the Shrubberies in Kenmare. A pair of gifted obsessives, they made just enough from these sales to buy more ink, paper, and other supplies. So it was that Will's father's club chairs came to be replaced by a Vandercook proof press. Where the rolltop desk once stood was now home to a pair of large vintage Hamilton cabinets filled with various fonts of metal type. Where before his father had stored first-edition rarities in glass-front bookcases, industrial metal shelves now housed cans of printer's inks, tympan paper, press oils, and the like. There were objects as large as a beautiful Jacques board shear they bought at an auction in the Berkshires and as small as intricate little reglets, quoins, and loupes. And paper, lots of drawers choked with a full-blown menagerie of paper. While my engagement with books had always been as a reader, learner, buyer, and seller, I'd never felt compelled to make a book. Marveling at their workshop—their biblio-laboratory, as Nicole called it—I sometimes wished it were otherwise.

He also kept his calligraphy pens and inks here, but rarely if ever used them anymore. Knowing his forgery days were behind him, I once asked Will why not throw that stuff out or give it to Nicole? "You're like a recovering alcoholic keeping a stock of favorite liquors around." He said he wasn't thirsty, and not to worry about it. For the most part, I didn't.

I suppose I should not have been surprised that Will had locked Slader's package in his fireproof safe overnight. But I was surprised by what, with the great delicacy only a person who has handled rare books and manuscripts his whole life displays, he pulled from the heavy-card mailer. Swaddled in tissue, which Will neatly unfolded and set aside, was a drab, nondescript pamphlet, a bit the worse for wear. The kind of ephemeral detritus most people would recycle with yellowed newspapers and outdated catalogs, or else use to line the bottom of a tiny birdcage. Its edges were somewhat tattered and its tea-colored cover was lightly spotted along the bottom with what looked like old water stains. At about half a dozen inches tall and maybe four and a half across, it was altogether unmemorable.

Neither Maisie nor I said a word when Will, whose own anxious eyes were dancing, looked up from the artifact and said, "Well?"

There was no reason Maisie should have known what her father was so restless, even edgy, about. As for me, early American literature—this was printed in Boston in 1827 by some Calvin F. S. Thomas, so stated on the front cover—was outside my usual province. Had it been an early recipe book or art monograph, then maybe. But I'd never seen this before and said as much to Will.

"Neither have I," he replied. "At least one that's not in captivity."

"Institutionalized, in a library," I explained to Maisie.

He carefully turned it over, and on the rear cover, framed by a border of repeated triangular ornaments, like stylized burnt conifers or ink-black sunrises, similar to that on the front, was an advertisement for "Book & Job Printing" by that same "Calvin Thomas of No. 70, Washington-Street, Boston, Corner of State Street." There was no indication on either front or back of who the author of this dreary-looking little chapbook, titled *Tamerlane and Other Poems*, was, aside from his or her being a Bostonian.

"*Tamerlane*," Will said, a tone of uncommon impatience cascading from high to low with those three syllables. "No chimes ringing, Meg? No *eureka*?"

The title did sound familiar, I had to admit. I remembered that Christopher Marlowe had written a play called *Tamburlaine the Great*, and knew that George Frideric Handel had composed an opera *Tamerlano* in the early eighteenth century. The British fantasy writer Angela Carter wrote an elliptical short story—"The Kiss," I believe it was titled—in which the Turkic conqueror was a character. But Marlowe and Handel were plainly no Bostonians, and Carter, a Brit, hadn't started publishing until almost a century and a half after this *Tamerlane* saw the light of day. Nonplussed, I had to admit I was drawing a blank.

"Well," he said. "Logic and reason dictate that this is an exceptionally high-quality forgery, the finest facsimile known to bibliophilic man, and not a genuine copy of the so-called Black Tulip of American literary rarities—"

So that was what the beautifully drawn flowers flanking Will's name on the letter envelope were meant to represent.

"—Edgar Allan Poe's first book. But if it's really and truly authentic, as he claims it is and it looks to be, though I have every reason not to trust him or myself, for that matter, this would join the ranks of only a dozen copies known to have survived."

"So you've seen one before, you're saying?"

"Seen, but never touched," he answered with unabashed and unwonted excitement. "I remember my father taking me to Philadelphia back when I was eleven, on a father-son field trip around Halloween to go to an exhibit at the Free Library. They were showing a copy of *Tamerlane* they'd just acquired through a bequest from a collector named Richard Gimbel. Our train trip and the nice hotel on Rittenhouse Square, where we had a fancy enough dinner that I was required to wear a jacket and tie, are a bit of a blur in retrospect. But one thing I remember clearly is my father pointing at the Poe displayed behind glass and telling me, 'Now there's a book I'll never possess, Will. That is a true unicorn. Never forget you saw this.'"

"Can I touch?" Maisie asked, and before Will or I could say no, she'd reached out and gingerly laid her fingertips on the cover, as if it were a sacred relic. Which, in some ways, I suppose it possibly was.

"Let's have a look, but then best put it back in the safe until I've had a chance to do some research," Will said, delicately lifting it and leafing through the first few pages of poetry.

"May I ask what Slader wrote you? It is Slader, right?"

"I don't see who else it would be, Meg," turning to the end to see there was no colophon, then paging through the twenty leaves—forty pages—of text. It was clear Will took this book seriously, unicorn or no. "Like I said last night, his Poe calligraphy is stunningly good, impeccable, and I don't think he was trying that hard."

"How's that?"

He set the pamphlet down again on the table. "The paper, unlike what I'm seeing here with this *Tamerlane*, isn't as period as it should have been. And the purplish color of the ink is entirely wrong. More Virginia Woolf than Edgar Poe. He knew I would know. If he'd wanted to, he could've fabricated a far more credible letter in dark brown or black ink and on period paper, but there was no point in bothering. That's what he's telegraphing me."

Maisie looked at Will as if he were speaking in a foreign language that needed to be translated. But he stared out the window and continued, for all intents and purposes talking to himself.

"You know, with Slader potentially active again, I'm going to have to be careful at work. Poe manuscript materials don't come on the market that often, but when they do, they go for big money. There was a previously unknown letter that came up at Christie's around five years ago, about 'The Tell-Tale Heart,' and it went off for a hundred and a half."

"That's a hundred and fifty thousand, Maze," I explained, and she raised her eyebrows.

"A holograph manuscript of one of his poems, 'The Conqueror Worm,' fetched twice that at a much smaller auction house up in New England."

"You haven't answered my question," I said.

"If I'm not mistaken, the record was set at auction for a two-page manuscript of a love poem he wrote right before he died. Hammered down at eight hundred thousand or so, and it was only the first half of the poem. That wasn't quite a decade ago. Imagine what it would bring today—"

"Will?" I asked, with an impatient frown.

Startled, he looked over at me, suddenly cognizant that Maisie and I were staring at him, and said, "I'm sorry, yes?"

"What does all this mean?"

"Like I said, he wants to meet. No doubt to discuss this book—this, whatever it is."

"When?"

"Friday."

Sometimes my husband exasperated me. I loved him, as the toady phrase has it, warts and all. Yet there were times, like now, when he could be unnerving, if not confounding. I had a hundred different arguments against his going along with such lunacy, not the least of which was that he would be leaving me and Maisie alone in the house. Divide and conquer, wasn't that the oldest trick in the book?

"And where is this meeting supposed to take place?"

Will scratched his temple, hesitated. "He seems to prefer meeting in nice old hotels. The Beekman Arms, at three."

"If you don't go, then what?"

"He'll persist. He's the definition of persistence, as you of all people know."

"You absolutely shouldn't do this," I insisted, aware he'd made up his mind.

He considered my words before countering, "I shouldn't, it's true. But I'm not left with a choice. Slader's not only persistent, he's clever. This *Tamerlane*? If it is authentic, it's either stolen or the rare book find of the twenty-first century. The twelfth known copy turned up in a New Hampshire antiques barn three decades ago."

"And if it's a forgery?" I asked, hoping my frustration that all of this was unfolding in front of Maisie wasn't overly obvious to her. Despite the girl's bravado, she was fragile and hurt.

"You've heard me say how the untutored eye is the forger's best friend? My eye is anything but untutored. Without getting into a more scientific analysis of the book, and despite the fact that, as I said, it shouldn't logically be right, every instinct in me suggests it could be genuine. The paper tone, its texture and weight and, what, frailty. This uneven darkness of the ink. The variety of vintage stains, tide lines along the bottom edges, and other flaws. And if that's the case, this is trouble because it's here now with no reasonable explanation as to why I possess it. The only provenance is a forged letter in Poe's hand. There's a reason Slader gave it to Maisie along a dark road where no one was watching," he said, then asked Maisie, "Do you remember if he was wearing gloves?"

"Honestly, I couldn't—"

"I'm lost," I interrupted. "Why don't we call the police, if you think it's stolen?"

Any mention of the police made my husband recoil. After his encounter with the law back when I first knew him, he steered clear whenever possible, even though I knew he hadn't relapsed into forging since. He'd confessed, done his penance, reinvented himself. Even as I understood his reluctance, I began to compass the vague outlines of Henry Slader's trap here. Was *Tamerlane*, to use a childhood phrase for a sophisticated ploy, a hot potato?

"Rather than the cops, I think it's the convict I need to consult with. Shall we go clear the table and wash dishes?"

"Let's do," I said, stifling my irritation.

"Speaking of which, did you move Ripley's bowls, Maze?" he asked.

Maisie said she hadn't.

"Would you mind keeping an eye out for them? And for Ripley too? They've both gone missing, it seems," he said, and as he spoke I noticed that the perplexed and perplexing look on his face was one I hadn't seen since the bad old days when Slader first surfaced in our lives, and when poor Adam, mysteriously friends with Slader, had been slain. Days which, other than unclouded memories of my brother, I'd just as soon consign to oblivion. After all, as I was reminded in the woods last night, not only did his murder remain unsolved, but any leads that might once have existed had now gone as cold as the headstone in the Montauk cemetery where he was buried.

If Henry Slader had lost some years out of his life while in prison, it appeared he hadn't lost his edge as a world-class forger and despicable yegg. Here he was again, as welcome as some sarcoma, as malignancy itself. I had been so keen on forgetting my encounters with the man, wiping him from memory, that I could scarcely picture him in my mind. But when I walked into the low-ceilinged, dark-wood-paneled tavern of the Beekman Arms, that handsome white-clapboard colonial behemoth at the center of Rhinebeck village, the oldest continuously operating inn in America and a place where George Washington and many other dignitaries had slept, I recognized him at once.

Pale as cod, head not shaven but shorn tight, angular in every way, spare but still strong, wearing a black sweater and jeans, he rose with a disconcerting grin to shake my hand, as if we were long-lost friends. Could he possibly have forgotten? Not about our hating each other, but about what he'd done to me years ago. When I placed my warm talon, my fleshy pincers of a right hand, in his and gently pressed, he winced. Almost imperceptibly, but unmistakably, winced.

We sat at a table that paralleled the venerable old bar, me on a Windsor-style bench that ran along the wall, Slader with his back to the daytime regulars drinking their beer. Before he could say a word of the speech he'd no doubt rehearsed, I asked, "So you've taken to assaulting girls now? In the guise of a ghost, to boot."

"Nothing of the kind. I just gave her the package, asked her to give it to you."

"She came home all scraped up, scared out of her wits, and you're saying you didn't push her over?"

Slader shrugged. "Didn't think she'd frighten so easily—"

"Your entire intention was to terrify her, you disingenuous bastard. Now you're going to insult her on top of that?"

"Please. To answer your question, no, I never laid a finger on the girl. If she claimed otherwise, you might want to talk with her about the perils of lying. It's something you know a little about."

There was no point, I realized, in pursuing it further, and I certainly hadn't come here to rehash ancient history. I would always loathe Slader, and he, me.

"That was quite some calling card you left," I said.

A waitress came by the table and asked what we'd like to drink. I ordered a Jameson. "Seltzer on the rocks with lime," Slader told her, then confided after she'd left, "Abstinence is one of the many bad habits I learned in lockup."

"No doubt. But the Poe. It's a blue-ribbon fake, I must say. Did you do it?"

Slader laughed, looked away with a cough, then back. I'd forgotten how dark his eyes were, ebony in this dimly lit bar. "You're the one who's apparently graduated to letterpress printing. Me, I'm just a hopeless, out-of-date calligrapher. A cursive dinosaur."

"I wouldn't call letterpress any less out-of-date than calligraphy. So if you didn't forge it, who did? And why put it in my hands? I don't want to have anything to do with the thing."

Slader thanked the server, crushed his lime into the sparkling water. "That 'thing' is worth north of a million, you know. On the right day, in the right auction room, I could see it going for two."

"Why not three?" I asked with a smirk.

"You're right. Why *not* three? Let the hammer drop where it may."

"Please."

"You think I exaggerate? There are a lot of well-heeled collectors out there who want this book, the Holy Grail of American letters. Not to mention libraries. Three would shatter all records, but it doesn't seem out of the question. All it takes is two determined bidders of means who are willing to chase one of the greatest rarities of them all."

Were it genuine, Slader wasn't altogether mistaken. For a copy in original wrappers, sky would be the limit in the rooms. I had done research before heading over and learned there are no known copies of *Tamerlane* inscribed by its author. The slim volume emerged into an indifferent world where it not only received no reviews but where, when its young author published his second book, *Al Aaraaf, Tamerlane and Minor Poems*, in 1829—a book that did gain Poe some attention, mixed reviews being better than none—some people even dismissed his claim that there had ever been an earlier edition of *Tamerlane*. What insult upon injury, for the public to ignore a poet's first book, then deny it ever existed to begin with. If that weren't enough, Poe himself seems not to have kept a copy. And as for *Al Aaraaf*, there appeared to be only around twenty survivors of the original edition of that book as well. Early Poe is a landscape of almost freakish rareness.

The first copy of *Tamerlane* to surface in an institution, I found out, wasn't until 1876, in London's British Museum, of all places, where it had been purchased in 1860 along with a batch of other American volumes. It now resides in the British Library. Eight American libraries possess copies—the Lilly in Indiana, the Ransom Center in Austin, the Huntington and Clark in San Marino and Los Angeles, the Free Library in Philadelphia, the Regenstein at the University of Chicago. Manhattan being Manhattan, the Berg Collection at New York Public has two, one with its cover intact, the other with no cover at all. Two copies are in private hands. And, to round out the census, the copy that had been housed in the Alderman Library at the University of Virginia—it bore a romantic inscription, now faded to near invisibility, from one Phatimer Kinsell "to his sweetheart" Mary Reed—went missing in 1974, and remains lost to this day. *Totus est*.

"Is it the one lifted from Virginia?" I asked, emerging from my stream of thought.

"That's a reasonable speculation, but no. Under infrared light there's no sign of the inscription that's unique to the Alderman copy. According to rumor, that was an inside job and whoever ripped it off, or paid for it to be lifted, doesn't dare bring it to market. Either way, not the same animal."

Before I'd left the house, Meghan was still upset about my meeting with this man who had attacked me. "It's deranged, your willingness to talk with him. You know what happens to the moth drawn to flame," she said. "What's the matter with you?"

However much I disliked Slader, however much I distrusted and resented him, I couldn't help but admire the knowledge he possessed. He could fairly be accused of many ills and iniquities, but ignorance wasn't one of them. Besides, if there was any chance the *Tamerlane* was real, it was imperative I get it out of our house. I even considered bringing it with me to give it back, but that same possibility, ironically, in fact precluded my doing so. Black tulips don't belong in bars. Part of me also believed, perhaps wrongly, that by keeping it in my safe for the short term, I might have more leverage in my discussion with Slader.

"Is it one of the two copies held privately? Stolen, in other words?"

Slader stared at the lime wedge in his drink, shaking his head.

"It's the thirteenth copy," he said, raising his eyes as he clasped his hands on the small table. His gesture and the cryptic look on his face conveyed a curious blend of self-assurance and, what, gravity, anxiety. In my few but unforgettable encounters with Henry Slader I had never seen anything on his face other than arrogance in its many forms. On the other hand, in times past we had never discussed such a legendary rarity.

"Well," I muttered, taking a drink of my whiskey. "If so, it's an historic find, one of the first magnitude, front-page newspaper material, but—"

"True enough," he interjected. "The last copy discovered was sold at Sotheby's thirty years back, and the eleventh copy came to public light a little over thirty years before that, in 1954, if I'm not mistaken."

"All very correct and interesting," I said, quite sincerely. Then, just as sincerely, I told him, "I still don't want to have anything to do with it, or you."

Undaunted, his full confidence returning, he said, "With me, I understand. But unless you destroy it, which I doubt you'll want to do, or turn it in to the police, which I equally don't see you doing, as I'm positive it would raise more questions than you'd be able to answer, I don't think you have much choice."

"You're wrong," I countered, and signaled the server for another round.

"By the way, did your lovely wife tell you about her little visitation the other night? Your adopted daughter isn't the only one who saw a ghost. She's just the one who screamed."

"I'm sure I have no idea what you're talking about."

"After all these years of wedded bliss, I would have thought you didn't keep secrets from each other," he sneered, leaning forward. "Well, of course, there's always that *one*."

My patience with Slader was running thin. Yet I had to admit that, while I was sitting alone with *Tamerlane* most of the previous day, in the wake of its tumultuous entry into my life, an old forbidden passion had been reawakened. I'd reread the accompanying letter that was so exquisitely, if perfidiously, rendered in Poe's distinctive script, and felt grudging admiration. Like shoplifters and adulterers and drug addicts, forgers do experience a contact high that rivals religious rapture, though they often come to regret their fleeting, immoral gratification. While I loathed the rotten part of my heart that was drawn to forgery, it would be a falsehood to claim it wasn't alluring.

For one as emotionally tortured as Poe, his penmanship was, particularly after he had graduated from his teens, quite methodical and legible. His words were spaced evenly, his baseline was often as straight as the raven flies, his letters angled to the right with ascenders pointed like a row of robust cypress trees bent a bit by the wind. If, as Poe himself believed, handwriting is a window into one's soul—"that a strong analogy *does* generally exist between every man's chirography and character will be denied by none but the unreflecting," he wrote—then the author knew his mind, based on the surviving evidence, given how infrequently he struck out words. Yes, sometimes whole passages were excised by his drawing neat vertical lines, angled a bit like a tepee with no top. But Poe was no James Joyce, who crossed out and rewrote most every phrase he set to paper, then crossed out the rewrites too. Edgar's handwriting suggested to me that his ideas came to him in strong steady waves. And this remained true, although his hand did evolve and change from the earliest to the middle and late phases of his writing life. His signature varied as well during different eras, from self-consciously stylized to childlike; rounded to angular; sometimes elaborately underscored, other times naked of ornament. He was something of a chirographic chimera.

"I'll be sure to ask her," I said finally. "But don't give yourself too much credit. Chances are, whatever you're talking about, she forgot."

"Doubtful, very," Slader whispered, with a cocksure smirk that made him seem a bit of an idiot, even though I knew he was anything but.

At that moment, as I looked this man in the eye, I was reminded of Hanlon's razor, a philosophical notion that states one should never attribute to malice that which can be adequately explained by stupidity. It occurred to me just then that, conversely, one ought never attribute to stupidity that which can be explained by malice. But for the Poe at home in my fireproof safe, I would have terminated our tête-à-tête right there and then. As things stood, I made my decision, and framed it in questions.

"Where did you get it?"

"You sure you want to know? It might implicate you."

"And what do you want me to do with it?" ignoring his remark.

Our drinks arrived. I took an ample swallow.

Odd and confounding, Slader lazily stirred the ice in his glass of seltzer with his forefinger, and as he did I caught him staring at my right hand. My instinct was to remove it from the table and place it in my lap where he couldn't see the consequences of his malicious act but, feeling peevish, I left it in plain view. Let him see, I thought, what he had done. Too much time had passed in the wake of my two straightforward questions, but I added nothing further.

He broke the strange, momentary spell, asking a question of his own. "You remember our mutual friend, Atticus Moore?"

"What about him."

"You used to be one of his best suppliers of high spots"—as crème de la crème first editions were known in the trade, books that helped mold literary history—"even when you weren't foisting forgeries on him." Before I could counter with accusations of my own, Slader raised his hands, warding me off. "I know, I know. I sold him stock myself, some of it golden, some not so much. But long before you consigned him your father's collection and shipped off to Ireland, you had always provided him with great material. I even bought something now and again when I could afford to—"

"Where is all this going?"

Slader half grinned, half leered, and as he did I noticed one of his front lower teeth was chipped. Prison legacy, I hypothesized. I also noticed one of the men seated at the bar kept glancing over at us, clumsily trying to eavesdrop. Heavyset guy with ginger hair, roundish face, khaki short-sleeved shirt, and cargo pants, more observant of me and Slader than any of the other barflies. Without so much as a thought, I winked at the man and, startled, he looked away.

"The obvious reason," Slader continued, "that he was able to continue buying all those expensive books and manuscripts, not just from you but from others, was that he had buyers with serious means."

"I know he was the main source for several large institutional accounts," returning my full focus to our conversation.

"True, but did he ever discuss his private collectors with you? And, in particular, one named Fletcher?"

"No, I always figured that was none of my business," I said. "What's this Fletcher's first name?"

"It *was*—past tense, mind you—one of those Yankee blue-blood monikers where the given name might as well have been a surname. Garland."

"Garland Fletcher," I said. "Never heard of him, or Fletcher Garland, for that matter."

"Fletcher's widow, Abigail, like Fletcher himself, has roots in Massachusetts going back ten generations or more. Well-heeled types. Super private. And, like her late husband, she's devoted a lifetime to collecting—a bit haphazardly, according to Atticus—New England antiquities, furniture, paintings, all sorts of other period pieces, many of them passed down through the family."

"Including books."

"Including books."

"Including *Tamerlane*."

He touched his nose, bared that chipped tooth again, before proceeding to tell me, in plausible, even credible, detail, how Poe's first published effort came into the possession of a Fletcher relative back in early-to-mid-nineteenth-century Boston and had remained in the family for nearly two hundred years. Because the thing had never changed hands, never been donated to a library or sold at auction, never so much as been appraised by an insurance company, and since the Fletchers hadn't seen fit to let the world know of its existence, it never found its way onto any census of surviving copies. As black tulips went, this was the most midnight black of them all.

"So what you're saying is that the widow Fletcher has decided to announce its existence to the world, and Atticus is the one anointed to put it on the market on her behalf. Or, more likely, you've stolen it from the Fletchers. Or else Atticus has, and you're supposed to fence it somehow through me."

Slader leaned forward in his seat. "Am I wrong in re-membering you as a much cooler cucumber back when you were younger? This rush to conjecture isn't becom-ing in one seasoned in the, how should I put it, murkier side of the trade," he said, his tone as flat as the face of a lake undisturbed by so much as a breeze. "That said, Will, there are elements in each of your notions that aren't entirely incorrect."

Double negatives, always the sign of a prevaricator. And I didn't like him calling me by my name. I did, however, need to hear the man out. As disheartening as it was to acknowledge the fact, Slader was dangerous to me in ways no one but he and I knew.

"Abigail Fletcher has no intention of putting *Tamer-lane* on the market. Nor will it be missing from her col-lection for long."

Now I was fully confused, but wasn't going to give him the pleasure of hearing me admit it. I drank the last finger of Jameson and waited.

"Think of it as being borrowed during the course of an appraisal of her collection."

"Appraisal," I repeated, as the ploy became clearer.

"Yes, by a trusted expert in the field. At the moment, its morocco solander box is right where it belongs on Mrs. Fletcher's bookshelf. Just the pearl hidden inside the shell has been temporarily appropriated while the lady herself is vacationing with friends in the south of France. Somewhere near Avignon, I think," he said, taking a thoughtful sip from his glass.

"You're mad," I told him. "That's plain theft. I won't be involved."

Slader slumped back in his chair, exasperated. "You re-member that business a few years back when a contractor who was installing a sound system, or maybe security, in a private library figured nobody looked inside all those handsome slipcases, so who would ever miss the treasures they housed?"

"A small wave of perfect Faulkners and other delectables hitting the market all at once—of course I remember."

"That, my friend, was plain theft," he said, his mouth sinking into a frown. "A decent idea badly executed. We're not amateurs who think it's all right to steal part of a library and leave behind a bunch of empty boxes. We're far more judicious than that. More disciplined, more circumspect. All we're doing is taking one thin volume and basically putting the same thing back."

"I see. Like that 1493 Columbus letter to King Ferdinand and Queen Isabella that was switched out from the National Library of Catalonia, then sold for a million by a couple of Italian rare book dealers," I said. "That scheme worked fine until the authorities figured it out, negotiated the return of the original. They repatriated it earlier this summer, you may remember, in a fancy ceremony at the Spanish ambassador's residence."

"Much better idea, but still a bad execution," was Slader's bland response.

"Bad execution, why's that?"

"Because it was discovered is why. The best forgeries are never discovered. You and I know for a fact that we each have work out there in the world that will never be run to ground. That's my definition of good execution."

Once a forger, I thought. I couldn't argue with the gnarly logic of his statement.

"But forget Columbus, forget Faulkner. The Poe isn't even on a very long-term loan. Just long enough until an exact copy can be made to take its place and go back in the book dungeon that is the Fletcher library. Which is why time's tight."

"For you, maybe. Not for me."

"That's where you're wrong," he said, brusquely no-nonsense. "You are aware that while our charming criminal justice system puts statutes of limitations on many, even most, crimes, murder ain't one of them. Some of the stories I heard under lock and key were fascinating. Men who'd been sent up for three to five years for some lesser misdeed would never see the light of day again if the cops knew other, choicer things they'd done back when. Gateway crimes. Things like you yourself have done."

Already knowing where Slader was headed with his desperado anecdote, I said, while trying to hide both my disdain and fear, "That's all fascinating, but what does it have to do with Poe?"

"Well, as I'm sure you know, he *is* credited with writing the first detective story and knew his fair share about murder, and not just in the rue Morgue."

Again, nothing for me to do but wait. Ginger-head had returned to his baleful staring in our direction. He had the look of a loner, one who spent many hours in a basement mixing chemicals or practicing magic tricks. If he was indeed trying to eavesdrop on what we were discussing, the bar was too noisy. Though I couldn't help but be curious why he was so interested, I forced myself to ignore him in order to concentrate on Slader.

"I have irrefutable evidence of your guilt in the case of your brother-in-law's—"

"You're deluded."

Slader revealed that chipped tooth once more. If I were a violent man, I might have wanted to knock it, along with some of the rest of his teeth, down his throat.

"We both know certain, shall I say, unwholesome aspects about each other's lives, but there are details we obviously aren't aware of. You, for instance, have no idea that I'm a pretty decent outdoor photographer. Or used to be, years ago."

I shook my head and offered him a disparaging smile.

Ignoring me, he continued. "When I used to visit Adam Diehl back in the halcyon days, I got some beautiful shots of the lighthouse out on Montauk Point, a lot of shorebirds, dramatic skies and waves."

"This is all terribly charming, Slader, but speaking of points, what's yours?"

"One winter morning, sometime predawn, I was out walking along the beach with the early-bird joggers. The sky was a weird green-gray. I took some stills of the rollers, some of gulls against the clouds."

"Very Ansel Adams of you."

"I also happened to get quite a sharp photograph of you leaving Diehl's bungalow. And another of you getting into your car, a silver Volvo that looked like it was ready for the junkyard. I had a bad feeling when I saw you speed off. So I made like a zephyr myself and disappeared."

"Wish you'd stayed disappeared," I muttered, then added, offhand, "One could ask what you were doing there at that hour."

"One could decline to answer," he said.

I gave this a moment's reflection, then pressed forward. "If you've got this so-called evidence, why didn't you turn it and me in a long time ago?"

"Because I invest for the long term," he said without the slightest hesitation, quietly, his brow wrinkling as he tented his fingertips under his chin. "You see, you lost me my friend and business partner, and in so doing you deprived me of substantial future income. What gain is there in it for me if you're languishing in the joint, taking advantage of the prison library and communing with the chaplain?"

The image made me laugh. "Sounds relaxing," I said. "You must have enjoyed your time on the inside."

"Won't say I didn't. One learns a lot behind bars. For example, when you run afoul of agreed-upon terms, you pay a price. We had an agreement, you and I. You compensated me for my losses and we both moved on. Then you blew that deal by stealing from me again."

I cringed inwardly, knowing he wasn't wrong. Years ago, I had purchased from Atticus a breathtakingly skillful forgery of some Arthur Conan Doyle documents— letters and a manuscript fragment—that I later learned had been fabricated by Slader. Driven by absurd rivalry, I forged a superior duplicate of his inventive original, and then, more brazen yet, I turned around and sold my forged forgery back to Atticus, thus rendering Slader's "original" valueless. High-wire madness and, convincing as the documents were, not a single word had ever been so much as a figment of Doyle's fertile imagination.

"I gave you one more chance to make things good in your beloved Ireland—"

"You knew it was impossible for me to start printing fakes on my boss's press—"

"—and you blew it again. That time you paid the price in three and a half fingers. And as it turned out, fate made the better investment for me. I got some good years of practice in seclusion while you've had plenty of time to hone your skills as a printer. So now you're going to deliver your next installment."

"I owe you nothing, Slader."

At that he flared up. "You stole my life, my livelihood. This is all on you, my friend."

"Such righteous anger is unbecoming in a blackmailer."

"If this deal goes as it should, it can easily be the end of the matter," he said, calm again, smoothing the palm of his right hand over the crown of his head. "Once and for all."

"You can't be trusted, no matter what assurances you make. And you know it."

"Was that finally a confession I just heard? How refreshing," he said.

"It was a statement of fact."

"To be sure. So my proposal is simple, modest, straightforward, and poses no risk to you or your family."

"You sound like a cheap insurance salesman," I tried, knowing I was boxed into at least hearing him out. Memory, being at times a mercurial monster, came at me just then from an unwelcome angle, as I recalled how this man's threats in Kenmare had proved to be anything but empty. "I'm listening."

"Good man," he said. "So then, you may or may not know that the fellow who handprinted *Tamerlane*, Calvin Thomas, wasn't a very experienced printer. Far less experienced than you. Eighteen years old, just like Poe was. There's no record that he printed anything more demanding than apothecary-shop labels, leaflets, maybe some calling cards, and so on before he produced the Poe pamphlet. Lowly jobbing work. Which is probably how the poor young poet could afford his services in the first place, assuming Poe even paid, which he likely didn't, though nobody knows their arrangement for sure."

"Yes," I began, "but Thomas didn't have to replicate something that already existed. All he had to do was produce a passable—" before realizing, to my dismay, that I was being drawn, despite myself, into Slader's fantasy.

"Thanks to a fabricator I've known since long before I met you, I can provide paper from the period. Or paper that'll pass close inspection as contemporary to the period."

Despite myself, I sighed. "Wove paper, not laid, right? Also, that text stock didn't look handmade to me."

He brightened at my question. "Of course, machine-made and the correct weight, which I think is around three or four mils. Even the wire-mesh pattern is right, which isn't that visible to the naked eye. It's impressive and, as far as I'm concerned, even harder to replicate than the meatier papers of the sixteenth, seventeenth centuries with their chain and wire lines and inherent natural defects."

"Also, no watermark."

"What papermaker," he asked, "with an ounce of pride would bother to watermark such mediocre stock?"

How I hated to admit it to myself, but I felt a little intoxicated. Not from the Irish whiskey but from this dialogue tinged with the sacred, like Lazarus rising from the dead, as well as the profane, all but erotic in its forbiddenness and secrecy. Still, I crossed my arms and said, "There are other letterpress printers far more qualified for your job. Blackmail aside, I still don't understand why you want me to do this."

Slader's answer was calm and immediate. "Because we don't trust anybody else to know just how unlawful this is and still move on it."

"That's an insult."

"Better to take it as the compliment it's meant to be."

I knew this was a crossroads in my life. But wasn't certain which path, if either, was more wisely taken. "Were I to do this, and I emphasize *were*, I assume I'd be printing with plates made from high-quality photographic negs."

"You assume correctly. The display type and ornaments on the cover need to match the original, as do the age wear and staining. They have to be identical twins for everything to work."

"But then, if I'm following you, wouldn't the original have to be degraded or changed afterward, to make it distinct from the copy that's going back into Mrs. Fletcher's case?"

"It can't be helped." Slader nodded and continued speaking to me but with his eyes trained somewhere past my shoulder, maybe at an imperfection in the wall. "A sad but necessary business. All you need to worry about, first, is to make a credible doppelgänger."

Trying to conceal my horror at the idea of damaging, even slightly, an authentic first edition of *Tamerlane*, I said, "You know as well as I do how important condition is to rare book people. Vandalizing the original makes no sense. It'll bring the value down."

"Ah, that's where you're wrong. With a book this desirable, condition's a bit less important than with most firsts. Possibly the most famous, most distinctive copy out there has a sizable ring-shaped stain on its front cover. Some whiskey drinker like yourself must have used it as a coaster a long time ago."

"I know the one you're talking about," recognizing the copy he described as one in a private collection in New York. A blessedly brief image of my father rose to mind, my father who, if he'd been alive, would probably have been friends with that collector, even as he would have disowned me for sitting here with the likes of Slader.

"None of the surviving copies is anywhere near mint, so let's not make ourselves crazy. I might add, just for argument's sake, that even a little defaced, a little imperfect, this *Tamerlane* deserves to be out in the world where all can admire it, instead of being locked in a vault that reeks of out-of-date eaux de parfum."

"What noble sentiments," was all I could think to say in the face of such sublime audacity. "You expect me to believe you're suddenly an idealist? A liberator of incarcerated rare books?"

"Even so," he came back, with a slight nod. "Now, you asked me earlier why we need you to do this, and I gave you an answer that was maybe a bit snide," he said, an unwonted look of optimism on his face. "My apologies. The real reason is we need someone intimate with the business, someone motivated by fear of being compromised. And someone who can work with us when an undiscovered copy—in fact, the only extant *Tamerlane* signed by Poe—surfaces for authentication before it goes up to auction."

"It's not signed," I said.

"Not as yet, true."

"Well, you can't be accused of pulling punches."

"That means you accept the offer, I believe."

Unthinking, I swirled my glass and lifted it to my lips, then took a sip of whiskey-scented air before realizing I'd already finished my drink. Setting the tumbler back on the table, I asked, "Is there any benefit to me in all this, beside your guarantee of confidentiality in other matters?" and as I did so, I felt as helpless as one who, after slipping on a patch of black ice while walking down steep steps, finds himself mutely in midflight, arms and legs flailing, knowing a bad injury, even death, awaits him. "And guarantees about the safety of my wife and daughters."

Slader offered a galling sneer. "There are several mouths to feed here, but I think that might be possible." After laying out the rest of his proposition, which was more generous than I might have expected—though I hadn't come here looking to enter into any financial deal, quite the opposite—he said, "By the way, I have a question of my own."

"That being?"

"That being, who in their right mind would name a child Maisie? Doesn't seem fair, given how poorly she fared in that Henry James novel."

"*What Maisie Knew*, you mean?"

"Lot of hate in that book, you know."

I didn't respond, in part because I didn't think it was a question seriously posed, but also because I didn't know the answer. Instead, I took out my wallet to pay for the drinks. "You'll be in touch?"

"Tomorrow," he said. "When your wife and young Maisie are out of the house to go fetch your older daughter, who, I assume, will be assisting you with the printing as ever. If you planned on joining them, don't. You usually stay home when they pick her up anyway, so that shouldn't be a problem."

Floored by the frosty confidence with which he made these statements, as well as their accuracy, I sat back, wondering how long he had been spying on me and my family. I looked past Slader and saw that the ginger-headed man who'd been watching us had settled up and vanished. Another drinker now occupied his stool.

"You've gotten older, Will. Set in your ways, given to routine. I know more about you and yours than you might care to imagine. For instance, I'm sure you'd have preferred that Nicole skip that art reception she's attending tonight, unfortunately scheduled on a Friday, when she usually comes up. But if you look at it from her perspective, the Saturday morning trains are less crowded and tend to run on time. Preferable for her, I think, no?"

"Goodbye, Henry." And with that I rose.

"Till tomorrow," he said, looking straight ahead at where I'd been sitting.

I left the tavern, which had grown noisier while we were there, and emerged from its merry gloom into the late afternoon light of the bustling village. After climbing into my car, a worse-for-wear minivan we'd bought some years ago, where I had parked it in front of the inn, I sat there with my hands draped over the steering wheel, thinking, or trying to think, about what had just happened.

One of my guiltiest pleasures as a boy, embarrassing as it is to admit from the distant vantage of adulthood, had nothing to do with pornographic magazines, violent comics, anything of the kind. No, when my parents were out of the apartment and I was left to my own devices, I loved nothing better than to secretly pull down a first edition from my father's collection and, against the rules, read the book cover to cover. I was careful. Knew not to hold an eighteenth-century octavo in contemporary calf wide open, but rather at a prudent angle so its hinges wouldn't be strained. Knew my hands had to be clean and dry, not something puerile consumers of porn needed to worry about. So it was I read my way, over several weeks, through a 1749 first-edition set—six volumes bound in sprinkled calf, with engraved armorial bookplates on each pastedown—of Henry Fielding's *Tom Jones*, looking for, and not finding, the dirty parts.

Driving home from Rhinebeck, recollecting this youthful indiscretion, I realized that I intended that night to read the poems in Poe's *Tamerlane* in their original binding, just as juvenile Poe himself saw them in print for the first time. No matter how jejune the poetry, how compromised the copy might be, reading the priceless pamphlet from a bygone epoch was the only way to make my experience meaningful to me. Why? Because this was how I might best begin to familiarize myself with the overall look and feel of its unevenly inked pages, the featherlight heft of it in my hands. Also, it would constitute a first step toward acknowledging and owning that I was in the midst of falling again from grace. It was a fall I suppose I had always known was inevitable. As warm wind from the open car windows swept around my face, I felt at once melancholy and ecstatic.

When she was four years old, Nicole could draw a perfect straight line. Before she was six, she could draw flawless concentric circles, even harder to do. By the time she was ten, she was able, without any help from her father, over the course of a snowbound week during winter break from school, to produce an admirably detailed pen-and-ink drawing replicating one of Piranesi's etchings of Rome. Not faultless by any stretch. She was no Piranesi, as she was the first to avow, and had never set foot in Rome, but her reproduction was as respectable as any copyist much older and more experienced might produce. It hangs, framed, in the guest bedroom at the farmhouse. That she didn't sign it as her own creation showed how mature she was from the beginning.

Given Will's gifts as a calligrapher, and the bond he shared with Nicole as they sat together at the kitchen table while he gently helped her hone her skills, I wasn't surprised at how steadily our daughter progressed as an artist. And given my own passion for art, we were happy to pass dreamy long hours in museums where she could make friends, as she liked to put it, with O'Keefe and Cézanne, van Dyck and van Gogh, Degas and Léger. With every visit, her knowledge grew by the leaps and bounds of a Matisse dancer. When it came to budgeting her supplies—pens, nibs, inks, paper, canvases—we were the epitome of indulgent. Nothing made me happier than to see her hazel eyes light up when she opened a fresh sketch pad and box of oil crayons and sat down to draw.

Nicole never cared about most things other girls her age craved. By middle school, her daily outfits consisted of paint-stained sweatshirts, cuffed jeans, and heavy black boots. She wasn't antisocial as such, was always an excellent student, but as she reached her teens, going out on dates, hitting movies, attending rock concerts were lower among her priorities than drawing, painting, learning lithography. In retrospect, it should have come as no surprise that she would want to treat even her own skin as a canvas. After a prolonged phase of lobbying, Nicole convinced me and Will to let her mark her entry into young adulthood with a de rigueur tattoo, though neither of us was thrilled by this idea that had consumed her as flame consumes kindling. She chose a lovely if fierce kingfisher, her favorite bird and spirit animal, perched on a branch, its blue crest like a shock of electricity, its eyes majestic, its long beak trained ahead as it prepared to impale a fish, or anything else it fancied. Since the kingfisher was inked on her shoulder, it remained hidden most of the time. To this day, embarrassing as it is to confess, her fearsome totem sometimes takes me aback.

When she emerged from the Maple Leaf onto the open-air platform in Rhinecliff, her kingfisher caught my eye, as Nicole wore a camisole with a blue-jean shirt tied around her waist. Even down here by the Hudson, whose low waves lapped against the rocks that paralleled the track, it was muggy from the rains, hot from a strong morning sun that had been cloaked behind clouds for much of the month. Nicole smiled at me while Maisie skipped over to help with one of her bags, and I thought to myself, though I'd never mortify her by saying so, what a beautiful young woman she had become. Quirky, yes; a little idiosyncratic, sure; but stylish in her own way. Her dark auburn hair was cut unevenly across her forehead and above her shoulders, no doubt by herself. As ever, no makeup, though she didn't really need any. She'd left her trademark black leather boots in the city, exchanged today for a pair of cordovan clogs. An aficionado of silver rings, she wore several on each hand.

"How was the trip?" I asked, hugging her hello, and we fell in step together walking toward the badly rusted stairs that led from the platform to the station.

"Three bald eagles today," she answered. "Down past Bear Mountain."

"Not half bad," said Maisie.

"And how're you doing, Maze?" Nicole asked, shifting her pack from one shoulder to the other. Nodding at the bandages on Maisie's arm, she added, "How's the other guy look?"

That was Nicole. Mince no words, take no prisoners. It wouldn't have surprised me if she'd expressed concern about Maisie's scraped knees too, even though the girl was wearing long pants today. My younger glanced at me for guidance, and Nicole didn't fail to spot that either.

"We had an unwelcome visitor near the house the other night," I said, and as we drove away from the Hudson inland toward the farmhouse, I filled her in, leaving the *Tamerlane* out of my account, figuring Will would prefer to do that himself. Changing the subject, I asked how her art opening had gone the previous evening.

"The paintings were great, the crowd was middling, and the wine was pure poison," she answered. "A few art-school pals were there, so that was good." She paused for a beat. "What about this so-called visitor?"

"Your father'll tell you about it when we're home," I replied, noting her frown and knotted eyebrows. "He can explain better than I."

After meeting with Slader, Will had holed himself up in the studio. It seemed that he'd set other printing projects aside so he could devote his time to a close study of the Poe pamphlet, whose rarity, I now believed, was less a factor to marvel at than to worry about. When he'd returned from Rhinebeck, I inquired, as tranquilly as I could after seeing such a perplexed look on his face, "So, then, is everything straightened out between you? You're giving him back the book?"

"Yes," he muttered. "No."

We sat facing each other across the kitchen table, a wooden bowl of purple grapes between us. He stared at the fruit, pulled a couple off their stems with his left hand, jostled them in his cupped palm, not looking up.

Impatient, I prodded, "You mean yes, things are resolved? No more of him lurking around the house in the dark? No more attacking Maisie?"

He leveled his eyes at me. Maybe I was misreading, but it seemed there was a look akin to pleading in them. Pleading, and warning. Then he blinked several times and was fully present again.

"How was it"—he sidestepped the subject, clearing his throat—"that Mary decided to name her daughter Maisie?"

"What? I have no idea—no, wait, it was Mary's favorite aunt's name, or something along those lines. There was also a raft of B movies, starring Ann Sothern, about a girl named Maisie who went on adventures. Why ask that, of all things?"

"Just curious," he said, tossing the grapes into his mouth, chewing, and swallowing. "Slader was, to answer your question, more reasonable than anticipated. According to him, he hadn't any intention of frightening Maisie, and swears he never laid a finger on her. Be that as it may, he won't bother her again."

"Then why the mask? Why accost her in the dark?" I asked in frustration.

"That was meant for me more than Maisie, strange as it may sound."

"I don't understand any of this. You can trust him if you want, but I don't know why you would. What's he want? Why give you that Poe?"

While my husband explained, I sensed I was being given a redacted version of the story. Maybe even heavily redacted. Rather than press him, though, I reasoned that any deliberate omissions were probably for the girls' well-being, and mine. There were those who, especially in our early years together, frowned on my implicit trust in Will. Some of them had reason not to trust him, but I was not one of them. As best I could manage, I let the matter go. Nicole was joining us, after all, and not just for the weekend but through the following last week of August to Labor Day. Unlike the past, when having the whole family under one roof wasn't out of the ordinary, now that our elder worked during the summer between semesters at college, such a stretch of time together was a luxury not to be taken for granted.

After a stop at the grocery and another to pick up a bottle of wine, the girls and I headed homeward. All three of us were in an upbeat mood. Her sister's arrival had raised Maisie's spirits, and together they overruled my habitual radio soundtrack of classical music, tuning instead to indie rock. As we neared the farmhouse, they were singing some superbly inane lyrics. All of us were laughing, so it was the more jarring to see a car parked in front that I didn't recognize, an older-model Chevy, I think it was, powder blue. Leaning against it was a man I didn't recognize, arms crossed over a distended belly, wan sun gleaming on his reddish hair. I instinctually braked, pulled to the side of the road. Phlegmatic if scowling, he turned toward us for a moment, then faced the house again.

"What's the problem?" asked Nicole.

"Is that him again?" Maisie said, trying her best to sound unafraid.

I turned their music down. "Not sure."

"Unless I misunderstood, why would he give the package to Maze when it was too dark for anybody to see him, but now come back in broad daylight? Doesn't make sense," Nicole said, then delicately added, "Think you're being a bit paranoid, Mom? That could be a delivery guy, maybe ran out of gas, something the opposite of sinister."

Her point was well taken, but didn't stay tenable for long. As I placed my palm on the gearshift to put the car back into drive, another man emerged from the front door of our house, shutting it behind him—which seemed odd; why was this stranger letting himself out?—and made his way down the steps and across the yard. Slader. The only time I'd seen him up close had been in a night-dark bedroom. He'd held a tiny flashlight in his teeth and a cleaver in his hands, and he'd been trying to kill my husband in bed next to me. But I'd have known that silhouette anywhere, night or day.

Fighting shock, I glanced at the rearview mirror and saw Maisie frozen in the back seat, mouth agape. Forward again, and there was Slader walking toward the parked car, lean and lank, swathed in defiant black in the summer heat, hands in the large square pockets of a leather jacket, chin against chest, with a dark-blue baseball cap. Looking neither left nor right, he went straight up to the red-haired man and spoke forcefully to him, clearly annoyed. I couldn't hear their voices through our closed windows, only saw scolding hand and head movements before the redhead climbed into the driver's seat, Slader went around to the passenger side of the vehicle and got in, and they drove off in a hurry beneath the dense overhang of boughs that shaded the lane. Too late, I realized that I ought to have written down its license-plate number.

Had the girls not been with me, I might have been impetuous enough to follow the car. Instead, I pulled into the driveway, my thoughts turning to Will.

"I know you're going to think I'm still being paranoid, but I'd appreciate it if you stayed here with Maisie for a minute while I check inside."

Nicole obliged, though I'm sure she would have preferred to accompany me. Truth was, I wished she could.
A terrifying memory of that bloody, barbarous night in
Kenmare was surging through my mind as I got out of
the car. But I had to think of my younger daughter, who,
brave demeanor aside, was still recovering from her own
trauma.

On the front porch, I opened the unlocked door and
poked my head in before entering the hallway. Other
than the kitchen clock's hollow ticking, the house was
hushed, noiseless.

"Will?" I called out, deliberately trying to sound un-
worried as I strode the length of the worn antique Ka-
zakh runner that lined the hall and into the kitchen. No
sign whatsoever that my husband, or anyone else, had
been in here. My forehead pulsed and palms grew damp
as I continued to the back of the house and knocked on
the studio door, which was closed. "Will? You in there?"

"Meg?" he answered. The preposterous nightmare
image of him splayed out on the floor, soaked in his
own blood, vanished the instant I opened the door to
find him sitting at his worktable looking through a small
drift of delicate, vintage-seeming paper, and jotting notes
in his binder. "You all right? You look like you saw the
proverbial ghost."

Terror gave way to anger. "What was Slader doing
here? That was Slader just now, wasn't it?"

Will closed the notebook he'd been writing in and
slipped the sheaf of papers into a portfolio. "It was," he
said, as he came around the table to put his arm around
my waist and usher me out of the studio back toward
the kitchen.

"You lied to me."

"How's that?"

"You promised he wasn't going to bother us again."

Will paused, took me by the shoulders, and said, "He didn't bother us, or didn't intend to. He meant to be gone before you were back from the station. Where are the girls?"

I couldn't help myself. Forcing back tears, I said as sarcastically as I could, "They're out cowering in the car, because he didn't bother us again. Why on earth you would allow that criminal into our house, our refuge, our sanctuary here, is beyond me—"

"Meg—Meghan," as that uncomfortable look of pleading and admonition loomed on his face again. "You've got to trust me that everything will be all right."

"I'll trust you, but you still haven't told me what he was doing here."

"Truth is, we're grown men who made terrible mistakes when we were younger. Now we're trying to make amends. It's that simple and that complicated," adding, almost as an afterthought, "From here on, the less you know about things, the better."

"The less I know, the better? Will, that maniac mutilated you right in front of me, and I'm supposed to just not ask?"

"The girls are waiting, Meg. Let's not upset Maisie more or ruin Nicole's arrival. Please, just let me do this my way."

Pull it together, I scolded myself, but not before warning my husband that if I ever saw Henry Slader inside this house again, I would go straight back to the city, taking both our children with me. Rarely was I this assertive because rarely did he give me cause to be. After our homecoming from the upheavals of Ireland and Will's troubles with the law that were a small but real factor in sending us there in the first place, our lives had been, I confess, uncommonly settled, unruffled. Friends might even have viewed us as boring in our contentment. We seldom argued. We loved our girls. Savored our work with books. Slader promised to poison all that.

"What's the matter? Why are you crying?"

Startled, we turned to see Nicole at the entrance to the kitchen, Maisie behind her.

"Your mother's nervous about the man who just left," Will explained, going over to give Nicole a welcoming hug.

After me, no one was closer to Will than Nicole, but still she said, "Who can blame her, after what that freak did to you. Not to mention Maisie."

"I understand, and I agree," he told her, told all of us. "But he's gone, never to return. I think Maisie would be the first to insist she's all right, no?"—at which Maisie, though still pale, vigorously nodded. "As for me, I'm here, quite unmurdered."

"Good," said Nicole, unsettled but clearly sensing it wasn't the right moment to press him further. "Let's keep it that way."

"Shall do. Meantime, can we consider having lunch? I thawed some chicken broth after you left," he said, knowing full well that his attempt to pivot to another subject was as transparent as that very broth, if not more so. "Tortellini in *brodo*'s still one of your favorites, right, Nicky? I want to hear about your doings in the city, where life seems to be a bit slower than up-country these days."

Over the course of that afternoon, the rhythms of family routine settled in again, uneasily but surely.

Taking advantage of the sunshine, Maisie hunted around the yard for the still-missing Ripley before giving up her search to join me in the garden pulling weeds and picking tomatoes, kale, and pole beans. For their part, Nicole and Will went to the printing studio, where he showed her the rarest book she'd ever seen. He had assured me earlier, while the girls were out on the porch catching up with each other, that *Tamerlane* and its unsettling presence in our lives promised to be transient. He went so far as to say that though we could never reveal its being here, we might, as bibliophiles anyway, consider that sheltering it, however briefly, was an awkward honor.

On his first point, I was grateful. On the second, I demurred. Yet for all my striving to convince myself that things were going to be fine, that we weren't living through an incipient calamity, there was no way I could explain why a small framed snapshot of me and my brother, taken when we were youngsters frolicking on a Montauk beach, was missing from the chestnut sideboard where family photos were arrayed in tabletop frames. Surely, Henry Slader had removed the memento. Other than our family, nobody had been inside the house.

Why do that? How well had Adam, whom Slader had impersonated for the unhappy benefit of me and Maisie, really known him? My brother had never mentioned Slader to me in the months before his death, though they were clearly acquainted. What was the purpose of stealing something with no intrinsic value whatsoever for anyone other than me, in that it served as a photographic prompt of a fond, faded memory? A memory of a time that had never been, in all likelihood, as happy as I preferred to remember it. Certainly not as content as my life had been in recent years, with the notable exception of Mary Chandler's passing, and now this reappearance of Slader, which felt like a foreboding of death in and of itself.

True to his word, while Meg and Maisie were out of the house, Slader had delivered paper that matched the 1827 original with breathtaking fidelity. Wearing a pair of the disposable nitrile gloves I often used when mixing ink, I painstakingly candled each sheet against the daylight, both the virginal stock and several leaves of the original *Tamerlane*. The new was harmonious with the old, the fake visually indistinguishable from the prototype—although, of course, Slader's paper wouldn't by definition become "fake" until I printed Poe's words on it. I marveled at its hue, texture, and weight, and told him as much. Once more, for a brief, surreal moment, I felt a weird kinship with this man, who, I'd grudgingly come to accept, was my equal in the dark craft of forgery. While I might have been overwhelmed by mistrust and ire, not to mention envy, I had come to realize each of us was a survivor of the other, each had shattered the other's life in significant ways. We had been diabolically competitive back in our heyday, even before we'd ever met. Had cut one another out of lucrative deals and had forged that same illegitimate cache of Doyle letters about the genesis of *The Hound of the Baskervilles*, word for fictitious word, plus, for good measure, composed a passage of that famous novel that never made it into the book. We had each managed to cause the other to be brought in for questioning about Adam Diehl's unsolved murder. I had deprived him of his covert business partner, maybe his lover; he had deprived me of several fingers on my right hand. He had suffered prison time that I myself might have seen had I not been much better at avoiding such indignities. At the end of the day, I had to admit, he was no worse a transgressor than I was myself. Had we been collaborators instead of competitors, God knows what satanic masterpieces we might have produced.

When I glanced at him across the drafting table by the sunny window, he was oddly smiling at me. He had smirked and grinned before, but I couldn't remember ever witnessing Henry Slader smile. That smile brought me back, like a dropped stone, to my senses.

The plates for front and back covers, which we unwrapped next, would have to be proofed on the Vandercook, their registration meticulously matched with the original. At first blush, they looked almost too perfect, counterintuitive as that may sound. In this, as in any forgery worthy of running the gauntlet of high-minded, keen-eyed experts, perfection was less compelling than the stab of the real. Just the right amount of imperfection was key to fakery's rising toward the believable. I would have to remedy its antiseptic newness by aging the decorative border surround just a touch, degrading the type here and there to look more like the Fletcher copy.

"Solid quality," I said. "Who made these?"

He looked past me out the window to where several deer stood at the bottom of the field, browsing low-hanging branches laden with heavy leaves. "Unwise question, man. Not to forget, the less you know, the better off you and yours will be."

Masking my irritation with a veneer of deference, I removed the text plates from their kraft-paper wrapping. Plates like these are heavy for their bulk and easily damaged if dropped. Anyone observing me might have thought I was handling precious gems, given how cautious I was in transferring them from their packaging to the stainless-steel shelves beside the Vandercook.

"Do you have any idea how hard it will be to make a decent copy of this pamphlet? It's delicate as can be, so unevenly printed in the first place, so damned inconsistent. This level of amateur work is beyond hard to replicate—"

"Make it of its period, of its day, and we'll be golden. Where's the original, out of curiosity?" he asked.

"I don't think I'll tell you."

He chuckled, glancing sidelong in the direction of my fireproof safe. "Suit yourself. Just don't lose it."

No need for me to respond.

"There's one more thing."

I glanced at my watch. Unless Nicole's train was late, Meghan and Maisie would already have picked her up and the three of them would be shopping in Rhinebeck by now.

"Don't worry. I'll be out of here in a heartbeat," he said. "I have just one other item I wanted to leave with you. Like the *Tamerlane*, this needs a virtual twin," and with that Slader produced from his satchel a stiff card envelope from which he pulled a letter protected in a clear Mylar sleeve.

Taking the handwritten document, I scrutinized the time-faded signature at the bottom of the leaf, which read, *Yr. Obt. St. Edgar A Poe*, underscored with the same wavy flourish I had seen on other Poe letters. A flourish that Poe himself, in his *Chapter on Autography*, charmingly referred to as being "but part of the writer's general enthusiasm."

"Your obedient servant, Edgar Allan Poe," Slader needlessly translated.

To my amazement and dismay, I was persuaded by its seeming legitimacy. Poe's even word spacing; his letters, well formed if larger and less legible than in later years; his rectilinear baseline; the basic consistency of his cursive—it was all there. Even down to the *A* being slightly smaller than the *E* and *P*, an idiosyncrasy I had read about that one graphologist rightly or wrongly interpreted as a subconscious snub to his foster father, John Allan, with whom Poe had a strained relationship, at best.

"Who's this recipient?"

"As you'll see when you read it, he was apparently an editor at a Boston newspaper. Looks like Poe delivered the book to him hoping for a review, a brief mention, any crumb of acknowledgment," Slader said. He explained that only the *North American Review* and *United States Review and Literary Gazette*—both of which had offices on Washington Street, conveniently near Calvin Thomas's print shop—had bothered to note *Tamerlane*'s existence in 1827. The letter's addressee, Theodore Johnston, appeared to be just one more literary gatekeeper who refused to waste a single drop of ink on Poe's modest pamphlet. When, Slader went on, the August issue of *The Boston Lyceum* came out that year, it included some remarks by one Samuel Kettell, who wrote of "a young gentleman who lately made his debut as an author by publishing a small vol. of misc. Poems, which the critics have read without praising, and the ladies have praised without reading." Assuming it was Poe to whom Kettell referred, the "young gentleman" was both mocked and unnamed.

"Pretty put-down," I said. "But Kettell might have been insulting somebody else."

"True, but since he listed *Tamerlane* two years later in his volume *Specimens of American Poetry*, acknowledging Poe as its author, some scholars think that the earlier reference was to Edgar."

I shrugged. "Old news. Anyway, by 1829, I suppose it hardly mattered since the thing had sunk into total obscurity. So what you're saying is that this letter was mailed along with the *Tamerlane*?"

"Mailed or, more likely, hand-delivered. I'm thinking hand-delivered since both Thomas and Poe had little money, and back in the day it would've been an awkward size to post. Poe was in the army, stationed at Fort Independence in Boston Harbor, but he might have gotten leave to go into town, and could've delivered it then. Who knows? Since the envelope's lost, if there ever was one, it's anybody's guess, but it was folded and tucked inside the pamphlet."

"Why did you remove it?"

"Because that's what I did."

Obstinate bastard, I thought, and moved on. "Is there any other known example of the book with a letter?"

"Nary a one," said Slader. "As Abigail Fletcher tells it, though she's by no means certain, Johnston was a relative of a relative, a hoarder who never tossed things out—"

"Seems to run in their blood."

"—and whose accumulation of books for review, broadsides, pamphlets, letters, and the like stayed in an attic for decades until her grandfather, or great-grandfather, went through the rat's nest and tried to separate the wheat from the chaff."

"To mix a metaphor," I gibed. "How do I know you didn't forge this?"

Unamused, Slader jutted his chin. "You don't. No matter, I want you to make a copy, if you're still adept. But with variations in the wording of the cover letter— which I'll leave to you—and the name of a different critic in the header, one that's close to the original. The information is in here," and he handed me a slip of modern paper with the name typed on it.

"I'm as adept as you," I retorted, wondering if it was true. "Just, I'm not doing that anymore."

"Until now. And let us not forget the gifted Nicole."

"Out of the question."

"I've got to go," Slader said. "You'll find everything else you need's provided, some small leaves for the letter, half a dozen sheets of cover stock. That gives you plenty for makeready, and enough for one good cover. Give me back any sheets you don't use or that get misprinted or ruined in trial runs."

"I can discard the waste sheets myself."

He smiled at me again. "One can't be too careful now, can one? Meantime, as we both know, the cover's an especially important component since, given the book's fragility, many people, including Abbie Fletcher, won't tend to open it up past the first page or two."

Realizing more time had passed during this delivery than planned, I offered to show him to the door.

"Don't bother, I can let myself out. It's not like I don't know the way."

Meghan's earlier cliché about me being a moth drawn to flame crossed my mind, now replaced by the more piteous image of a moth drowning in printer's ink. Of course, I scolded myself. Of course he'd been lurking around inside the house when we weren't here. Scoping out my family, invading my private life. It wasn't like we had a security system. Besides, hadn't he managed to sidestep the one we'd installed at the cottage in Kenmare, when he broke in and attacked me? I wouldn't even put it past him to have had something to do with Ripley's disappearance. Sure, she was a wise old lady inured to the elements, but she rarely strayed far from her food bowl—and, for that matter, her food bowl itself had never strayed either. Compelled as I was to ask him how long he had been trespassing, I said instead, "Go right ahead," and as he turned to leave, I asked, "When do we meet next?"

"How long, on a fast track, will it take to finish and deliver?"

Gazing out the window as I made quick calculations about setup, first-pass proof, performing any necessary adjustments, second pass if needed, then final print run, folding, binding, I told him, "If all goes smoothly, by Thanksgiving."

"Sorry, that won't do. Let's make it a week from today," he said.

"Ridiculous. Ink needs to dry."

"Use a hair dryer. We've both done that with calligraphic inks, right?"

"Printing ink is more viscous. The heat can cause alligatoring, even bad crackling," I countered, noticing that the deer had disappeared into the woods below the house.

"I'll be at the Beekman Arms next Saturday afternoon at three," he said.

"Will your ugly ginger-head friend be there shadowing us again?"

"Cricket wasn't shadowing us," said Slader, without so much as a blink. "He was just enjoying a drink like everyone else."

"Cricket?" I rolled my eyes.

"He'll be there if it's useful to me for him to be there. Otherwise, he's already done the work that's necessary to our Poe book, so it may be time for him to disappear."

"He made these engravings? Or pulled the paper?"

Slader let out an exaggerated sigh, tapped on his wristwatch, and said, "One last thing. Now that your daughter will be here, I want her to deliver the goods."

"Absolutely not," I snapped. "She can't be involved."

"You and I should never be seen together again. She's the only one who can do it," he finished, and abruptly left the studio.

I called after him, "That's not going to happen," but he didn't respond. Even as I shouted a second time, I heard the front door close.

Like it or not, Slader had me trapped. Many times over the years I wished I hadn't been compelled to remove Adam Diehl from our lives—Slader, not Diehl, had been my true nemesis, though I hadn't known it then—but never had I regretted it more than now. Nicole make this contraband delivery? Even shadowed by her incognito father? Impossible. Meanwhile, any plans my wife had made to celebrate our daughter's arrival for the holiday would have to be postponed. Or at least curtailed. What was more, I'd be forced to explain to Nicole in as roundabout a way as possible what was going on here.

How I wished I could keep her out of it. But, painful as it was to confess, my ability to distinguish dark blues, grays, and blacks had been diminishing in recent years, and I couldn't confidently rely on my own color vision. I badly needed her help with mixing the exact shade of ink, an apprentice task she was used to doing. She'd nicknamed herself "blind Milton's daughter" as a way of alleviating any self-consciousness on my part when she was assisting me with coloration on far lesser, more innocent projects. Equally important, though very much a task she was not used to doing, I hoped she could assist me with aging the faux *Tamerlane* cover. To be sure, this wasn't why Meg and I'd supported her decision to go to art school, but I wasn't unaware that she might have picked up fresh insights to offer beyond my old-school methods. She had already studied techniques for staining and scumbling, as well as precision scratching to produce an aciculated surface—all the tricks in the book. Tricks, however, not designed to be applied *to* the book.

Nor did it help that Slader had nearly crossed paths with Meg and the girls, and that rather than starting this unholy project from a place of even the most tenuous calm, I'd been thrown into an even deeper inner chaos. When I assured them there was no reason to worry about Slader darkening our door again, and swore that all was well and I was quite unmurdered, I was grateful to hear Nicole respond, "Good. Let's keep it that way."

Early the following morning, having skipped breakfast, I fortified myself with strong black coffee and got down to work. My first step was to prep the press in order to run off test proofs on modern paper of a weight similar to Slader's—I needed to get a feel for the plates and the bite of their type. When I heard a knock on the studio door, I knew by its confident timbre it was Nicole. I invited her to come in and shut the door behind her.

Without so much as a *Beautiful day out*—it was—or *How did you sleep?*—not awfully well—she asked, "So what exactly are we doing?"

Ambivalent as I was about the way she phrased her question, and all the pitfalls it implied, I told her, "As I hinted yesterday when I showed you the *Tamerlane*, I've been commissioned to make a facsimile of it for a client."

"Client?" she mildly scoffed. "I thought this guy was your enemy."

"He was, is. But without getting into our whole tortured history, I owe him this favor. When it's finished, he and I'll be square."

As far as Nicole knew, her much-loved father had never failed to be straight with her. While her little sister's twilight run-in with this stranger, and her mother's manifest fear of the man, surely worried her, she didn't question my commitment to make as perfect a replica—the word *forgery* was expunged from my spoken lexicon—as possible. Not that Nicole was some ingenue. Far from it. I knew that, like a treed cat on a slippery limb, I would have to be careful not to make any false moves with her. How much easier my life had been before Slader reentered it. A week turnaround on this project was short, yes, but on the other hand, it couldn't be over with quickly enough.

"Let's get you squared then," Nicole said, slipping on an apron and standing close beside me at the press. Nor did it take long for my collaborator to weigh in. "That ink's all wrong, you know," holding up a trial sheet of the first signature of the book.

"Of that I'm aware."

"Let me look at the original again."

I had her put on a pair of the nitrile gloves—she thought in order to protect the slim volume; I knew it was to avoid fingerprints—and gave her the combination of the fireproof safe.

"That's new," she said. "Granting me access to your sanctum sanctorum? Feels like my sixteenth birthday all over again, when you gave me Sir Arthur's fountain pen."

"Nothing's in there I can't trust you with," I said, knowing that my earliest forgery, a purported 1897 missive from Doyle to his brother, Innes, confessing he had fallen in love, despite being married, with an impossibly desirable woman named Jean, was the only conceivable exception. Nicole and Maisie would one day inherit the more licit, truly authentic treasures in the safe, including (to name but an eclectic few) my first-edition set of *Lolita*, in which Nabokov had used colored pencils to draw two butterflies; my 1742 *A Journey to the World Under-Ground by Nicholas Klimius*, an imaginary voyage into the hollow Earth, which Mary Shelley read when writing *Frankenstein* and Roderick Usher kept in his own library; my rare *The Tale of Peter Rabbit*, privately issued in 1901 by Beatrix Potter herself after a succession of blind-minded publishers rejected her illustrated manuscript. Granting Nicole access to my rare-book repository somehow seemed a lesser extravagance now that the *Tamerlane* was housed there.

She carried it over to the window and, putting on the pair of tortoiseshell glasses she'd started wearing this past year, studied it page by page, quipping, "This Calvin Thomas was no Hans Mardersteig."

My daughter and I both believed Mardersteig was the best letterpress printer who ever lived—not just in the twentieth, but in any century. I even owned a handful of masterworks produced at his press, the Officina Bodoni, and I sometimes studied these for inspiration.

"His inking is light in places," Nicole continued, "pale, then too heavy, smudgy in fact, elsewhere. I'm going to make notes for each page, then break them out into which rectos and versos are inked differently for all the signatures."

Hearing this, I couldn't help being proud Nicole had learned to notice such details by working at my side. Even problematic solace was solace. As I test-printed plates, she mostly sat with *Tamerlane* by the window overlooking the long meadow, observing details that distinguished each of the forty pages in the book. Though she paused briefly to take a walk with Meg and Maisie, I myself spent the full day snarled in layout computations, plate adjustments, the algebra of counterfeiting. Sunday was gone in a trice with nothing usable printed, all prep.

The next morning, after apple and buckwheat griddle cakes from a recipe Maisie found in one of Meg's antique cookbooks, Nicole and I went through her detailed census of how certain pages were variously inked. The bottom third of several were so spotty they were a bit difficult to decipher, she said, then gave me a list of

worn or broken letters, like the one on page fourteen
that read,

> We walk'd together on the crown
> Of a high mountain, which look'd down
> Afar from its proud natural towers
> Of rock and forest, on the hills—

so that I'd make sure not to fill in that first imperfect
O in the second line to match the complete letter at
the beginning of the fourth. On the interior half title for
"Fugitive Pieces," the first three letters were so over-inked
that anyone giving the words a hasty glance might make
out the title as "Ficitive Pieces," a prophetic misreading
of sorts. Meantime, if Edgar's poetry was, as he himself
admitted in his preface, hobbled by "many faults," callow
Calvin's inexperience was more palpable yet. Nor did
his printing show any signs of the promising genius scat-
tered here and there in Poe's verse.

"Let's have a look at the binding and imposition," I
said. "Seems to be a simple three-hole pamphlet stitch,
if I'm not mistaken—as elementary as the printing."

"There's more than one signature, and they're side
sewn," she observed, squinting at where the thread was
visible beneath the wrapper.

"Without taking it apart, which we're not about to do,
I think it was printed in three signatures—no, four—and
maybe a half-leaf signature interleaved between the others. We'll need to sort that out and replicate this deckling
on the same fore edges as the original here."

Nicole nodded and added to her notes.

By late Monday, having run off three partial copies
on different proof papers, I was ready to get down to

the nitty-gritty of mixing, and aging, the ink. I had never shared my process with Nicole, even though we had spent years doing calligraphy and copying together, skills at which she all but equaled me by the time she was a few years older than Maisie. Not wanting my daughter, who could have worked miracles in the art of fakery, to be tempted to travel the road down which her father had gone—though look at her now, I marveled with shame—I hadn't let her in on my youthful experiments with oxidizing ink with ammonia, or else adding gum arabic to my mixing pot, then further adding sodium hydroxide, one fussy drop at a time, with a pipette. Granted, these were old-fashioned techniques. Back-in-the-day ruses. Not unlike tricks I'd read about in accounts of the Hofmann forgeries trial in Salt Lake in the 1980s, where it was proved that iron gallotannate ink works marvelously well when used to forge documents on antique paper. Indeed, paper from the very period in which *Tamerlane* was printed.

I explained all this to Nicole, who soaked it in like one of those flat Japanese origami toys that, when dropped into a dish of water, explode into three-dimensional swans or steamships or swimmers. As a student at Cooper Union, she'd already had plenty of exposure to the way dyes, paints, and inks were prepared throughout the history of Western art. And her internships for the past couple of summers as an artist's assistant had taught her plenty about the relative merits of sturgeon versus rabbit-skin glue, for instance, or—more to the point—manganese black versus iron oxide black versus bone black. She'd regaled us with such arcana over many a dinner after work in the city, and once again she took her turn at sharing her newly gained expertise with me.

"People don't realize how many different kinds of black there are," she said.

"You know, Poe himself called it the 'no-color.'"

"That's one way of looking at it, black being the absence of all color."

"He was referring to purity and impurity, as I recall, good and evil."

"Interesting idea, but it doesn't get the ink mixed." Together we laughed, then she went on, "I just mean in the spectrum, every other color is contained in black. For me, it's the richest, most dynamic color of all. In terms of wavelength, black takes them all in, doesn't let any of them go."

"How greedy of it," I joked.

Arching one eyebrow, she agreed, "Well, it does feed on other colors. That's why there are different blacks—it all depends on their appetite. Like flamingos."

"Flamingos?" My turn to arch an eyebrow.

"You know, how their feathers are pink because of all the shrimp they eat—"

"Sturgeon and rabbits and shrimp, oh my."

Scowling at my feeble humor, she said, "As for *Tamerlane*, all we have to do is nail just the right black."

That was my daughter. It still surprised me that, through all the inevitable adolescent tantrums, all the wing stretching as she fledged into her own brilliant colors and tested adult flight, we remained closely bonded over what we both loved.

And so we pressed forward. The more Nicole and I shared information, the more we labored side by side that week, the less this task felt like the wrongful act it was. It morphed, rather, into a rewardingly difficult father-daughter assignment, and at moments I almost forgot what we were in fact doing—but, alas, never entirely.

I wasn't sure how much thought Nicole had given to our printing project, but at night, in bed with Meghan, I knew her mother was quietly seething about the matter.

"Why are you doing this?" she asked me around midnight, midweek, just as I was about to turn off my bedside lamp.

"Doing what?" was my lame dodge.

"It's bad enough that you're making this fake—"

"Meg. It's a facsimile."

"—but to willfully drag Nicole into it?"

How I wished I'd extinguished the light and pretended to snore before she began with her questions. "Nicole's not being dragged into anything. She always helps me."

"Helps you with legitimate book projects, with Stone Circle. Not this."

"Since when is making a facsimile illegitimate?"

Ignoring me, she said, "You should just tell Slader the jig's up. You have to stop. If you owe him money, we can figure out how to pay him."

"I don't owe the man a penny—"

"Whatever it is you owe, nothing's worth your back-sliding and, yes, dragging Nicole along in the bargain."

"I can't argue with you," I said, after a moment during which my conscience gnawed at me, then reluctantly offered to ask Nicole not to continue in the morning. "It has to be her call, though," I finished, uncertain whether I would follow through with this pacifying offer. The cold truth of it? Nicole was far more dexterous than her father, and I was all too aware that folding, trimming, and sewing the pages, as well as adhering the cover, lay ahead of us—me. Besides, the girl was nobody's fool. She knew that the difference between a top-flight facsimile and a forgery was a game of but a few negligible degrees, rather like the difference between cold water and hard ice.

Awakened not by screams or by worries about Will but by a chorus of birdcalls out the window and sunlight streaming into the bedroom, I experienced my first taste of serenity since that night last week when Maisie was assaulted and our lives were infected by Poe's juvenilia. Glancing at the bedside clock, I saw I'd slept in. A bowl of granola had been set out for me downstairs, along with fresh-cut fruit and a pitcher of milk. A half-finished pot of hazelnut coffee sat on the stove, ready to be reheated. After lighting the gas burner, I switched on the radio, as I did by rote every morning. Bach's *Well-Tempered Clavier* further brightened my mood. It seemed a safe risk to feel at peace.

While the coffee warmed, I walked partway down the hall toward the printing studio but, seeing its door was shut, decided to leave my husband and daughter to their dialogue about *Tamerlane*, to let Nicole find her own way to making the right decision and bowing out. Back in the kitchen, I went to the fridge for juice and saw Maisie's handwritten note moored beneath a magnet shaped like a hen wearing a polka-dot kerchief.

Morning, Meg, it read, *Rode the Bomber over to hang out with the twins. Back after lunch. xoMazey. PS. Will be careful so don't worry!*

Easier asked for than done. Still, we had agreed at a family meeting, with Nicole serving as informal negotiator, that Maisie would be allowed to go to town alone—"It's barely a village," Nicole pointed out—but only during daylight hours, even though Will had installed new batteries in her headlamp. Given Slader had already revealed himself, it seemed unlikely he would threaten her again. Further, because he had convinced—or else coerced—Will to print the *Tamerlane*, it wouldn't have been in his best interest to do so. I poured milk on my cereal, sat at the table. Nothing, I told myself, was going to spoil the feeling of tranquility that settled over me this morning, like a vessel becalmed, its sails slackened, after days and nights of rough waters. Mawkish as it seemed, I felt Bach's clavier underscored my thoughts.

Naïveté is its own undoing. I knew as much. Just, it felt good to forget for a brief half hour. My enveloping serenity was erased in a heartbeat when I heard a knock at the front door. Not loud, not insistent or threatening. Tentative, which was somehow all the more unnerving.

On the porch, as I feared, stood Henry Slader. I pulled open the door and demanded, "What the hell are you doing here?"

"I won't be long," he said, staring past me into the house.

"Have you done something to Maisie? Is she all right?"

Confusion swept across his face. "How should I know? I haven't seen her. That's not why I've come."

"I'll get my husband."

"No, that's not why, either."

"What is it then?" I felt at once furious and terrified. "You're not welcome here."

Ignoring my self-evident remark, he gave me a paper bag with cord handles, stating, "This is yours." I looked inside and saw it was the missing framed photograph of me and Adam on the beach.

"Why do you have this?" Though I'd suspected him of the theft myself, my shock was so deep, I spoke the words almost before I realized I'd formulated the question.

"I took it without thinking when I was with your husband last Saturday," Slader replied. "I thought it'd make me happy to have it, but it doesn't."

"I'm glad to have it back, but I don't understand. What—did you know my brother?"

Slader tilted his head, like an inquisitive dog, albeit a shorn albino one, and gave me a look tinged by an unsettling combination of frustration, glumness, and hostility. "Your husband knows the answer to that question. You should ask him sometime."

"I will," I said, floored by this odd encounter.

"Meanwhile," he went on, regaining his composure as impudent self-assuredness spread across his narrow, bleached face, "you need to understand it's in everybody's best interest that you don't interfere with the work he is doing right now."

Across the yard, parked at the side of the road, was the same pale-blue Chevy that I'd seen when my girls and I had returned from the Rhinecliff train station. This time, no one was waiting for him by the car.

"Has he said how it's coming along?" he asked.

"No, and I don't want to know."

"Suits me," Slader said. "Just, as I say, don't get in his way. I'm tying up loose ends, and don't need you or anybody else impeding my progress."

Was that a threat? Sarcastic, while again realizing just how much this man confused and frightened me, I told him, "Thanks for returning what you stole. If you ever come here again, I'll call the police," and shut the door in his face. After bolting it, I leaned my back against its cool oak, as if that would somehow keep him at bay. Unable to quell my curiosity, I hurried into the living room and peeked from behind the curtain in time to witness Slader climb into the car and, unlike before, get behind the wheel and drive off by himself.

Maisie, I thought. I needed to go to her friends' house at once and, making excuses, pick her up. Placing the photograph back where it belonged with the others, I went to the kitchen and grabbed my wallet and car keys. I scribbled a note, *Back shortly*, left it on the table, turned off the burner, and rushed out.

Her closest friends were Celia and Janine Bancroft, twin sisters her own age. So it was toward the Bancrofts' house I drove. As I passed the stretch of road where I believed Maisie had been ambushed by Slader, I slowed, wondering which thicket of bushes he'd been hiding in. Also, despite myself, I couldn't help but ponder what on earth his connection was to Adam. How bizarre for Slader—who else could it have been?—to have impersonated my brother with that photo mask I found in the woods. Weird too that he filched the picture of Adam and me, and weirder yet that he returned it in person. It would have been much easier for him just to throw it out, knowing no one would be the wiser. Had he apologized? It happened so unexpectedly, I wasn't sure one way or the other.

One thing I did know, as the woods gave way to a few houses on either side of the lane and I made several turns that would take me to town, was that I intended to ask Will what he knew about Slader's relationship with my brother. My deep well of grief over Adam's unsolved murder had been tapped again. When Will was finished with this vexing, this galling project of his, I would ask if he knew more than he'd let on about that bloody night in Montauk. Well-trod terrain, but maybe there was some small detail he'd remember that might open the cold case again. All these years I'd believed that Henry Slader had gotten away with murder, persuading myself that the prison time he served for assaulting Will doubled as bad-karma punishment for what I believed he'd done to Adam. Now I began to wonder.

Bikes littered many of the yards in the sparsely populated hamlet. A field-hockey goal with torn netting and no players in sight stood, a bit forlornly, in one yard across from a small church whose steeple was sorely in need of reshingling. An overturned russet wheelbarrow and Adirondack chairs with peeling yellow and orange paint occupied another. Here was a skinny teenager in jeans and sleeveless T-shirt bent under his open car hood; there, an elderly woman on a shaded porch, dozing in her wheelchair. And everywhere, the kaleidoscopic greens and flower-laden beds of deep August. Somehow, this interplay between games and work, youth and senescence, left me feeling more restless than when I'd left the farmhouse. I shook my head, concentrated on my driving.

To my relief, Maisie's old-fashioned Black Bomber stood upright on its kickstand in the Bancrofts' driveway. Finding myself reluctant to put my worries on exhibit in front of her friends, I drove down the mile-plus curve of road to its dead end, then parked next to what appeared to be the foundation of an unbuilt house. Nettles, blooming loosestrife, and an extended family of weeds were its only inhabitants now, together with a clan of fieldmice, or voles, rustling in the concrete fissures. Cutting off the engine, I got out of my car, walked over to an old guardrail that had been placed at the terminus of the road, and sat down on it to think. Behind me somewhere in the woods I could hear a stream trickling. Overhead, a family of finches peeped without a seeming care. No houses were in sight, though it was clear that when the developer paved this road some years ago, there had been every intention of lots being surveyed on either side, and homes built. While bucolic all the same and calming in its solitude, this shaded spot struck me as a place whose promise was unfulfilled, a place the past had somehow let down.

I shook my head and studied my hands clenched in my lap. Ease it up, Meg, I chided myself. Life's a sine wave, and you're nowhere near the bottom of the trench. Nicole's a healthy, luminous, smart young woman. Maisie's a brave and tenacious survivor, safe with her friends. And whatever Will is doing, it's something he has to see through for reasons of his own. He's been a paragon as a husband and father these many years. Nothing really is all that dire, surely, and the chances were good that I was projecting my own disquietude on these abandoned acres of cul-de-sac woodland. Noticing an empty gin bottle and discarded beer cans in the underbrush, I realized this must be a high schoolers' partying site, a moonlight parking spot for lovers. So at least it was a locus of some sort of happiness, however secretive or fleeting.

A soft crunching roused me from my reverie. Not footsteps but the unbroken, smooth, rolling sound of tires over pebbles on pavement. When I snapped my head up, my eyes refocused from the folded hands in my lap to a car a couple hundred feet up the road from where I was parked. Its engine cut, it glided quietly to a halt. Sun and shadows on the windshield made it impossible for me to see who was in the car, and though I had only seen Slader's—or whoever's—Chevy from the rear, its pale-blue color was identical.

Unthinking, I gulped in air, got up from my corroded perch, and weighed whether to climb over the guardrail and run into the woods toward the stream or wait where I was, stand my ground. I patted my jeans pocket and, reassured that the key was there, considered striding the dozen paces over to my car, turning it around, and driving toward, then hopefully past, him, or them. If I bolted, I could be chased. If I tried escaping in the car, I could be blocked. Just when I needed to be clearheaded, my thoughts became a thicket of panicky, worthless non sequiturs. Caught in a paralysis of fear, I stood and stared down the road.

Movement, then. The door on the passenger side of the car opened. But rather than Slader or anybody else stepping out to return my gaze or confront me in some way, I saw a bulky shape, brown like burlap, fall from the opened door onto the macadam road, where it lay motionless. Now I took several steps forward, trying better to make out what was going on. For about the time it takes an orchestra to tune, nothing further happened as I gaped at this uninterpretable tableau. Overhead, the family of finches, which had fallen silent, began to chitter away again. Up much higher, circling like weightless black rags in the rich blue of the sky, several crows squawked.

The car door was unhurriedly pulled shut from inside. I squinted hard but couldn't make out who was in the driver's seat. Time passed; no one moved. Certain the driver could see me, his rapt and helpless audience, I began to wonder if the whole performance might not have been for my benefit. Panic thinks its own thoughts. Had Slader somehow followed me after our brief encounter on my porch, only to dump what appeared to be a body on the road, a body that surely must have already been in the car when he returned the photo of Adam? Logically, I knew that the form lying on the ground was far too bulky to be my daughter. If not Maisie, then who?

Before I could puzzle my way further toward any explanation, the Chevy's engine started. With dream-like fluidity, it began backing up slowly, so slowly it felt like an arrant taunt, never stopping to turn around, and soon enough receded from where I stood aghast. The license plate that should have been visible above the front bumper was either missing or had been obscured. Again, how I wished I'd been astute enough to have taken down the number when this same car, which now disappeared around the long tree-choked curve, was parked in front of our house.

The creek burbled, indifferent. A breeze meandered through the uppermost branches of black cherry and ash trees, indifferent. My breathing was shallow and fast. I badly wanted none of this to be happening.

Rather than run down the road to check on whatever it was that had been shoved from the mysterious car, I climbed into the relative safety of my own and, hands quaking, managed to start the engine. When it came to life, its mechanical hum and the sudden accompaniment of incongruous harpsichord music on the radio helped snap me out of my liminal fog. I turned the vehicle around and drove at a crawl, scanning up ahead in case the Chevy driver decided to return, hoping my imagination had skewed something innocent toward the sinister, until I was alongside the heap on the side of the road.

It was a wasted hope. The body, for it was a body, lay crumpled on its side, facing away from me. An adult, a male in a dun suit. As I weighed whether to step out and look more closely, it occurred to me that no one I knew had this man's anemic copper-colored hair, curly to the point of being wiry. He was broad shouldered, somewhat heavyset. The skin of his ankles—he wore run-of-the-mill brown walking shoes but no socks— was purplish white. His torso didn't rise and fall, which meant he wasn't drugged or semiconscious. One of his livid hands was raised, clawlike and rigid, inches above the pebbly ground. Remembering now the man Slader had argued with when the girls and I'd returned from Rhinecliff, I wondered if he wasn't the same. Was this what Slader had meant by tying up loose ends? I stared for a long minute, paralyzed myself but, unlike the body, breathing. A fly, in stops and starts, traversed the rim of his blue left ear.

That was it for me. That was enough.

Even then I knew I wouldn't be pleased, an hour from now, a day, maybe forever, by my decision to leave this man where he'd been unceremoniously ditched but, shifting my eyes from his corpse, I glared ahead and, deaf to any wiser angels, drove away.

Queasy and faint, I told myself I had to get to a phone immediately—in my haste, I hadn't brought my cell—to report what I had just seen. But I pressed on, knowing that if I pointed my finger at Slader, he wouldn't hesitate for a moment to implicate Will and rain fiery hell on my whole family. The sporadic front yards I'd passed earlier were even less populated now than they had been. Both the teenage auto mechanic and the nodding grandmother had moved along, which was good. No eyes meant no eyewitnesses. Maisie's bike was gone as well, also a relief since it meant I didn't have to encounter her here, and chances were she had already headed home. So far as I knew, not one soul had noticed me drive through this rural neighborhood, and by way of excusing my absence from the house, I visited a bakery in Red Hook, where I bought a fresh carrot cake, Nicole's favorite and my own. Inevitably, on my way home I found myself being followed by a police cruiser for half a mile before it turned onto another road. Should I have called an ambulance? No point, I convinced myself. Judging by the color of his flesh and rigidity of his limbs, the man had been dead for some time before being abandoned. There was nothing for it. I breathed in and out.

To my relief, no powder-blue car was parked anywhere near the farmhouse. Will and Nicole were still back in the studio working as I entered the kitchen, removed my note, and threw it away. When Maisie came flying down the stairs two at a time, my queasiness returned. Was she about to confront me? Had she somehow seen me or even Slader drive by the Bancroft house?

"Maisie, there you are," I said, numbly smiling.

"Meghan, there you are," she teased. "Oh, look what you brought home. What, no raisins?"

"They only had plain today." I felt my pulse beginning to slow again, now that I was back in this familiar world of daughters, cookbooks, apples and oranges in a yellowware bowl on the granite counter—the ordinary, everyday, mundane things we surround ourselves with in the hope they'll somehow protect us from different, harsher worlds. "What's doing with the Bancroft twins?"

Picking up one of the apples and taking a healthy bite, she said, "They're going out on the water this Saturday with their dad, sailing down to Pollepel Island to see the ruins of Bannerman Castle. And I'm invited. OK for me to go?"

I nodded, told her yes, so long as the weather held and she promised to wear a life jacket as always. Life jacket, I thought. How immoral, how illicit of me was it to realize, just then, that the poor fellow with the wiry hair who lay lifeless on the side of that deserted road seemed, for a brief moment, to be so far away as not to exist at all?

Ripley had been missing for a full week by the time Nicole and I began printing finished sheets of our *Tamerlane* on the Vandercook press. My daughters had ventured with me out beyond the tall grass surrounding the house, well past the verge of woods, absurdly calling her name and making various tongue clicks and kissing sounds to catch her attention. Being half feral and very much not a dog, she didn't respond. While I couldn't shake the nagging suspicion that Slader's abrupt entrance into our lives and Ripley's equally abrupt exit weren't coincidental, I was damned if I'd give him the satisfaction of accusing him. I remembered all too well how he'd mistreated a poor hound back when he was bedeviling me in Ireland. Besides, maybe Ripley had, as strays sometimes do, just moved along to freeload elsewhere. Or perhaps she'd fallen prey to a coyote. Still, I found myself glancing out the windows, hoping to catch sight of her as she skulked in the green, altogether aware that Saturday was only a few days away and other, more urgent matters needed my undivided, undistracted attention.

Despite my promise to Meg, I hadn't found the courage to come clean with my unsuspecting daughter. Hours passed as Nicole and I, like surgeons hovering over a patient, checked and rechecked plate placement and ink distribution on the rollers, and held our breath as blank sheets of chaste paper rode the cylinder and emerged with Edgar Allan Poe's poetry impressed, with perfect imperfections, on their surfaces. It was as if we were superintending a time machine, ink-smudged demigods—the idea made us smile, me guiltily, she with delight—fashioning not something new from old, but old from new.

Now and again, I had Nicole retrieve the fragile original for side-by-side comparisons of this or that page. Immodest or not, we both thought the likeness to the Fletcher copy was very strong, though we had to wonder if any two of the dozen, or rather baker's dozen, copies were identical matches to their siblings. I strongly doubted it. But to find out would take a small corps of amenable rare-book librarians to bring their individual copies of *Tamerlane*, along with the two privately owned ones, to an agreed-upon bibliographic bunker where they could be set side by side and painstakingly compared. Imagine the logistics of such a scene, imagine the scholarly jockeying. Imagine the insurance costs and white-gloved guards. Like a convocation of the forty-three surviving Fabergé eggs, if nowhere near as visually alluring, nor as astronomically pricey. Point was, any differences between our *Tamerlane* and the one Calvin Thomas published in

June or July not quite two hundred years ago were, to my mind, of little consequence. One could not fully cast the other in doubt, I believed. And unless our copy was scrutinized in the bowels of a cyclotron, which would probably never happen once it was tucked safely back into the obscurity of Mrs. Fletcher's solander case, I felt certain it could withstand close examination.

Nicole had mixed a perfect iron gall ink. Slader had provided impeccable plates and paper. The print job went swiftly without a hitch—I'd long since learned how to work the press with one of my hands maimed—once we had everything readied. And though we used all the available cover stock in order to get one that was more than respectable, that piece of the puzzle had fallen into place as well. Time had come to bind our book.

"We can guesstimate the binding thread," I told Nicole.

"It's not visible to the naked eye anyway," she agreed, running her silver-ringed fingers through her choppy pageboy hair. "Just have to go with the right weight and a natural off-white color. Line up the three stab holes and sew it with this stitch I found online from the period. Shouldn't be an issue. I'll handle that myself like we do with other books."

"Our Achilles' heel here is the paste," I ventured.

Nicole disagreed, and as she explained that recipes for glues and pastes had hardly changed in centuries, I was once again reminded that, notwithstanding my every effort to steer my gifted daughter clear of the precincts of forgery, she possessed more of the counterfeiter's mental and physical tools than perhaps even I did. Fortunately, she seemed not to have developed the dark and essential frailty that all forgers share

Hubris. All these years I thought I'd finally shaken it, as one shakes a nasty flu. But it had been a revelation to me, working on this Poe project—look, even that white-collar terminology has about it the tangy scent of hubris—how deeply embedded it was in me, how there was no shaking such an alluring demon. Yes, alluring. Because the hubris I refer to is imbued with a kind of dark joy, a joy that comes from the admittedly amoral satisfaction of hornswoggling so-called experts, of beating the system. But amoral or not, I had been doing my best to hide my bleak yet real happiness while laboring beside my daughter, all the while hoping she would read my passion as having to do only with being together, teaching and learning, working at our craft in a good cause.

We would have *Tamerlane* ready to deliver on schedule. The letter was another matter. While I felt dirty after my every encounter with Henry Slader, this was a rare instance when I wished I knew how to contact him so we could talk about not just the letter but his intention to present the only known signed copy of Poe's first book to the literary world. It was, I'd come to believe, hubris taken one step farther. Indeed, over the precipice. Credulity abounds, especially among the greedy. But it must be stretched with care, not bent so much that it risks being broken. While a heretofore unknown autographed copy would generate a lot of excitement, it would also beg for skepticism, especially in a book this desirable. Poe himself hadn't allowed his name to be printed on the cover, instead choosing coyly to assign authorship to an anonymous Bostonian.

While Boston was indeed his birthplace, why had Edgar done this? I had come to learn that conjectures were plentiful. Creditors from unpaid gambling debts needed to be dodged, as did Poe's foster father, who was furious with him for the gambling losses he'd racked up before leaving the University of Virginia. Even joining the army was, for Poe, a cloaked affair. Lying about his age and name, he enlisted as twenty-two-year-old Edgar A. Perry a month or two before *Tamerlane* was published. Nor is it certain the printer Thomas ever knew the poet's real name. Poe's twofold desire to remain anonymous while at the same time seeing *Tamerlane* enjoy critical and public acclaim, or at least notice, was problematic, to say the least. No, the unsullied *Tamerlane* was sufficient for our cause. Were it up to me, I'd revel in the discovery and leave it at that.

Being charged with forging a letter and faking a signature was preferable to being charged with a far graver offense, however. Feeling every bit a character out of one of Poe's tales of ratiocination—I was missing only a meerschaum and tapers that might throw "the ghastliest and feeblest of rays"—I slipped out of bed around midnight on Thursday and crept downstairs to the studio. Door locked behind me, I retrieved my box of nibs and pens from a high shelf and began scribing, on modern paper, trial runs of the master's hand.

A forger's calligraphy has much to do with confidence, which encourages the proper flow necessary to mimic the original, and muscle memory, which gives the practiced forger the ineffable ability to inhabit, if you will, what's going down on the page. Consider an amateur pianist, who must think about notes, scales, time signatures, and fingering. The handful of true players, by contrast, have so mastered these mechanical aspects that they *become* the very music they play. All that's left is to imbue it with life and soul, to expound upon the

composer's intentions while bringing one's own story-
telling genius to the keyboard. This is why Meg loved
the *Goldberg Variations* when played by Glenn Gould
or Murray Perahia, but didn't care for performances by
other renowned pianists. The notes were the same but
the accounts differed. Similarly, with literary forgeries,
the shapes of letters, impress of nib, tint of ink, were
essential building blocks. But wizardly forgers, the rare
virtuosos among our small community of misfits dead
and alive, had to inhabit the writer at hand so fully that
they truly, for magical minutes, *became* the author.

My muscle memory was intact, it seemed. While Poe
had not been my forte in the past—Henry James, Arthur Conan Doyle, W. B. Yeats had that questionable
distinction—I'd studied his handwriting carefully and
even launched inscribed copies of *The Narrative of Arthur
Gordon Pym of Nantucket* and *Tales of the Grotesque and
Arabesque* into an unsuspecting, quite welcoming world,
where collectors snatched them up. I even had the audacity to autograph the *Pym* in both Edgar's and fictional
Arthur's hands—Poe purportedly forging the latter on a
lark—which should have been a tip-off but wasn't. The
book is out there somewhere even now, treasured by its
proud owner, who may or may not know that, with the
exception of a single authentic one the author inscribed
to a mysterious Mary Kirk Petrie, there are no recorded
copies of *Pym* actually signed by Poe, Pym, or, for that
matter, Roderick Usher. Cheek and whimsy I didn't lack
in my prime.

Confidence, now, was another matter. It had been
twenty long years since I'd penned anything in the hand
of somebody other than myself. When I swore off producing forgeries, I'd made a pact not only with Meghan

but with myself. I was alone in knowing just how much
I managed to get away with during my active years, and,
like any disciplined gambler, I was wise enough to leave
the table at the top of my game, cash in my chips, and
turn my back on the business altogether. Tonight, in order
to save my hide, I was forced, as it were, to put my skin
back in the game. While admittedly I had enjoyed the
printing aspect of the job, as I sat at my drafting board,
with my gooseneck lamp trained on its surface, I felt
nothing akin to the joyful self-assurance I used to feel
when holding an illicit pen—assurance I badly needed
to write this short missive in the master's early hand.

The house was quiet as a sepulchre, as Dickens put
it, though it might as well have been Poe. My window
was cracked open to let in the rich nocturnal air. Every
so often, an unseen creature or errant wind rustled,
sounds that would normally arouse curiosity but which
this night merely chafed my already frayed nerves. Time
passed—how much, I didn't know since I kept no clock
in the studio—as I shifted on my stool, assaying again
and again certain lines of text that I found problematic.

"—. . . *I will wait anxiously for your notice of the book
in the hope it pleases*—" I found difficult, for instance,
to reproduce in part because of the lovely complexity
of Poe's *pl* ligature. His *p* initiates simply enough on a
gently curving upstroke, followed unbroken by a longer
stroke below the baseline and back up to the apex, yet
not tracing the exact route of the downward line. Then,
without pausing at the looping stroke that doesn't quite
connect with the stem, a slightly thickened cuplike curve
moves off to the right and slants upward to form part of
the *l*, which is completed by another downstroke that
resembles a kind of needle's eye. What took young Poe

less than a wink of time to dash off, thinking only about what he was writing, not how, took me three dozen attempts to replicate even half convincingly.

Anxious and discouraged, I noticed my hands and forearms had become clammy, which didn't help matters. I laid down my pen, walked over to the back door, and descended a few stone steps to stand barefoot under the stars and cool off while massaging a cramp in my thumb. The night sky, Poe's "sable divinity," was cloudless. The Milky Way was a brilliant frosty brushstroke across its dome. In times past, I would have felt soothed by Ripley's gentle rubbing against my calves as she purred. But I was, I thought, very much alone. When I rubbed my palms against my sweatpants, took several deep breaths, and turned to go back inside, I was startled to see Nicole standing in the doorway.

"What're you up to, burning the midnight oil?" she asked in a low voice, stepping aside as I entered.

"Are the others awake?" I asked her.

"No, I don't think so. I couldn't sleep. Thought I saw light on the grass downstairs coming from the studio windows, so I came down to investigate."

I walked over to my stool, sat, and scrutinized my most recent effort.

"You didn't answer my question."

In her words, I could hear her mother. While I'd always felt close to Nicole and knew we had a bond solid as steel, I needed to remember she was also Meghan's daughter. Not to mention, I might add, her own person.

"There's one last part of the Poe project I need to finish," I admitted, trying and failing to fathom some way of getting around telling her the whole dirty truth. "He wants a letter to be replicated to go with the facsimile."

She pursed her lips, blew out a small, scoffing burst of air. "No big deal, right? That ought to be a cakewalk for you."

"I appreciate the vote of confidence, but Poe's not the easiest to render. More to the point, I don't seem to be on my game tonight."

Joining me at the drafting table with a sympathetic frown, Nicole removed her tortoiseshell glasses from their perch on top of her head, put them on. "What's supposed to be copied?"

To confess that my heart sank on hearing her request would be to oversimplify my reaction. I had taught my daughter the venerable art of calligraphy from her earliest days, and by the time she was nine or so, she was already trying her hand at Gothic, Chancery, and Humanist script, as well as more modern styles such as those used by the great William Morris, father of the British Arts and Crafts movement, who, I told her, revered calligraphy as an expression of the humanity of the craftsman and truth of his materials.

"You mean, humanity of the craftswoman and truth of her materials," she amended.

She had learned from the beginning how to cut reed and quill pens, developed her nib vocabulary to include terms like *shoulder* and *shank*, which had nothing to do with cuts of meat. Around the age of ten, she graduated to copying the handwriting of famous authors and statesmen, scientists and movie stars, and could also make damn good knockoffs of old *Garfield* and *Peanuts* comic strips. Did I make a point of telling her that we did these copies for practice, and never for the purpose of hoaxing or deceiving anybody into thinking they were genuine?

Emphatically, I did. And did Meghan underscore that decree even more often than I? A foregone conclusion.

All this being said, I secretly basked in her gifts, marveled at the subtleties of her prowess, and was somberly relieved when in her teens she turned more to plastic arts, to painting and printmaking. Not that forgers don't lurk in the shadows of those disciplines too—indeed, for every faker of literary artifacts there must be ten score fine art forgers. A hundred score. But I always believed Nicole would not follow this path.

Now, the rueful, pitiful fact was, I needed her help. Whereas Poe seemed to have been right-handed, I was a lefty. This would never have impeded my ability to make a persuasive forgery in times past, as I'd developed a surgically precise method of replicating the writing of all manner of authors, including such famous lefties as Lewis Carroll and H. G. Wells, along with your basic Western canon of righties, without smudging the wet ink with the side of my trailing hand. My practice attempts tonight were botched by smearing. Much as I hated to admit it, I no longer believed myself up to the task. At the same time, though I cringed inwardly at breaking my promise to Meg, I also needed to conceal from my daughter what the purpose of the letter truly was. My mind darted in every direction, trying to formulate a valid excuse to involve her, even as I showed her the original Poe letter and quietly pointed out what were, to my mind, the gnarlier issues that had to be surmounted. Any relief I felt that Nicole could make this forgery—like it or not, the word was back in my private lexicon now—while remaining blind to its meaning was matched by dismal guilt as I watched her practice her strokes and produce first drafts that were, I thought, frankly better than mine.

Still circling around the point, I told her that in his later years Poe sometimes copied his own wording in business letters. Once, in 1842, when he was trying to sell "The Mystery of Marie Rogêt," he pitched it to magazine editors in Boston and Baltimore at the same time— although at different prices—and a paragraph in each of his cover letters was almost verbatim. Both Joseph Snodgrass at *The Visiter* and G. Roberts at *The Notion* rejected the story. William Snowden at *The Ladies' Companion* in New York finally agreed to run it, and while the cover letter Poe presumably sent is lost, who knows but that it wasn't identical to the others?

Nicole said, "Good on Poe. Why reinvent the wheel?"

"Why indeed? But we ourselves are going to need to alter just a few things once we're ready to move to Slader's period paper." I pointed at the name of the recipient of Poe's *Tamerlane* cover letter and said, "This Theodore Johnston needs to be changed to another name. Date will be different by a day or two. Contents should stay essentially the same, but we'll alter a couple of words here or there with others that have a correct period feel."

"And Poe feel?" she added, without missing a beat. Startled by her tone, I glanced up from the letter. I couldn't remember a time when Nicole had given me such a strange, concerned look. In this low light, her unblinking eyes appeared quizzical. Not a countenance I was used to or relished. Even her tattooed kingfisher seemed to be fixing its inky eye on me.

Softly, simply, she asked, "Why?"

Her question might have devastated me, but I hadn't the right to be devastated. My daughter was no naïf, and I wondered if she'd already seen through my week of ruses anyway.

Just as softly and simply, I replied, making it up as I went, "Because the man who commissioned it—"

"Henry Slader."

"Actually, another long-ago acquaintance in the trade, Atticus Moore—Slader's his courier—wanted it to be as exact as possible. But to avoid any chance that it might in fact be mistaken as a forgery of the original, he asked that details be altered to something similar but different enough that there'd be no confusion. Thomas Johnson is the name he proposed. I haven't bothered researching it and imagine it's entirely fictitious. This way the facsimiles of both the *Tamerlane* and its accompanying letter could be used for educational purposes."

"What about these originals then? What happens to them?"

I persuaded myself that Nicole was curious, not accusatory.

"If I understood correctly, I gather the owner up in Boston may be considering putting them up for auction," I said. "Though they seem to cherish their anonymity, so I'm not sure how their identity will be protected. Possibly subterfuge."

"It'll be auctioned through your house?"

Knowing Nicole had a keen capacity for sussing out truth from lies—a trait genetically passed down from the barrister grandfather she'd never met?—I honestly told her I hoped so, even as I hoped I wasn't blushing in the wake of my other half-truths. "It would be a high-water mark in any auction season, so of course I'd love for us to handle it."

"But surely you wouldn't want this Slader to have any involvement, right?"

"As I say, Atticus's anonymous client is the owner, and he is acting as representative. He's a member of every distinguished antiquarian book association there is."

"That may be, but he doesn't seem to have good taste in couriers, if you ask me."

I chuckled. "I didn't ask, but you're not wrong."

"Well," she concluded, looking back toward the drafting board and antique paper that had an almost imperceptibly gray-green cast to it in the lamplight, "how many tries do I get to do this right?"

"We have three matching sheets," I said, grateful to get back to the work at hand. Seeing the resolve on her face as she removed all of the silver rings from her fingers and set them aside, I asked, "So you're up for this?"

She was, and then some, as it happened. Her second attempt proved to be the best of the three, although any of her drafts would have passed muster in the eyes of most antiquarians. As I had already done with proof passes, rejected pages, and other discards from the print job, I shredded the two lesser Poe letters and placed the keeper, along with the original, in the safe next to the *Tamerlanes*—one the first, one the faux. Slader had demanded I give him back any foul matter, my discarded pages, but I didn't trust him any more than he trusted me. No, they were better off burned to curlicues of blackened ash in the fireplace out back, then stirred with a stick into oblivion. By destroying the documents myself, I was assured they would never resurface.

After thanking Nicole for lending an accomplished hand, I said, "Maybe we ought to try to get a little more shut-eye before the sun comes up?"

Together we turned off the studio lights.

"You realize, I hope," she said, "that you could have done a better job at it than I did."

I disagreed. "Either way, I don't think we should let Slader in on our switch. If he doesn't like the letter, I'll take the fall, whatever that might mean."

"Let him do it himself," said Nicole, and we silently left the studio and went back upstairs to our rooms.

Meg shifted a little when I slipped into bed, muttered a few incomprehensible words in her sleep before turning over. I don't know if Nicole managed to fall back asleep, but her father certainly did not, for hours on end. Friday would be spent painstakingly aging both the forged *Tamerlane* and its ersatz accompanying letter that Edgar Allan Poe had never written to any Thomas Johnson, fictitious or otherwise. My thoughts about the best ways to accomplish this churned away, until I finally dozed off just as the soft white disk of sun was climbing through the treetops outside.

The problem was this. The man on the road did exist. Just because he was dead did not mean he didn't exist. Just because I didn't know him did not mean he didn't exist. My yearning to shunt him off to the edge of my consciousness, to suppress if not possibly even forget him altogether, had held for a day or so, but couldn't hold longer. I was witness to a crime. Or the aftermath of a crime. By going out of my way not to report it, had I become an accessory to murder?

Since my family was slow to get up, I busied myself with breakfast—baked fresh bread from aging spotted bananas, resurrection metaphor there?—and reasoned whoever had driven his victim to that desolate lane and dumped the body onto the road must surely have seen me, or at least my car, not two hundred feet ahead. But what if they hadn't? What if they'd been blind to anything beyond the wretched act they were performing on an otherwise postcard-lovely summer day? Or, all right, what if they noticed me but weren't in the least alarmed by the presence of a lone woman, one who stood frozen with confusion and fear, just far enough away to be unable to change the course of what transpired? Was it possible I wasn't viewed as sufficiently important to bother with one way or the other?

Will finally recognized the change in me at dinner last evening, but fortunately—or maybe unfortunately— he'd been so wrapped up in his own problems with that damnable Poe job that all he said was, "You seem miles away."

The girls had gone out to the garage to adjust the chain tension on Maisie's bike, spend a little sister time together, while Will and I finished with dishes.

I smiled, or rather winced, and shook my head. "Nothing of the kind."

"Maybe I'm projecting," he added. "Wouldn't put it past me."

In a single fleet moment, I decided to tell him what I'd witnessed, then backed away from the idea. Part of me didn't want to hear his advice about how I should or shouldn't proceed. Another part reminded me that I had no proof that Slader was behind the wheel, and to make such a claim was to allege, in so many words, that my husband was working with a murderer. Maybe even a two-time killer. Even worse was my confusion about Slader's filthy intimation that Will knew about his relationship with my brother and had hidden it from me. I hardly needed to remind myself that the man was a provocateur and disrupter and, what's more, a liar.

"What I want," I vented, though not raising my voice, "is for you to finish what you're doing and get Henry Slader out of our lives."

"Believe me, Meg, this is not how I'd hoped to spend our last full week of summer with the girls," he said, setting down a dish he'd been drying before placing both his palms on the stone counter, head lowered, leaning forward like a reluctant marathoner stretching his muscles. "Saturday afternoon he'll have what he needs, and that should be the end of him coming around."

"Yes, it should. But I'm beginning to wonder if there will ever be an end of Slader in our lives."

Yet now, this morning, as I stood at the same kitchen counter, it occurred to me that going to the police and reporting what I'd seen might be a better way to rid us of this forger and stalker. I could say I was too traumatized to report it earlier. Could set things straight so I didn't have to spend another minute with this bleak, grimy cloud hovering over my head. It might even provide a path for me to tell them about Slader's theft of my photograph of Adam, which in turn could open my brother's murder case to fresh scrutiny.

Reality set in, however, when I imagined the questions they were bound to ask me. Questions like, What were you doing on that dead-end street? Did you recognize the deceased man? If not, then how is it you recognized the powder-blue Chevy? Its driver, you say, is a friend of your husband? Not a friend, you say? What is his relationship with your husband? May we ask where your husband is right now? You say he's meeting with the man you saw in the powder-blue car, tomorrow afternoon at the Beekman Arms? What time did you say they're scheduled to get together? And if, as you claim, this man your husband's meeting with stole your family photograph and returned it to you undamaged, what charges do you think could be pressed against him after the fact? While we're at it, why haven't you reported any of this before?

I felt as pinned as a butterfly on a black velvet mounting board, in a display case with one-way glass where I could be seen but couldn't see out. Maisie's sudden appearance in the kitchen saved me from these swarming questions.

"Smells good in here," she said. "Can I help?"

"Would you mind cutting up some melon?" I asked, forcing myself to turn away from my morbid thoughts and pay attention to the present.

After breakfast, Will and Nicole returned to the studio, while Maisie came along with me on an errand for the bookstore. A couple of weeks earlier, our shop had purchased the library of a collector we'd done business with over the years, who had passed away after a brief illness. He was a widower with no next of kin, and the attorney charged with settling his estate found an unpaid invoice of ours among his papers and called the shop, asking if the volume might be returned. He further asked if we would be interested in making an offer on the rest of the library, which, of course, we were.

So Will had joined me—this was before Henry Slader reentered our lives—and one of my senior staff, who'd taken the train up for the day, to go through the collection and tally up what we thought would be a fair price. Buying libraries is one of the bread-and-butter ways booksellers replenish their inventories, and while several other dealers were also invited to bid on the whole lot, ours proved to be the best offer. The sole caveat was that the winning bidder had to remove not just the obviously valuable volumes, but every last scrap of printed matter in the house.

"Toss out whatever you don't want to sell, or give it away," the attorney said. "I hope you make a profit on the rest. But it all has to go so we can clear out the house for sale." We agreed and set about making arrangements to pick everything up before the end of August.

The collection was a bit of a hodgepodge. As often happened when we bought a library under similar circumstances, where an executor or attorney was trying to expedite the dispersal of property so an estate could be closed, this one was a combination of musty magazines and out-of-date catalogs, cheek by jowl with some genuinely desirable first editions.

On the drive over, I filled Maisie in about all this, telling her we were meeting with two of my colleagues she liked, Cal and Eliot, who had driven up from the city in a van and would be taking the bulk of the library back down with them. "This collector kept his books all over the house," I said.

"Even the bathrooms?"

"Do you and Nicky have a stack of books in your bathroom?"

"Even in the bathrooms," she said, answering her own question.

"The guys are going to pack everything that's not in the library, which is where I'll need your help. I need to sift through the better items there so we can take them back to the house for some preliminary pricing before we head to the city," I said. "Some of the books are pretty old and fragile, so I'll need for you to give me a hand boxing them as carefully as possible."

Today's work was just the kind of "bibliophilic triaging"—Will's tag for sifting the gems from regular stock and recyclables—that my husband loved to help with, and I was sorry this Poe business precluded his coming along. He possessed a sixth sense about which books might have an authorial inscription inside, and was a walking encyclopedia of "issue points," the typos and other arcane details that made the difference between a copy being the true first edition or a later printing. He also knew more about relative rarities than anyone else I'd ever met. Whereas many a book person might prefer, say, a pristine first edition of Jack London's *The Call of the Wild* in its handsome pictorial dust jacket from 1903, it was the far less famous *The Sea-Wolf*, published the following year, which—if it was in its legendarily rare dust jacket—would launch Will into an ecstasy. Even torn, even chipped, even in pieces. Pure ecstasy.

No slouch myself, I welcomed the distraction of being in my favorite milieu—rooms filled with books—with Maisie at my side. The library was in an old Carpenter's Gothic near the river, just north of Tivoli. When we pulled into the drive, my colleagues were already waiting in their van. They were quite a pair—one a short, prematurely balding lapsed academic, the other a skinny urban book geek who looked every bit the heavy-metal devotee he was. Both greeted me with friendly deference even as they showered Maisie, who was adored by the bookshop staff, with greetings.

"So, Maisie, what's the good news?"

"Having fun up here watching the grass grow?"

We were greeted by a friendly border collie, followed by the collector's neighbor, a ponytailed woman in her sixties whose dress and manner suggested to me that she'd been something of a wild child in her youth. Batik tunic of reds and browns cinched at her waist. Moccasins on her feet, bangles on her wrists. Nicole would have loved to sketch her.

The attorney overseeing the estate was running behind, she informed me, and had asked her to let us into the house so we could begin packing. The books remained on their shelves, just as they had been when I'd visited this place a couple of weeks before. I asked the others to get started with boxing the lesser volumes of paperbacks, Modern Library books, runs of periodicals, and the like, while I concentrated on the library room, where the collector had kept his best material. Given that he had bought a number of books from us over the years, some of the volumes I pulled down were like old friends. His interests had run the gamut, but he'd been particularly keen on nineteenth-century American literature as well as mostly modern science fiction. I went through his collection, now and again handing Maisie a book by Nathaniel Hawthorne or Philip K. Dick, which she wrapped in heavy tissue and stacked in boxes we'd brought with us. The neighbor woman, meanwhile, carried on a mostly one-sided conversation to fill the silence. Doing my best to focus on what was at hand, I exchanged pleasantries with her about the strange weather.

"Your neighbor was quite an intriguing collector," I said, in passing. "His two areas of interest are an unusual pairing."

She told me about how he loved haunting book barns and out-of-the-way small bookshops all over New

England, then continued with a lament about mortality and how much she was going to miss him. "At least he died peacefully. Pity he outlived the rest of his family," she said. Admittedly, I was only half listening, but when she mused, "Did you hear about that awful murder over near Taghkanic, or was it Ancram?" I glanced sidelong at her where she was staring out the window.

"I hadn't," I said, briefly frozen with a large book in my hand.

Don't ask anything, I told myself. Let her spin her yarn and see what she weaves with it. Meantime, I handed Maisie the quarto of Dante's *Purgatorio* illustrated by Gustave Doré, which seemed afield in this library—unless the owner considered Dante a science-fiction writer, not an entirely absurd notion.

"They're still trying to identify the body. Found him partly eaten by dogs or coyotes, they said on the radio."

"How awful," I managed, catching my breath.

"You all right, Meg—Mom?" Maisie asked. The second time I'd heard that question in recent days. Nor did I miss that she had referred to me as her mom in public.

"I'm fine," I lied. "It's just that I had a similar worry when you were late coming home the other night and I thought I heard a coyote."

"Oh, my," the woman said to Maisie, wide-eyed. "Were you attacked by coyotes?"

Sensing possible jeopardy, my daughter glanced at me, Dante still in hand, and said, "No. They just come around our house sometimes."

The woman returned her gaze to the clouds outside, saying, "It's our own fault. We keep intruding on their habitat, what do we expect?"

Fortunately, the lawyer arrived soon after and scuttled any further exchanges about killings and coyotes. He presented me with a letter of agreement stipulating that the sale was final and everything was sold "as is," which I signed after making out a check in the amount agreed upon.

When Maisie and I left—my colleagues stayed on to finish with their own packing, which was going smoothly—we took half a dozen boxes of books with us. At home, we carried the cartons inside and set them down in the study. I wanted to confer with Will about an inscribed H. G. Wells, *The Invisible Man*—just what my husband had become these past days—complete with a hand-drawn caricature, which I sensed might be the diamond of the lot. The collector's one flaw was that he hadn't been "condition-conscious," as we say in the trade, but the Wells was an exception, a gorgeous copy, and Will would see that at once. Anything, I figured, to bring him back into our blessedly, bookishly, unassuming routine.

"Have you had enough of your mom for one day, or would you like to come pick some vegetables for dinner?"

"I'm good to help," Maisie said, and we took down baskets hanging from the kitchen rafter and set off toward the chicken-wire-fenced garden, a short distance from the house. The sun was still strong though the afternoon was waning. Maisie picked peas while I gathered Swiss chard. I looked back uphill toward the printing studio and saw Nicole standing by the window, oblivious to me and her sister, holding a sheet of paper up to the light. Will stood behind her, peering at what was written or printed on it, and together they seemed to be engaged

in discussing some detail. On any other day, with any
other printing project, the vision of them there side by
side would have stirred a deep contentment in me. But
not today, not this project. My thoughts began to darken
anew, as I realized that no one in my family had been
untouched by this recent upheaval—Maisie maltreated,
Will coerced, Nicole impelled, myself conflicted—when
I heard a familiar cry.

Neither the yelp of a dangerous beast nor some
pampered pretty kitty meowing for a bowl of cream.
Instead, the feral mewl of a cat who seemed to have in-
vented her own quirky way of vocalizing—somewhere
between a squeak and a snarl—given she spent so little
time, as far as we could tell, in the company of others
of her kind.

"Where is she?" Maisie exclaimed, dropping her
basket.

"Ripley?" I called out.

Sure enough, there she was, lolling at the garden gate,
insouciant as the day she had adopted us. Maisie lifted
her up and got scratched for the effort.

"She's back," she said, with the broadest smile I'd
seen on her face in days. "Where have you been, you
bad thing?"

I picked up Maisie's basket and we climbed back to
the house. The news of truant Ripley's return would
bring a smile to my husband's face too. Little or nothing would make me happier, I thought, briefly allowing
myself to believe that the weight of these last perverse
and wayward days might soon lift, much like the pewter
skies that had reigned over most of the summer. Then I
remembered the man on the road. While there was nothing I could have done to save his life—he had already lost

it—I might well have somehow prevented the indignity of his body's being mutilated. I may not have known him. But I'd owed him that simple consideration, and horror had overwhelmed my humanity. How I would live with myself, going forward, was impossible to fathom. Yet there was no going back.

Early Saturday morning was overcast. Whether pearl or ash or some other shade of gray, I'd have to ask Nicole. Either way, overcast seemed fitting for the task I faced. So I thought as I poured my coffee before retreating to the studio to have one close final inspection of my handiwork. My and my daughter's, I should say.

Sometime in the moonless night I had come to the firm resolve to deny Slader one of his primary demands. While his point was well taken that some differentiating damage was needed to make the new Fletcher copy distinct from the original, and that a couple of trivial fabricated flaws in the true thirteenth *Tamerlane*—a couple of closed tears, some soiling that wasn't there before—couldn't depress either its intrinsic or auction value in any catastrophic way, I'd become adamant about not forging Poe's autograph in the pamphlet. No matter how good the forgery, how seductive it would be to potential buyers—just fancy possessing the only known signed copy—I was convinced it would raise suspicion. Suspicion that wouldn't enhance its stature and worth, and might even ruin both. Why take the risk when this correct, incontestable copy was already such a rare bird in hand? It had also dawned on me that while my reputation at the auction house was golden, or at least gold-plated, and my past as a confessed forger was all but forgotten, I was the last person to be entrusted with the authentication of a unique signed *Tamerlane*. Surely, it would doom the whole scheme.

As I set out down the hallway to the printing studio, I heard a knock at the front door. The rest of the household was still in bed, so I reversed course back through the kitchen and down the front foyer, wondering who the devil would come around so early on a weekend morning. I hoped it wasn't some local with bad news about Ripley, especially now that she'd just resurfaced. While our road was seldom traveled, she had no fear of traffic and there was no training her to stick to the relative safety of the fields and woods.

I opened the door to find two men on the porch, each plainclothes but displaying a badge. Stomach churning, though I knew that I hadn't broken any laws—it would be my word against his if Slader claimed I was knowingly harboring stolen property—I bade them good morning and asked what was up. Since they weren't smiling, neither did I.

"I'm Detective Moran," said the older of the two, casually dressed in jeans and a worn burgundy hoodie, unshaven, and hardened around the eyes. A man unused to sleep. "And this is Detective Bellinger. Sorry to bother you at this hour."

"No problem. You like to come in?" I asked.

"That's all right, thanks. We were just wondering if that car over there is yours," pointing at our silver minivan, really the color of a dirty quarter, sitting in the driveway.

"Yes, that's ours," I said, and stepped out onto the porch where I set down my cup on a wicker table by the door. "Is something wrong?"

Moran said, "Probably not, but I wonder if you or anyone in your household drove it two days ago near"—and went on to describe a neighboring village I recognized as being where two of Maisie's friends lived.

"I was here working, so I know I didn't," immediately regretting my having offered them an excuse they hadn't asked for. Why sound guilty when I wasn't?

"Any other individuals in your house possibly?"

"I don't think so," I said, realizing I'd hardly been out of the house since I began work on the *Tamerlane*, and had been pretty inattentive to my family's doings. What also came to mind, as I shifted my weight from one foot to the other, was Slader's passing comment in the Beekman Arms about how surprised the authorities would be if they only knew the unsolved crimes of those they'd imprisoned for lesser misdeeds. Be calm, I warned myself. You're a free man, under no scrutiny. Still, it astonished me to think that if these detectives had any idea they were questioning someone in the midst of producing a million-dollar-plus forgery, they might want to pursue another line of inquiry altogether with me. "I know my daughter rode her bike there to visit friends," I continued, serenely feigning concern. "The Bancrofts. My wife drove into Rhinebeck that day to pick up groceries. What's this all about?"

"You are aware there was a murder in the county recently and that the victim's body was disposed of on an abandoned road in the area in question?"

At once horrified and relieved—horrified by the slaying, relieved it had nothing to do with me—I blurted, "No, my God. I can't believe Maisie was near there."

"That's your daughter?"

"One of my two daughters, yes, but what does any of this have to do with our car?"

"You're not under suspicion, so don't worry," the other detective said, breaking his silence. He pulled a small accordion of paper from his pocket, unfolded it, and showed me a scanned color photograph of a headshot, asking, "You know this person?"

Face unevenly round as a pomegranate, wiry reddish beard, the blue filmy gimlet eyes of a vulture behind wire-rim specs, a once-broken nose. He was sporting a flat tweed cap similar to the one my father sometimes wore up here in the country—an Ascot, I think he called it. He did seem familiar, but I couldn't place the guy.

"I don't, I'm afraid," I told them. "Is this the victim or the suspect?"

"We don't yet have a suspect," was Moran's circuitous answer.

The half-closed front door behind me now opened and, somewhat to my dismay, Meg stepped out onto the porch. "What's going on? I heard voices down here."

Startled, I said, "Meghan, these are Detectives Moran and—"

"Bellinger."

"—Bellinger, and they say there's been a murder over in the Bancrofts' neighborhood. I hadn't heard about it, but I've been preoccupied this past week."

She coughed, said, "When I was over near Tivoli the other day picking up books for the shop, a woman mentioned she'd heard about it on the news. I thought she said it happened in Ancram, though, or Taghkanic."

"As I was telling your husband, we're sorry to bother you so early." Moran turned to her. "Someone not too far from where the body was ditched thought they'd seen a silver minivan in the neighborhood that afternoon."

Meghan gave me a nervous glance, then acknowledged, "It could well have been my car they're talking about. I went by our daughter's friends' house to check on her, but when I saw her bike there I just drove on without stopping. Ran some errands in town and came back home here."

They showed Meghan the same photograph they'd asked me to look at. After giving it an even closer perusal than I had, she shook her head. "Sorry, but I just don't know this man, officers—"

"Detectives," Bellinger corrected her.

"—and I hope you'll believe that none of us had anything to do with this."

"Of course not," Moran said, a warm if only partial smile of sympathy on his face. "That was never really in question."

"All we were wondering was if you might have seen something suspicious when driving there. I gather you're sure you didn't, correct?" Detective Bellinger asked Meghan.

"I'm sorry," Meg said with a shrug. "I wish I could help."

"All right then. We'll let you get back to what you were doing."

"If you happen to think of anything, remember anything at all, please get in touch," and with that Moran handed her his card. "Have a good one."

"You too," Meg and I said at almost the same time, as we watched them walk back to their unmarked sedan.

In the kitchen, I asked my wife about that strange look she'd given me when Moran spoke with her. She seemed oddly more thrown off by their presence on our doorstep than circumstances warranted—after all, neither of us had murdered the man in the photograph.

"All I know," she said, her voice tight as a fist, "is that nothing's been right, nothing, since Slader showed up. Now I have to get Maisie's sandwiches ready for her sail with the Bancrofts. They're picking her up within the hour."

I warmed my coffee with some from the pot. Meg may not have been leveling with me, not to mention with the detectives, but I was hardly in a position to question her further, so set off again toward the studio to press forward with my *Tamerlane* obligations

The minute I closed the door and stood alone in my sanctuary, a slow epiphany came over me. Now I wished I had studied the headshot as carefully as Meg had. Was it possible the man in the photograph was a young Ginger-head—Cricket, Slader had called him—as baleful as ever in pre–middle age, though perhaps more gimlet-eyed back in the day, wearing a full beard that was later shorn? I was aware he had a professional relation with my nemesis, but God only knew if it had abruptly ended, or, if so, why. While it was clear Slader hadn't been acting in

a way that could even slightly be construed as normal, I
never had the sense that his hectoring and threats were
those of a murderer, despite my willingness to let others
carry on with their suspicions about his possible involvement in the Adam Diehl case. I glanced at my partly fin-
gerless hand, as I'd done a thousand times, and still didn't
believe he had intended to kill me. Had he wanted to
accomplish that two decades ago, he would have brought
the cleaver down on my head or heart, not my hand.

Curiosity about any of this was neither immediately
useful nor helpful. Indeed, I understood that any curiosity I might have betrayed on the front porch would, in
turn, have invited the detectives' own further curiosity.
As I opened the back door to let in the fresh morning air,
I cautioned myself that it would behoove me to remain
circumspect—that is, dumb as dirt—with Henry Slader
when it came to the question of Cricket's fate.

I opened the safe. Put on, as always, nitrile gloves.
With great care, I pulled out the original and—let me
admit it to myself if no one else—the exquisite forgery
of *Tamerlane*. As I set them side by side on the clean
surface of my worktable, I experienced a moment of
uncouth pride. Pride of a kind I hadn't viscerally savored
in many a year. Yes, I knew this wasn't an achievement
about which I ought to have felt anything but revul-
sion, not to mention shame for collaborating with my
daughter. But I couldn't suppress this moment of, what,
gutter joy. I turned the pages with the kind of satisfaction only Calvin Frederick Stephen Thomas, born two
hundred ten years ago to the month, must surely have
felt when he held his first finished copy. By now I knew
the book intimately and turned to Thomas's most egre-
gious typesetting error, where the printer had misread

Poe's manuscript of "Dreams," one of the shorter verses
following the title poem, and set the nonsensical

> —have left my very heart
> Inclines of mine imaginary apart
> From mine own home,

rather than the poet's intended "In climes of my imagin-
ing." I felt a twinge of fraternal pain for youthful Calvin
and wondered why he never produced another book,
fading into pleasant obscurity while Poe rose to tor-
mented fame. But then, to be sure, our *Tamerlane* must
by design keep its fabricators wrapped in an even greater
obscurity, while its prototype should make headlines.

My transient pride flickered, faded, and snuffed out.
What replaced it was the far less fanciful knowledge
that this was nothing to be proud of, in fact, and that
I had the unpleasant task ahead of handing the thing
over to Slader.

Since I was firm in my decision not to add an inscription or autograph in Poe's hand on the pamphlet,
work on *Tamerlane* was done. Before heading back into
the kitchen to wish Maisie a good time sailing the river,
I pulled both twice-folded letters from the safe—the
poet's original and Nicole's—and studied them with
a magnifying glass. In each, the paper, ink, and script
matched the other. Satisfied, I stowed the fakes in my
fireproof safe, where they could be retrieved that afternoon for delivery downtown. Then I did something
impulsive. Rather than place the originals alongside the
copies, I pulled down a hardcover reference book of
monotype ornaments from a high shelf of other seldom-
perused volumes and tucked *Tamerlane* and Poe's missive

inside. Pamphlet and letter, which I'd preserved in a fresh archival polyester sleeve, were thin enough that when the reference book was closed, their presence, secured inside its many pages, was imperceptible. While a safe, I told myself, might be broken into—I'd noted Slader's glance in its direction when he was here—a monotype reference book, in this case concealing a purloined letter, was invisible to even the most prying eyes. Shelving the volume back where it belonged, I recalled a time, as a boy, when I hid from my father my first forged letter using this very trick. I had been inordinately proud of that letter back then, before I stashed it in my father's library in the second folio volume of Samuel Johnson's dictionary, figuring no one would ever bother to look there. I figured right. The dictionary was long since sold, but not before I retrieved my Doyle document from its hiding place. So it was that my first foray into the art of forgery, an imaginary log of my maiden voyage, survived to this day.

Nicole and Maisie were chatting away at the breakfast table when I returned to the kitchen. A place was set for me with jam and a scone. Maisie's lunch was packed in her bright-pink backpack, which sat open on the counter, but Meghan was nowhere to be seen.

"You all ready, Maze?" I asked.

"They'll be here in a few minutes," she said, nodding.

"Got sunscreen?"

Nicole answered, "She's got enough in that pack for a transatlantic voyage."

"Where's your mother?"

Nicole rose from the table, went to the counter, and zipped up Maisie's pack for her, saying, "She ran into town to do weekend shopping, told me to tell you not to worry."

Worry I did, though. Meg hadn't been herself since well before those detectives paid their unwelcome visit. After she returned from checking on Maisie the other day, she'd been edgy, distracted. Dearly as I wanted that weird glance she gave me on the porch to be meaningless, I knew she wasn't being straight with me about something. Yet how could the pot deem the kettle black? Hiding my distress, I responded, "All good."

"She told me to say she'd be back long before you needed the car for your meeting at the Beek," Nicole finished, just as one of the Bancroft girls knocked on the front door.

Nicole and I accompanied Maisie out front, where I shook hands with the twins' father, whose leathery chestnut tan was reassuring evidence he spent many hours on the water. We exchanged cell numbers and off they went, Nicole and me standing side by side on the lawn, waving goodbye as if we were happy figures in a Norman Rockwell painting. Walking back indoors, she offered to take one last look at the *Tamerlane* before it was to be delivered, but I told her I'd examined it earlier.

"If you're satisfied, so am I," she said. "Think I'll hike down to the woods and do a little nature sketching. Light's beautiful this morning. After all the brash abstract paintings I've been surrounded with this summer, it'd be a nice change of pace for my eyes."

"Good idea," I told her, then almost, but not quite, began to raise the issue of Slader's inappropriate demand that Nicole deliver the Poe.

"You all right?" she asked abruptly, hands pushed into the pockets of her jeans, mildly frowning. Before I could respond with a blithe falsehood, she went on. "You're

not, and it's understandable. Tell you what, I'm coming
with you this afternoon to Rhinebeck."

Mind reader, I thought. "No, your mother would
never allow it. Neither will I."

"What time do we leave? Two thirty?"

"You're not coming."

"I'll be back and ready by two fifteen," she finished,
glancing over her shoulder as she walked away. "You'll
go in, I'll just wait in the car."

"Nic, you're already more involved with this"—but
she'd already left the room. I stood there for a while,
wondering where Meghan had gone off to, wondering
whether Slader would approve of the copies, wondering how I got myself into this nightmarish mess. The
screen door to the studio slammed, and I watched out
the back kitchen window as Nicole strode down the
meadow. She wore a wide-brim straw hat her mother
had given her years ago and a shoulder bag full of pencils and oil crayons, no doubt, and carried a sketchbook
under her arm. As the forest enveloped her, I exhaled
and turned away.

Upstairs, alone in the master bathroom, I glimpsed
myself in the mirror above the antique porcelain sink
and was taken aback by how slovenly I looked. Rusti-
cated not in a pastoral sense but wretched as a runaway
convict. I showered—hadn't for a couple of days—and
shaved—hadn't for a few. Was it possible my hair was
grayer now than a week ago? No wonder Nicole had
expressed worry.

To kill time before my meeting in a few hours, I
settled in the study to pore through some of the rarer
books Meghan had retrieved near Tivoli. I made my way
through a dozen of them stacked on the table, penciling

suggested prices on slips of paper, as I often did for her if time allowed. Since most of the titles were familiar to me, it was easy work for a seasoned bibliophile and balm for an uneasy mind.

When I opened her first edition of H. G. Wells's *The Invisible Man*, however, I was bowled over. Had I been paying attention these past days, I never would have left it sitting on the table, though Meg was not at fault since she'd mentioned it with great excitement. Its issue points were correct, with the first page wrongly numbered 2. The requisite pages of advertisements were present at the rear of the volume. Its red cloth binding, stamped in gold and black, was bright and square, unusual for this title which had been, coincidentally, published the same year that Arthur Conan Doyle supposedly wrote my confessional letter to his brother, Innes. While I didn't recognize the recipient of Wells's inscription, what made it exceptional was that above the presentation, the author had added a pen-and-ink drawing of the invisible man himself, replicating in caricature his image from the front cover, seated comfortably on a chair in slippers and robe, lifting a cup to unseeable mouth, headless and handless. Twenty thousand, I thought, just for openers. I could hardly wait to give Meg the good news, maybe clear some of the downer clouds that had been shadowing us all week.

Rapt as I was with the Wells sketch, I only half heard the studio screen door slap shut at the rear of the house. At first, I didn't give it much thought, assuming Nicole was back early from her walkabout—that was quick; had she changed her mind?—and so continued perusing the book, trying to figure out the name of the recipient who had inspired the author to draw this elegant doodle. Thinking Nicole might lend her sharp eye to the exercise, I rose from the table, *The Invisible Man* in hand, and made my way toward the kitchen to show her. Our small world had been Poe, Poe, and more Poe since she'd arrived upstate, so I thought this would offer a nice respite.

"Nic?" I called out.

No response, so I walked toward the studio.

"Nicky? Got something I want to show you."

The door was ajar, so I nudged it.

"Nicole, you here?" I asked more quietly.

But the sunlit room, redolent of an odd fusion of ink and flowers, was empty. The back door was open with just the screen shut. I gazed down the slight declivity of the field studded with mustardy goldenrod and saw one of the same lone whitetails near the forest edge, browsing, as ever. Unseen, a prop plane droned like a steel mosquito somewhere overhead. The clock ticked in the kitchen down the hall. No sign of my daughter anywhere.

Paranoia abruptly kicked in. An image of Henry Slader, pasty as a nightwalker, shot through my imagination. He himself had boasted about trespassing in this house when we weren't here. Maybe he'd let himself in again, thinking the place was vacated—what with the car gone, Maisie off with friends, and Nicole in the woods—and was lurking inside. Clutching the Wells as if for dear life, I searched for him downstairs, room by room and, coming up empty, bounded up the flight to the second floor to make a circuit through the girls' rooms, our master bedroom, even checked both baths. Slader was nowhere to be found. Had a daytime ghost of wind, a freakish microburst, shoved the screen door open enough so it smacked into its frame, even though the leaves outside weren't so much as rustling? Fantastical idea, one for an H. G. Wells tale. But this wasn't some damn work of fiction.

Then it clicked. The noise I'd heard hadn't been made by somebody entering the house at all. If it was Slader—I could almost feel his malign presence now—he might stealthily have entered the printing studio while I was appraising books and allowed, on purpose or not, the screen door to slam when making his escape.

The Poe treasures. In an icy sweat, I rushed back to the studio. As I glanced up at the folio of monotype ornaments that I'd used as a kind of smuggler's Bible to hide the originals, I was relieved to see it appeared undisturbed, exactly as I'd shelved it earlier. My fireproof book safe was locked, per usual, but knowing I shouldn't trust appearances, I dialed the combination, opened the door, and peered inside to see that the *Tamerlane* forgery and facsimile letter were just where I'd stowed them. A cursory search of other compartments in the safe confirmed nothing else was missing either. Had I simply imagined the whole thing? Given the insomnia and strain of the week, it wouldn't have been out of the question. For safekeeping, I set *The Invisible Man* inside before closing and locking the safe again.

After looking behind me to assure myself that nobody was nearby watching, I reached high and pulled down the manual of monotype ornaments to double-check my impression that it hadn't been tampered with. I carried it over to the worktable, set it down, carefully opened the large volume. And of course, of course, despite my self-reassurances, I should have known—both *Tamerlane* and the Edgar Allan Poe letter had vanished. Like a fool, I climbed a stepladder, pulled out books shelved adjacent to my ornaments volume, and looked through them, one after the other, on the off chance I'd misremembered where I had stored the Poe gems. From the topmost rung of the ladder I peered at the dusty back of the top shelf that abutted the wall, hoping somehow they might have fallen out. But it wasn't to be. I could have yanked every last volume from its perch, could have turned my studio inside out, but the bald truth of it was that the thirteenth Black Tulip was gone.

I knew the authorities would have taken the body away. What I hadn't anticipated was that no evidence remained of its ever having lain there in the first place, stiff as a sculpture. No yellow police tape dangled from nearby branches. No dried blood discolored the ground or grass. As I looked farther up the road toward the guardrail where I'd been standing when the incident happened, a wave of hope passed through me. There was a fair to middling chance the driver might not, after all, have seen me from this vantage where he'd briefly parked. Not only was the distance greater than I had originally thought, but the trees there cast heavy dappled shade over the terrain. Maybe, just maybe, I'd blended into the shadowy scenery, inconspicuous, unseen.

Breathing a tentative sigh of relief, I drove to the end of the road, where I proceeded to turn around. I sat with my arms crossed and replayed the incident in my mind. On the radio, a Saturday morning opera was airing, a Benjamin Britten work unfamiliar to me. Lots of atonality and jagged rhythms gave the music an overarching mood of angst. Appropriate, maybe, but I was already struggling with plenty of atonal notes in my own inner soundtrack and hadn't any patience for music this morning.

I cut the engine, and with it the radio, so all I could hear were the same families of untroubled birds as before and, faintly, that nearby rippling brook. Arms crossed again, I recalled sunlight glancing off the Chevy's windshield, which further buttressed my growing conviction that I'd been an unseen witness to the grotesque, coldhearted act. Not that this necessarily exonerated me or lessened my feelings of guilt. But what it did mean was that my original reason for leaving Maisie and Nicole at the kitchen table, more or less on the spur of the moment before Will came out to join us, seemed no longer tenable. My nebulous plan had been to come here, confirm for myself that Slader had done what he did to intimidate me into silence—just as everything he'd done since reentering our lives was meant to threaten us into cooperation—then go straight to the police to confess I'd lied, and let the chips fall where they may.

Now that plan collapsed. Maybe Will was on the right path after all. Do what Slader wanted as a kind of long final farewell before getting our own lives back on track.

So, yes, the man on the road did exist, or had. But that didn't mean *I* did, or had. While somebody may have spotted a minivan in the area, my excuse for having been here was tight as piano string. I'd heard criminals often revisited the scenes of their crimes, and while I didn't consider myself a criminal, I did realize it behooved me to get out of here, never to return. As before, I covered my tracks at home with a domestic excuse, one I'd already planted with Nicole.

"Where the hell have you been?" Will demanded, when I walked in the door.

Not wanting to lie more than I already had, I hedged. "Excuse me, but everybody in the county decided to do their Labor Day shopping all at once," I told him as I pushed past to set down grocery bags on the kitchen counter. "Why are you so upset?"

"You and the girls had gone off in different directions, so I was here looking through your books in the study when I heard the door bang shut in the studio—"

"Slow down, Will. Please."

He placed his hands on his hips, looking less enraged than resigned. "Long story short, somebody broke in during the last hour and stole the *Tamerlane*."

"What? Yours or the original?"

"The original, unfortunately," he said, a note of despair clotting his voice. "What's more, I'd hidden it where I was sure nobody would ever bother looking."

"Slader?" I asked, knowing the answer already.

"That's my hope," he said. "Otherwise, I'm in some serious trouble."

I resisted telling him, *You're already in serious trouble*, asking instead, "Did he take anything else?"

"No, I don't think so. But, you know, Meg, he had to have been spying on me somehow when I stashed it where I did. There's no damn way he could have intuited such a thing."

Will walked over to the window and stared hard down the wide slope to the forest edge. "I suppose with a pair of decent binoculars—," he mumbled.

"Maybe it's time to turn Slader in," I said, well aware he couldn't really afford to do that without bringing down all manner of trouble on his own head, indeed on Nicole's and mine as well. Still, it needed saying.

He didn't respond, just kept searching the perimeter of woodlands past the garden's rustic deer fence.

"Where is Nicole, by the way?"

"Outside drawing somewhere."

"You think she'll be safe doing that?"

"He already got what he wanted—or half of what he wanted—so I don't see what point there'd be in his bothering Nicky," he reasoned. "On the other hand, I'm not sure any of us is really safe until I give him what he came for in the first place. After that, we'll see. And as for turning him in, I think we both know what a slippery slope that would be. Let me fulfill my end of the bargain, Meg."

I hummed in reluctant assent before we both went quiet.

"Agreed?" he finally asked.

Nodding that I did while thinking I probably didn't, I let the matter drop. My sense of balance wasn't as stable as I was used to. Hoping to change both subject and mood, I asked, "You were saying you looked at those books in the study? See the Wells?"

"It's wonderful," he exclaimed, turning toward me with a strained smile. "Given how things have been disappearing around here, I put it in the safe. Meantime, I managed to get a few other books priced—at least gave you and your team my two cents' worth."

Saying not a word, I took a few steps over to Will, slid my arms around him, held him close. We had hardly touched in the last week and he felt warm and familiar against me. "We'll get through this," I whispered.

He kissed me, then said, "Let me help you put these groceries away."

When Nicole walked through the back door into the kitchen not long after, her news sundered our momentary reprieve.

"Question," she announced, with no greeting of any kind. "Have Maisie or any of her friends been camping in the woods? Like thirty yards into the forest, past the stone wall?"

The probability of Henry Slader's having secretly set himself up in the woods was both terrifying and made perfect sense. "What did you find?"

"Not like there's remnants of a fire or anything. But somebody's been hanging out for sure. The ground cover was matted like maybe there'd been a sleeping bag used for a night or two. And there was an old stool closer to the edge of the field. I sat on it and you could see the back of the house clearly, even though it was camouflaged by barberry bushes."

"Any empty seltzer bottles?" Will asked with an uninterpretable smirk.

"No, but I did find Ripley's food bowl. Left it on the back porch."

Will and I looked at each other. "That explains how he knew where you'd hidden the *Tamerlane*," I said.

Nicole unconsciously finger-tousled her dark jagged hair, a nervous tic of hers, silver rings palely flashing in the sun, and asked what had happened. After I filled her in, Will looked at the wall clock. "I need to go soon. Nic, our earlier plan may need to be scratched. I don't think it's wise for you to come along."

This was news. "You mean to the Beekman Arms? No way," I fumed.

"It was my idea, don't blame Dad," Nicole told me, before Will intervened to explain that Slader had demanded that she, not he, was to deliver the Poe materials.

"Why?" I asked my husband, glimpsing fleeting surprise on our daughter's face. "I don't get it."

"He said we shouldn't be seen together again. And while I don't disagree, there's no feasible alternative. Besides, by breaking in here today, he tossed his rules out the window." Will shook his head at Nicole. "I still don't think you should come.

"I still think I should," she insisted. "I'll stay in the car while you make the delivery."

My husband shrugged, hands in his back pockets. He was willing for her to go along, but neither of them knew what I knew about the mystifying blue Chevy, the murdered man, and their probable connection to Slader. "It's risky enough that your father's doing this, Nicole. I know he has to. You, on the other hand, don't."

"I rarely contradict you, Mom, but tell you what," she said, turning to Will. "I'll drop you off at the inn, then drive around nearby, maybe do an errand. When you're done, just call my cell, then take a left on 9G, and walk past the old church—"

"The Terrapin?"

"—and head to the fairgrounds, where I can pick you up. This way, I'm there but not there."

Flummoxed, seeing no better alternative, I reluctantly agreed. Nicole ran upstairs to change clothes while Will disappeared to pack the facsimile *Tamerlane* and letter. When they left, I couldn't help myself. Sitting at the study table, surrounded by far less valuable and historically less important books than Poe's fragile pamphlet, I broke down in tears.

These, these were the books I'd always cherished my whole life, I thought. Not so precious, so priceless that blood might be spilled over them, or lives wrenched out of their usual orbit. I wondered if Poe, given the gothic darkness of his tales, wouldn't have been weirdly flattered, morosely heartened somehow, by the magnetic desires his first book generated in the hearts of men so many years later. No, that wasn't right. He would have been horrified, I thought, and comprehending. After all, Poe had a profoundly empathetic side to him that helped sustain his darkest visions. For all of Roderick Usher's human failings, his literary creator still pitied him at the moment of his downfall.

Brushing away my pathetic tears, I also recognized that this was not the end of *Tamerlane* in our lives. No matter how much I wanted it to be otherwise, this was only a fresh beginning. And by fresh I mean rotten.

S lader was sitting at the same table as before, facing the wall, when I slid in opposite him on the bench. He had already ordered seltzer with lime for himself and—tellingly, as he must have guessed I'd never allow Nicole to meet with him—a Jameson for me. I took a sip and marveled at how spruce and rested he looked—not unkempt as I might have expected of one who'd spent recent days and nights bivouacking in the woods. His pate was alabaster and appeared as if he never exposed himself to sunlight. Made me wonder if it hadn't been his accomplice, Cricket, who'd been spying on us instead of Slader.

"Where's your daughter?" he asked, as he brought his gaze up from the table, where his hands were lightly wrapped around his glass

"Where's the Fletcher *Tamerlane* and letter? And why did you break into my house for it this morning when it was you who shoved it into Maisie's hands in the first place?"

"Questions begging questions," he calmly observed, leaning back in his chair with a pseudo-exasperated sigh. "And no answers, none that you'd believe. Call it insurance, call it leverage. Besides, it's not like I took something that wasn't mine."

"Yours?" I said, smiling at his audacity.

"The far more immediate concern is where's your *Tamerlane*? You know, in the scheme of things, it's as important as the genuine article."

"Scheme of things," I scoffed, knowing it was useless to rebuke him any further for trespassing. The man was immune to such criticisms, and knew full well I wasn't about to report him to the authorities.

"This is part of the reason I wanted your Nicole to deliver the goods. My sense of her is that she's much more levelheaded than her father. But anyway, yes, scheme of things," he all but hissed. "Abigail Fletcher returns tomorrow night from her vacay in France, and her lovely new *Tamerlane* needs to be tucked into its solander bed before then. Not that she'll necessarily look for it, but one never knows."

I furtively scanned the bar—more packed with regulars and tourists up for the holiday weekend than when we last met—half hoping to see Ginger-head sitting there, morosely quaffing a beer.

"If you're looking for Cricket, his work was done so I sent him home."

Slader's tranquil demeanor as he made this statement nearly convinced me that he was telling the truth, and that his platemaker or paper fabricator, or whatever it was Cricket did, was not the man in the detectives' photograph. Otherwise, the word *home* was quite an icily diabolical euphemism.

"I hope he got there safely," was the best I could muster without opening up another line of inquiry I had no interest in pursuing.

Ignoring me, Slader said, "I noticed you failed to autograph the original. Cold feet?"

"You know as well as I do that would be a fatal mistake. In the scheme of things."

He rolled his eyes. "It would raise the value by a quarter million, easy."

"What it would do is invite such an array of klieg lights and criticism that my guess is it'd lower the value by that much, if not more," I said, hearing the bone-dry authority in my voice, although not knowing with certainty I was right. "At auction previews, Poe scholars would come out of the woodwork to challenge its authenticity. I think there's a strong chance it would have to be withdrawn from sale, or else, if it did go off, the thing might be bought in at the low reserve. Atticus knows as much, I'm sure."

"It was Atticus's idea in the first place."

I took another swallow of whiskey. "I think you're lying," I countered. "Atticus isn't that unsophisticated. But whoever came up with the idea, it's a nonstarter."

Contemplatively, Slader drummed his fingers, again staring downward. "What about instead of Poe's name, a simple inscription," he proposed quietly, as if speaking to himself. "*From the author*, for instance. Or, *With the author's respects*. That was done all the time during the period, as you know. It's not like Jane Austen ever actually signed her name in any of her novels."

"You prove my point. Austen's name was never even printed in any of her novels during her lifetime."

"Well, so, *From the author*."

"Look, it's marginally better, all right?" I said, aware I was offering an opinion that might encourage him. "But if you're married to the idea, it's best you do the work. Trust me."

That brought a raspy chuckle from Slader. "Trust you."

"I'm like a magician who stopped doing his sleight of hand twenty years ago. I know the mechanics backward and forward, but the dexterity is lagging."

"Cry me a river."

"Poe autographs aren't easy either," I continued, disregarding his taunt. "It's one thing to copy out a letter. If you mess up, you chuck it and do it again. But to risk ruining a seven-figure book with a botched signature?"

"Your daughter's up to it, though," he said, tilting his head a little, looking at me hard.

A knot cramped my stomach.

"Oh, yes. A little birdie told me she was with you most of the time when you were working on the Poe book. If the birdie isn't mistaken, it seems she had a hand—pardon my pun—in scripting the letter."

"Your birdie can go to hell."

Shaking his head, amused, he grew more serious. "I'm not married to the autograph, especially if it's going to raise eyebrows. The idea was just to make it sufficiently different from the Fletcher copy that there's no way she could claim it's the same one, all right?"

"I understand," I said, rethinking my argument.

"Let's table that idea for the time being. Meanwhile, show me your *Tamerlane* already. If you did a good

enough job, Abbie Fletcher won't be of much concern
to us."

I pulled out the plain rigid photo mailer in which I'd
carried the forgeries of both book and letter. Pushing
aside my drink to clear space, I set it on the small table.

"You sure you want to look at it here?" I asked. "Light's
not very good, and what if somebody notices or, worse
yet, spills their drink on it."

"Let me ask you a question," he said. "Are you happy
with the finished product?"

Now it was I who chuckled. "Nothing about any of
this makes me happy, all right?"

"Tell you what let's do," a hasty smile revealing his
chipped tooth. "Finish your drink and let's go into the
hotel library where we can have a look together. Nobody's ever in there but bored children playing on the
floor, and I didn't see a single rug rat when I came down
earlier—or, that is, when Cricket did—so we should have
the room to ourselves."

"You said Cricket had gone home."

Shrugging, he paid cash for our drinks while I took my
last sip of Jameson, realizing that he must be staying at
the inn, maybe under Cricket's name, rather than sleeping in the woods below my house. Who knew but that
he'd been dividing his time. All I wanted now was for him
to approve of the work Nicole and I had done—though
I'd never admit her part—and for me to find out what
was supposed to happen next. Move this along toward
its endgame.

Following him, I noticed he averted his face from the
security cameras situated above the bar, so I did the same.
We ducked through the doorway and entered the hotel
lobby, which was blindingly bright by comparison with

the pub. To our right were the registry and staircase. To the left of a large fireplace flanked by antique muskets on the wall was another doorway that gave on to the library. Despite its floral wallpaper, it was, I thought, perhaps the least lively library I'd ever set foot in, and quite appropriate for our unsavory needs. We made our way to a card table at the end of the room, beside a window, and sat next to each other. Without a word, Slader opened the mailer and gently pulled out the pamphlet and accompanying letter, then withdrew them from a Mylar sleeve like the one I'd used to protect the originals.

"Nice touch," Slader said, waving the sleeve in the air with a crisp plastic crackle. "Why shouldn't these be treated with the same dignity as the others?"

I couldn't help feeling like a fidgety pupil whose homework was being scrutinized by the most loathed teacher in school. Preposterous image, to be sure. Especially when the fact of it was that I found myself sitting with a convicted felon, a violent criminal who was now intimately and expertly examining a professional forgery—hardly schoolboy stuff—that had been manufactured with felonious intent. I looked out the window facing the center of town, where people were going about their business, largely oblivious to how fortunate they were, warm sun on their faces as they strolled past the lush beds of flowers and ornamental shrubs in front of the inn. Slader was silent as he methodically paged through the *Tamerlane*. He'd pulled a flat flexible magnifier the size of a credit card from his wallet and lowered his head to where it almost touched the paper to get a closer view.

Many minutes passed, and as they did I reflected on what a lonely trade it was to be a forger. The forger was

customarily his own audience, with no one but himself
to look to for praise or criticism, even for a simple acknowledgment. Not unlike an unknown poet, though
even the most obscure of poets can share verses with
neophyte friends and fellow bards. It was such a rare
moment, this, to sit with a respected, if hated, fellow
counterfeiter and await an adjudication of the work my
daughter and I had fabricated.

When Slader finished, having at last studied the back
cover by holding it up to a bar of sunlight and slowly
tilting it back and forth to catch the sheen of the ink, or
lack thereof, he set it down on the card table and said,
"Superb, man."

I didn't thank him.

Next was the letter, about which I had more qualms,
because naturally I'd had far less control over its production. Could a forger's daughter, not even knowing with
certainty she was making a forgery, produce an unsur-
passable work—one that Slader, an artist near the top
of our esoteric field, might sign off on? He held it up to
the sunlight, then turned it upside down and squinted at
the baseline and middle zones of the letters and words,
their ascenders and descenders. He even touched the
letter to his nose to make sure any ink smell was gone.

"Well?" I said, impatient. "Good to go?"

He looked me in the eye and nodded. "You're a very
intransigent person, my friend. You know that?"

"So my wife tells me."

"First, where are the proofs and rejects? You were
supposed to return them to me."

"I shredded them into confetti, then burned them.
You want the ashes?"

Ignoring my question, he continued, "Also, I'm not going to ask why your daughter didn't change more of the text, because I don't think it overly matters."

Horror-struck by his mention of Nicole a second time now, I considered contradicting him, insisting I'd done all the work myself, but thought it best to wind down our discussion. Anyway, for all I knew he had telephoto pictures of her scribing it in the middle of the night.

"He sometimes didn't, in point of fact," I said.

"Besides," Slader continued, "since there aren't to my knowledge any other surviving examples to compare it with other than Fletcher's, it's hardly a concern."

"Well, on that point we disagree," lowering my voice as a hotel guest wandered into the room and, seeing there were only books and two preoccupied men here, left. "If Mrs. Fletcher hears the news, which she probably will, she'll compare her letter with this one, which will surely be reproduced in the auction catalog, and red flags might rise."

Slader adjusted himself in his chair, ran a palm over his head. "Maybe you're right. Maybe it would be best if the *Tamerlane* was discovered without any letter, and came to auction sans accoutrements, no autograph, just the pure goods—"

"I never knew you had the capacity to listen to reason, but it's heartening to see."

Ignoring me, he played out the rest of his idea. "It's not like the letter couldn't turn up later, all by itself."

"That would need a clever backstory—how it surfaced, naked and alone, after almost two centuries out of the public eye. Twinned with *Tamerlane*, it wouldn't need explanation."

A genuine look of amusement broke on Slader's gaunt face, prompting me to realize I was arguing both sides of the matter, and was doing it because I didn't want Nicole exposed. But it was more than a little too late for that.

"You know as well as I," Slader said, "that forging plausible narratives to bolster our documents is half the joy of operating in the foggy heaths of history, imps of the perverse doing our thing, as Poe might've put it. We've claimed the right to revise the past as we see fit, and so we do. We change facets of the world to fit our own agendas. No big deal, and half the time we're never even noticed. I'd go so far as to say half the time people don't have any definite recollection of what actually did happen. Fact and fantasy carry equal weight, as far as I'm concerned."

Out of the blue, I told him, "You're a strange guy, Henry. Not that I disagree."

He looked at the *Tamerlane* with a blank expression, then began to busy himself with putting it back in the sleeve. "I'll take that as flattery, coming from the likes of you. But enough fucking around. I need to let Atticus know the work is done."

"Give him my regards," I said, changing the subject. "Before everything went south, in no small part because of you, he used to be a friend."

"How touchingly sentimental," said Slader. "Any bad blood between you is your fault alone. If you want to mend fences, why don't you tell him yourself? He's on his way from Providence. Should have been here by now."

Aware that my daughter was driving around Rhinebeck, waiting for me to finish, I checked my wristwatch, surprised at how late it had gotten. "That may have to wait for another time. Why's he coming, anyway?"

"Would you trust any of this to the post office?"

"Understood," I said. "So my part is done, right?"

"Part of your part."

Though I knew it was coming, the way he uttered that quartet of words—stern but without inflection or the slightest pause—left me breathless. It reminded me once more, as if I needed reminding, that Slader had me in a lethal bind. If I wanted my life, and my family's well-being, to return to how it had been before Maisie's scream cut like a scythe through the tranquil evening air, I had no choice but to cooperate.

"All right," swallowing rather than speaking my two paltry words. "So you still intend to bring it to auction?"

"We do," he said, sliding the pamphlet and letter back into the stiff mailer.

"Next year? Year after?"

Defiant impatience spread across his face.

Finding my voice again, I said, "I'd assumed you might want to give the Fletcher woman time to settle in with her new copy. Make sure no suspicions are raised."

Slader fully frowned at me, held up the mailer. "This is her *Tamerlane*, her Poe letter addressed to somebody whose name is slightly different from what she remembered—a difference the old girl will blame on the shortcomings of a faulty memory—and she's going to be perfectly content with it, just like she was before."

"So what do you have in mind?" I asked, though wanting to flee Slader rather than hear any further plan that he, in his calm amorality, might hatch.

"Atticus will be the final arbiter, but my understanding is that the book will need to be 'discovered'"—he bracketed the word with finger quotes in the air—"within the next few days so it can go up for auction around the anniversary of Poe's death."

Candid incredulity was what I felt. "Slader, get real. That's early October. You don't have any idea how impossible that would be to arrange on such short notice."

"The seventh, to be precise," Slader said, rising from his chair. "Falls on a Sunday this year, so maybe you can schedule it for the Friday night before, in honor of Quarles"—the pseudonym Poe used when he published "The Raven."

I needed to get away from Slader so I could think. Standing, I found myself drained. "That would only make a tight schedule tighter. There's not enough time to research, write, photograph, and print a new catalog for distribution by then."

"Maybe rival auction houses would have a different response, given how rarely this book surfaces. Commission's not the only reward for handling it. The prestige—"

"Don't be presumptuous, Slader," was my response to his empty threat. "I know how my business operates. Either way, I'd have to consult with the house. We could probably put out a press release, post the lot online, and print an addendum."

Rather than respond, he changed direction. "Look, this is good work, both book and letter. Atticus will have his own ideas how to proceed, and might agree with you—who knows? For me, the sooner it's sold and profits divvied, the better. As for you, you should go find your daughter. I've seen her drive by here on West Market Street twice already, and she's probably getting worried. Pass along my compliments on her handiwork, if you will."

I didn't dignify his remark with a response, but just asked, "When will I hear from you next?"

"When you hear from me next."

That was enough of Slader for one afternoon, so I turned away and strode past the shelves of books that seemed to be a lending library of sorts, made up of tatty, well-thumbed volumes abandoned by transient visitors at the inn. They were, I mused, a sorry lot.

Outside, I blinked in the strong afternoon sun and headed along Montgomery past the repurposed Baptist church and stately Victorian homes set back from the broken sidewalk, phoning Nicole as I made my way toward the county fairgrounds.

"Done?" she asked, after the first ring.

"In a manner of speaking."

"Tell me where you are and I'll pick you up."

True to her word, she found me standing alone at the entrance to the grounds, where only a week before, thousands had converged to ogle champion cows and chickens, sheepshearing and tractor pulls at the annual county fair. Maisie used to be partial to pig races and caramel-covered apples but had lately outgrown such trivialities. Were the fair still going, I thought as I climbed into our minivan, I would have liked nothing better than to disappear into its old-timey diversions as a way of erasing Slader from memory.

"Home?" Nicole asked, sensitive to my lousy mood.

"First I'd like to go throw some stones in the river."

"In it, or at it?"

"Either way works."

"That bad?"

A fair question, I supposed, since the fact of it was that by committing a venial crime, with my daughter's help, unwitting or not, I had lessened my exposure to the accusation of having perpetrated a mortal one before she was even born. A mortal one, I should add, that seemed no more tangible to me now than it did then, no more real. Intangible or unreal or whatever, it was nothing I could ever discuss with Nicole.

"Actually, it went well in retrospect, insofar as such a meeting could be said to go well. I just don't like Henry Slader, and the feeling's mutual. But for what it's worth, he does know rare books better than most anybody I've ever met."

"Rare books or forgeries of rare books?" she asked.

"One doesn't preclude the other, as far as knowledge is concerned."

"So did they fly? The facsimile, the letter? Sorry, I shouldn't ask, but there it is."

"He said to say as much."

"You really want to go down to the river?" she asked, putting the idling car in gear.

"Why don't we do something a little more celebratory," I said. "Let's head back into town and drop by that wineshop across from the Beek. Pick up a bottle of a really excellent red for your mother. Not like it's been a picnic for her this past week, with us holed up in the studio, the hermits of *Tamerlane*."

"I'm pretty sure they stock some nice Barolo from the Piemonte region."

"Listen to you," I said, as we retraced my steps back to the center of Rhinebeck.

In the shop, Nicole, whose college education apparently included advanced wine tasting, looked through the stacked cases of Côte d'Ors, Bordeaux, and Riojas until she found offerings from northern Italy, which she began assessing. As she did, I couldn't help staring out the windows at the imposing white inn that rose several stories across the street, on the off chance of catching a glimpse of Atticus Moore. Assuming Slader had told me the truth—in this instance, I saw no reason for him to have lied, other than maybe to keep in practice—my once-close friend would be arriving, and probably lodging, there sometime soon.

I remembered back to the time, the lowest in my life, when my early, extensive, and brazen habit of creating forgeries caught up with me and I was arrested. This would have been the mid-1990s, when I was in my middle thirties. Reimbursing dealers and collectors the money they'd paid, along with heavy interest in some cases, to avoid lawsuits and other legal quicksands, was difficult to bear. But having to apologize to Atticus, my closest mate and patron in the book world, was personally devastating. He was rightfully angry and hurt. And it was only by the grace of residual friendship and my full restitution of his losses that, over time, we were able to patch things up. It was to Atticus that I sold most of my venerated father's rare-book collection when Meghan and I decided to get married and decamp to Ireland to start over. Atticus ended up deceiving me in turn—my moment for anger and hurt—only later to make his own apologies by sending me more money, surely, than he really owed me. We were even. But our friendship was fractured. That I was the one who messed up first always left me feeling, unfairly or not, that our convoluted downhill path had been my fault, not his. While his name came up in passing now and then, at either auctions or book fairs, we hadn't spoken for over two decades.

Now he was back in my life, I gathered, and it was clear as high-proof gin that we found ourselves together on the wrong side of virtue.

"What do you think of this one?" Nicole asked, breaking my reverie as she held out the bottle of wine she'd selected.

"I'll defer to you," I said. "Why not get two bottles?"

"Splurging, are we?"

"The label looks eighteenth-century and I like the eighteenth century."

"It's vintage," she said, "but not quite that vintage."

Outside on the curb, as we strolled toward the car, I saw him. Or thought I did. Nor was I surprised, since this isn't that populous a town even on a holiday weekend swarming with city people here to bid farewell to summer. His hair was silver, longer than he used to wear it, leonine. While his age showed, he still had about him a kind of limber, prosperous appearance in cream trousers and dark-blue blazer. Were he done up instead with waistcoat and breeches, and perhaps a cape thrown in for good measure, he might have passed for a Georgian-era gentleman. He walked now with a cane, although from my vantage across the street it looked to be more of an affectation than for any medical purpose.

"You know that guy, I gather," Nicole said, as he turned up the sidewalk toward the wide front door of the inn, where, no doubt, he'd be meeting with Slader.

I glanced at her. "Used to."

"Atticus, isn't he," she continued, without a pause.

"How do you figure?"

"Doesn't take an Auguste Dupin to put it together. When you wanted to come back to town, and not only that but to a wine store right across from where you'd just been, I figured you weren't quite done here."

"I suppose you're right," I admitted. "But tell you what. I think I've seen more than I expected to see, and enough's enough. Let's go home."

"You're sure?"

"He'll be in touch with me when and if he sees fit."

Nicole and I got into the car, she at the wheel as before.

"Dupin, eh?" I said. "You've been reading your Poe."

"I mean, I studied him in school. But I've been rereading his tales in bed this past week," she said, pulling away from the curb to head home. "Black tulips or no-color tulips, Poe's the man. Conan Doyle himself knew that Sherlock Holmes wouldn't exist without Poe's Dupin. Think about it. I know Holmes is your all-time favorite, but they're both eccentric, both cocky as hell in their way, and they're both brilliant at deduction. Magically, surreally so. They're shamans in tailored suits. And Monseiur G—, the prefect of the Paris police? He matches up with that dense Scotland Yard guy—"

"Inspector Lestrade."

"Right, Lestrade."

"So who is Watson?"

Without pause, she said, "Poe's unnamed narrator, obviously."

Having been a lifelong Conan Doyle devotee, I knew he'd made a rather backhanded acknowledgment to his predecessor in the very first Sherlock Holmes story, *A Study in Scarlet*, when Watson mentioned to Holmes, "You remind me of Edgar Allan Poe's Dupin," at which the great sleuth scoffed, "Dupin was a very inferior fellow

... very showy and superficial." I sometimes wondered if Doyle wasn't betraying some anxiety of influence with that, demeaning a literary forebear's detective in order to make room for his own, though it is true that, many years later, in a 1912 poem in the *London Opinion*, he wrote

> *... As the creator I've praised to satiety*
> *Poe's Monsieur Dupin, his skill and variety,*
> *And have admitted that in my detective work,*
> *I owe to my model a deal of selective work.*

Not by any means great verse, but honest and respectful.

Straight-faced, I teased my daughter, "So how do you explain why Holmes smoked a clay pipe or a briar root in the Conan Doyle stories, and a calabash in the movies, while Poe's Dupin is always puffing a meerschaum?"

"Details, details," she said, and stuck her tongue out at me.

While I had no right to feel good about things, Nicole lifted my mood. A custard of clouds was gathering out west across the river, whisking over the mountains, which would make for a memorable sunset. After her day of sailing, Maisie would be cheery, if exhausted. Meghan, I hoped, might find herself calmer now that the *Tamerlane* materials were out of our farmhouse. Everything, I almost convinced myself, was going to be fine.

M oran again. This time by himself. After a prelude of apology for disturbing me once more, especially on a lovely Saturday afternoon, he politely asked if he might have just a few more minutes of my time. Did he actually say, "Murder investigations run on their own schedules, and sorry to say they don't much care about ours"? I was so rattled by his reappearance that it's possible I might have thought that to myself. Either way, I invited him inside.

As I led him toward the kitchen, I couldn't help but glance at the photograph of me and Adam on the beach. An object that surely preserved the fingerprints of Henry Slader. We sat down and I offered him ice water or maybe some apple juice, same as I'd proposed to Maisie on the night this all started.

"Thanks, I'm fine," he said.

I did fill myself a glass of cold water, then sat across from the detective, doing my utmost to betray none of my nervousness, though I felt dull arcing electricity run up and down my spine.

"Something came up since I was here earlier that I wanted to ask you about."

"Progress with your murder case?"

"Not so much. Just that it's come to light that you were caught on camera driving on the same cul-de-sac where the body was discovered the other day," he said flatly, looking at the dried herbs and Amish baskets hung from the hand-hewn crossbeams along the ceiling.

"Camera?"

"No one was there filming you, as such," he explained. "And it's not like there are security cameras, which is a shame. Turns out one of the residents we questioned has digital wildlife videocams mounted on his porches front and back to tape, you know, foxes, fishercats, black bears, whatever goes bump in the night. Nature lover, all very innocent."

"I see," I said. "So the camera runs in the day too, and it recorded me driving by."

"That's right."

"But I already told you that I went over there to check on my daughter."

"You did," he said, his eyes now focused on me rather than the decor of the kitchen. "That perfectly explains your earlier trip. What I'm wondering is—well, two things. First, I'm wondering why you drove there a second time."

"That's easy to explain—"

"Second, and more important, I'm wondering why so much time elapsed between when you were caught on the camera headed in the direction of the dead end, and when the video shows you going by the other way, driving back toward the main road that would lead to town or home. I'm sure there's a logical explanation, Mrs.—"

"Meghan is fine."

"We're just wondering what the explanation might be."

His use of the plural *we're* unnerved me, probably just as it was meant to do. "Am I under some kind of suspicion? I haven't done anything."

"I'm sure you haven't," he said. "We're just wondering if you might have more information than you've given us."

Knowing this was a crossroads moment, one in which it would have been best to tell Moran what I'd seen, instead I stuck with my story. Because I was now convinced that Slader, or whoever, hadn't noticed me down by the guardrail, I felt surer than before about the plausibility of what I'd already stated for the record. Some small embellishment was now necessary, I gathered, so I told the detective that though I didn't have any wildlife cameras mounted on our porch, I too was a nature lover.

"It's a peaceful and meditative place," I said.

"It's peaceful right here, I'd have thought," Moran countered, looking out the window at the serrated forest canopy below.

"Yes, but I live here. Sometimes I want to get away to think."

"Got it," he said, eyes back on me. "So you're saying the second time you went there was to meditate again?"

"The second time I went there was to make sure I remembered everything exactly the way I'd told you and your partner."

"I see. And was it?"

"Exactly the same," I said, feeling the confidence of a liar who was certain of getting away with her fabrications. "May I ask you a question?"

"Shoot," he said.

"If that wildlife camera taped me, wouldn't it have taped the murderer's car too?"

Moran shook his head. "Maybe, maybe not. The guy had wiped the card in his camera before we got there, so he had jack left from the day in question. There's another ingress road to the dead end, and it's even less populated than the one your daughter's friends live on. No cameras there, wildlife or otherwise. The perp possibly used that one. We don't know."

"Too bad," not knowing what else to say.

"Got that right," he agreed, getting up from the table. "Well, sorry to have bothered you again. A piece of advice?"

"Of course," I said, as we walked back to the front door.

"Since we haven't collared this perp, you might want to steer clear of that location."

"What about my daughter Maisie?"

"Well," he said, "it might be better if she stayed away too, just until we identify and catch our suspect. Chances are, he'll never go there again. But we've advised the residents in that neighborhood to be vigilant and lock their doors."

Watching Moran stride down the steps and across the front yard to his sedan, I came to the realization that my decision not to tell Will what I'd witnessed might not have been a good one. I'd seen how crazed he was with the Poe job, how intimidated by Slader, whether or not he admitted it to himself. But I needed to confront him. Get the truth from him about why he felt threatened. If he'd been making forgeries behind my back all these years since we returned from Kenmare, I needed to know. If there was some secret they shared from the deep past, something Slader knew that would bring Will down, then I needed to know that.

In the interim, I wasn't oblivious to Moran's having hinted, however obliquely, that I myself hadn't been ruled out as a suspect. Or at least as a person of interest. Were he to accuse me, any protest I might make that, no, it was somebody else, in a pale-blue Chevy, who dumped the victim's body while I, innocent as a child, merely looked on, wouldn't wash. My moment for that had passed.

Maisie was dropped off by the Bancrofts, windburn coloring her cheeks and forehead, full of stories to share about tacking and jibbing and manning the tiller. When Will and Nicole parked and came inside, she was regaling me with a tale about spotting a seven-foot sturgeon lazing on the waves—"all spiky like a dragon monster"— which caught the attention of her sister, who asked if Maisie could draw it.

"After she changes," I said, asserting some motherly authority, wondering if anything in the Hudson grew to that length. Maisie ran upstairs, two steps at a stride, as Nicole presented me with bottles of fancy wine. "What's the occasion?"

"Family reunion," said Will. "We haven't had much chance to sit down together this week, so I thought it would be good to revel a little."

"Thank you," I said, touched by the thought, if beleaguered by my earlier concerns. "How did your meeting go?"

Will got the corkscrew out of a drawer and opened one of the bottles, while Nicole reached down three etched-glass goblets from the cupboard, elegant inheritances from a mother-in-law I never knew.

"So far as such a meeting could go well, it went well," he said, pouring the dark-red wine and handing me a generously filled glass, and another to Nicole, who swished it around in the bowl of the stemware, nosing its bouquet with the confidence of a sommelier.

"Prosit," she said, as our goblets lightly chimed.

We chatted for a few minutes about Nicole's wine savvy, but I finally had to ask if Slader had admitted to breaking in here to steal the *Tamerlane*.

"In point of fact, it was his *Tamerlane* all along," said Will. "The issue was briefly raised, as quickly dropped, and, with both copies in his hands, along with both letters, I think he's finished with such skulduggery."

"So, that's it? No more Slader?"

I noticed Nicole fidgeting with her rings. It was never a good sign for my resolute, unusually coolheaded daughter to display a case of nerves.

Will set his wineglass on the counter. "I think so, yes. But Atticus Moore is in town, and this entire exercise, as I understand it, was to make it possible for the original *Tamerlane* to come up for sale."

"I don't even want to know what that means," I told him, caught off guard by the unexpected presence, not to mention possible involvement, of Atticus. He was the closest friend Will ever had, in or out of the trade, and was the first to forgive Will after the forgery scandal broke. Though Mary Chandler and Atticus lived and ran their bookshops in different cities, I always appreciated how the elder bookman helped her from afar, shared customers and leads on archives or book collections with her. Success of the kind Atticus had achieved in his long career can sometimes breed callousness, but in his case, from my limited vantage, I saw it generating only largesse, certainly when it came to Will and Mary. He appeared to have been an honest broker when it came to paying Will's part of the profits from the sale of his father's books and manuscripts. Why they stopped speaking years ago, I never understood. Bookselling, though, like any vocation, can breed as many antagonists as comrades. Years back, on a visit from Ireland to the States, when I sold the last shares of my bookstore to Mary and her then-partners, I enjoyed spending Thanksgiving with Atticus and his family, and was sorry his relationship with Will had soured. Sorry, above all, for Will.

"That's fair," he said, startling me from my reverie. "I can't say I know what it means either. What I can say is that if Atticus and I could somehow come to a rapprochement, it wouldn't be the worst thing in the world."

All four of us helped make dinner that evening. Will and Maisie grilled local duck, leeks, and portobello mushrooms out back, while Nicole and I made a fresh walnut pesto with basil from the garden, prepared an heirloom tomato salad, and together sliced the first Cortland apples of the season to make tarts. Around the table, as a ravishing sunset of corals and tangerines painted the walls, we ate our feast in higher spirits than any of us had been in during the twelve days of what I privately thought of as the Henry Slader siege. While we were not precisely held prisoner by his army of one, our movements—mine, at least—had morphed into the self-conscious, looking-over-the-shoulder variety. We'd been living on tenterhooks and finally, that night, we all put our worries aside.

During dessert, Maisie produced a pencil sketch that Will said looked just like an Atlantic sturgeon, prehistoric with a spatulate snout. "That's a pretty rare sighting," he said. "They're endangered, you know."

"Nice drawing, Maze," Nicole added.

Afterward, we all watched an early Hitchcock movie, *The 39 Steps*, which, though part of it is set in the Scottish Highlands and our innocent protagonist is running from both police and murderous spies, made me nostalgic for Ireland. Ancient arched bridges over frothing creeks, moors shrouded in mists, old stone houses in picturesque valleys. Maybe we could visit over Christmas later this year, I thought, as on-screen a gyrocopter joined in the noir manhunt for our fugitive hero. Maisie had never been to the land of my birth, and Nicole, conceived in our cottage in Kenmare, and therefore, to my mind, an honorary Irish lass, would soon be too far along in her busy life to want to join us. I was so deep in my musings that I drifted in and out of the film's plot, but was relieved to see that poor Richard Hannay, Hitchcock's wronged Everyman, would in the end prove cleverer than either the authorities or the ruthless espionage ring bent on capturing or killing him.

When we retired for bed after our memorably uneventful evening, I raised the Ireland idea with Will, who readily agreed. "It's months away, so if we plan ahead around Nicky's semester break—"

"Let's ask them both in the morning?"

"Let's do," he said, kissing me goodnight before shutting off the light on his bedside table and falling asleep.

I read a little before setting aside my book, extinguishing the lamp, and drifting toward sleep myself. Outside, all was quiet but for the periodic hoot of our nearby owl. An image of the Flying Scotsman express train rocketing across the black-and-white landscape of the film was what I remembered last, until some hours later, how many or few I couldn't guess, I woke, not fully, and thought I heard a faint, distant thump. Not distant, downstairs. Then, another thump or thud sounded, softer than if the owl had brushed its wings against a window on the first floor.

Fully awake now, I lay still and listened. Will's breathing was deep and steady, and I resisted waking him as I knew he badly needed the rest. Naturally I thought of Slader, but from what my husband had said earlier, it seemed improbable he would have reason to trespass again.

Time passed, my pulse slowed. Old houses, I knew, are percussion instruments in their way, making all manner of creaks and moans and ticks. Especially farmhouses such as ours, with a nineteenth-century laid-up, drystone foundation, in which there was no end of heaving and settling. Was it the same kind of wishful thinking I'd experienced the evening that Maisie was waylaid, when I imagined her scream was that of a coyote or a snared rabbit in death throes? Maybe so, but because we had locked every door and window, I began to second-guess myself. How long I continued to listen, I couldn't say. But whether it was minutes or half an hour, the next thing I knew, sunlight was streaming into the room and my husband was gone from our bed.

The others were stirring when I came downstairs. All three were beaming. They had specially made a breakfast of pancakes with blueberries.

"What's the occasion?" I asked, sitting down at the table as Maisie poured coffee into my cup. "Why all the smiles?"

Nicole had been chosen, it seemed, to answer my anticipated question.

"Christmas this year in Ireland," she announced.

"Unanimous decision," added Will. "When we're back in the city, I'll start working on logistics."

"Including a passport for me," Maisie said, failing to contain her excitement.

After breakfast, I began a cursory search around the downstairs rooms of the house to see what might have caused those noises during the night. The doors were still locked. None of the windows had been tampered with. Not a single book had been moved, so far as I could tell, in the study. Nothing had fallen off a shelf; no picture had come loose from its hook on the wall. I couldn't fathom so much as a shadow of explanation for what I'd heard.

"Need help?" Will asked, coming up behind me. "Looks like you lost something."

"My mind."

He laughed. "That makes two of us. But, seriously, what're you looking for?"

While I didn't want to ruin his upbeat mood, given that he'd been suffering as much as—actually more than—the rest of us this past week, I explained about the nocturnal noises.

"I hate to say it, but that makes no sense," he told me, matter-of-factly. "The only person we know who's been audacious enough to break in here—"

"You mean crazy enough."

"Audacious, crazy, whatever—the only one who would do such a thing is you-know-who. Problem is, he already got what he wanted and he's satisfied with it. And while we can call him crazy, he's methodical, even businesslike, if rough as a buzz saw around the edges. He has no earthly need to be back here creeping around in the study."

That gave me an idea. "Ripley was in your studio last night. Maybe you forgot to let her out?"

"As you know, whenever Ripley gets stuck indoors, she clues us in with some full-throated caterwauling, not just a quiet thud. Consider it a nightmare and leave it at that."

Will was right. I had to acknowledge that I'd been so anxious the slightest thing out of the ordinary made me more jumpy than it would have in normal times. For all I knew, I might've heard those same witching-hour noises in summers past and never given them a second thought. What was incumbent upon me to do was pull myself together.

Disappearing is a dangerous business. A naked leap into the unknown, it promises an escape from adversaries, an exodus from life's woes. But it's also a confession, an abandonment of the very people who have stood by one's side, defended one against all odds, believed when others refused. Running away from my troubles, no matter how bad they got, hadn't crossed my mind for many years. How could it have, when I was married to a wonderful woman, with two magical, inimitable daughters, and a past of secular sins buried so deeply they were never likely to be lifted into the dreary light of day again, despite Slader's harassment and threats? Sins, I should say, that I had willfully suppressed and all but forgotten until these past weeks, out of the habit of living a life free of wrongdoing. Or, mostly free.

So why even ponder such an act of cowardice, forsaking everyone who ever mattered to me? Why give even a fleeting thought to disappearing—maybe inventing a new identity and slipping into the aether—when I knew it was nothing more than a craven fantasy?

Because the invisible knots that bound me were tightening. Because every move I made in order to extricate myself seemed only to bind me all the more. And because I had to admit to myself that each day that followed Maisie's encounter with Adam Diehl's spurious ghost, his twilight doppelgänger who'd come to exact revenge on her father, saw me make one mistake after another, though I'd been convinced I was doing everything right. But I could no more undo what I'd done than run away from what lay ahead.

After I got off the call and slipped my cell phone into my pants pocket, I looked around, as if emerging from a deep sleep, to find myself standing in the middle of the field below my house. Then I remembered why I was here. In an impromptu effort to keep my conversation with Atticus Moore private from my family, I had wandered past the garden, halfway to the edge of the woods. Because the signal was often stronger outdoors, neither Meghan nor Maisie—Nicole had run to town briefly on an errand of some sort—if she happened to look out the window, would think I was up to anything unusual. That is, unless rather than rejoining them in the farmhouse I simply put one foot in front of the other and marched off into a missing-persons file, not unlike what Agatha Christie did back in the 1920s after learning her husband, Archie, had fallen in love with another woman.

Poor Agatha, I thought. How must she have felt when she later learned that a thousand officers and fifteen times as many volunteers took part in the desperate search to find her? Even Arthur Conan Doyle got involved, presenting a spirit medium with one of Christie's gloves in the hope of tracking her down. When she was finally located eleven days later at the Harrogate Hydro, a luxury hotel spa in North Yorkshire, she claimed to have no memory of how she got there or what had happened, but clearly she had staged the whole disappearance to shame her gallivanting husband. Either way, a dangerous business. And it didn't save her marriage.

My story would run along different lines, I thought, watching a swallowtail butterfly flit over the tall grasses. No worried armies of police would bother to hunt for me. Nor would my disappearance generate international media attention. Unlike Archibald Christie, whose infidelity drove his wife over the edge, Meghan hadn't done me the slightest wrong. On the contrary. And rather than landing in some run-down New Age spa, nursing my misery in a fugue state, I could imagine myself winding up in a holding tank somewhere far upstate, having had too many Jamesons in a blue-collar bar near the Canadian border, say, and looking more suspicious than circumstances otherwise warranted.

No, I thought. When you run away, people are rarely mistaken in viewing you with mistrust. Why flee if you've done nothing wrong? And the only people I would end up hurting were those who deserved it the least. Deserved it not at all.

So rather than light out into the woods, I followed the meandering path of the butterfly toward the garden, contemplating my exchange with Atticus.

"Why didn't you come over and say hello?" he'd inquired, speaking as if two decades hadn't passed, his tone of voice altogether amiable, that of the Atticus I'd known for many years before everything went south during an overseas call from Kenmare to Providence. A call during which the unthinkable—at the time, in any case—became clear to me, and Atticus's unsuspected collusion with Slader reared its hideous head.

"I suppose I could ask you the same question," I told him.

"You were with your beautiful daughter, and I didn't want to interrupt the two of you. Besides, I knew that after I met with Henry, I'd be calling you today anyway, so thought it best to let life take its course."

I opened the rickety gate and lingered inside the garden. Persistent rains had made for a tough vegetable season this year. Meghan's harvest of tomatoes, I saw, was barely half its usual size, and many of the lower leaves on the stalks were yellowed, with brown spots not unlike the coloration of the wings of the butterfly that presently abandoned me.

"So how do you see life taking its course, old friend?" I'd said, without an ounce of sarcasm shading my use of the word *friend*. What I imagined we needed to negotiate was far too weighty to be polluted by quips, jabs, posturing.

"That is going to depend on certain contingencies, some of which are out of my hands. How, by the way, is Meghan doing these days?" he asked. "From my provincial corner of the universe in Providence, I have to say how impressive she is, with her book business flourishing the way it has over the years."

"That's kind of you to say, and I wholeheartedly agree. But as for how she's doing these particular days? Not so well, as I think you might expect. Before Slader burst into our lives, she and the rest of us were doing fine—"

Atticus's response was quick and crisply intoned. "Slader's insane antics had nothing to do with me, but I apologize for any of his misbehavior that upset your family."

"He needn't have leaned so heavily into the faux-gangster angle, terrorizing my girl out of her wits. I probably would've cooperated without all the hysterics."

"You'll forgive me if I doubt that," Atticus replied. "But his behavior toward Maisie was unforgivable, and I've given him a piece of my mind about it. Now we're at a different place, and you won't be having to deal with him if I can help it. We need to talk, alone, as you've probably guessed. Much as I'd love to see Meghan and your girls, I think it's best we get together in a more neutral environment than over there at your finca."

"That works in theory," I agreed. "Forgive me, though, if I wonder whether meeting with you could result in my ending up like Slader's accomplice, Cricket?"

"What or who is Cricket?" he asked with such manifest puzzlement that I believed he had no idea what I was talking about. "Actually, no, please don't tell me. I don't want to know. In answer to your question, you needn't worry about 'ending up' like anything, aside from quite a lot better off than you already are."

Having no idea how to respond to this claim, I waited.

"Do you know the old hotel they renovated overlooking the river, down near the train station in Rhinecliff?" Atticus continued, interrupting the silence. "Adjacent to an iron footbridge over the tracks?"

"I know the place," I said.

"The hotel bar is quite empty during the daytime, especially on a Sunday, and there's a shaded porch patio just off the bar that looks out on the Hudson. All very civilized. Can you be here in an hour?"

Now, standing among the waning summer plants, I picked one of the last of the cherry tomatoes, whose earthy scent was a reminder of how richly peaceful life had been two short weeks ago, before my earlier sins had caught up with me. I popped the tomato into my mouth, bit into its warm tartness, and closed the garden gate before hiking back to the house.

Meghan was in the study going through more of the volumes in the collection she had bought. How I wished I could simply sit down with her and trade thoughts on Mark Twain's *Celebrated Jumping Frog*—a debut markedly different from what Poe had experienced, one that brought its author widespread success not quite forty years after *Tamerlane* came out. The copy she was examining, with its fat gilt leaping frog on the front cover, looked a little the worse for wear but, still, it was always a good book to have in stock, if only because it wouldn't remain there long. When, instead, I informed her that I was going out for a little while, she understandably replied, "Please, tell me it's not Slader again."

"As I've said before, I honestly believe he's gone from our lives."

Not one to mince words, she gibed, "As you've wrongly told me before," then asked whom I was meeting with. At the mention of the name Atticus I could see a quick flicker of hopefulness pass across her face. "Well, maybe that's a good thing."

"Do you know whether Nicole's back from town?" I asked.

"I think so, yes. Heard the car pull in ten or fifteen minutes ago."

"All right," I said, throwing on a light jacket. "Promise I won't be gone long."

When I went to the garage and climbed into the car, my mind lingering on Meghan's optimistic look, I was jolted by Nicole in the passenger seat, plugged in to one of her devices, listening to music, while reading "The Masque of the Red Death," for all intents and purposes lost in her own world. Had she got it in her head to come along with me, having somehow overheard my conversation with Atticus? I knew that wasn't physically possible. Even as I'd deliberately strolled down into the field, fifty yards, sixty, from the house, I had been careful to keep my voice low as I spoke with my Providence confidant from a lifetime ago.

"Fish?" I said, after she told me what her Poe soundtrack was.

"You don't know Phish? Next-generation Grateful Dead."

"No, and I also don't know what you're doing in the car."

She pulled out her earbuds, shut her book, and said, "I know you're more used to Mom's classical longhair stuff"—indeed, Meghan had been sorting books to Vaughan Williams or Delius, I could never tell the difference—"but, trust me, Phish and Poe go well together."

"I'll make a note of that," I said. "Meantime, you'll pardon me but I'm going to have to ask that Phish and Poe and you get out of this car. I have to go somewhere."

Nicole turned toward me, her hazel eyes now serious. "So I gathered."

"Well?"

"Well, that's why I'm sitting here."

"You can't come along," I said, with as much finality in my tone as I could muster. My daughter was as stubborn as she was smart, and I doubted there was much I could concoct that would dissuade her from joining me. She was one of the three primary reasons I couldn't flee from the labyrinthine mess I'd gotten myself into, one that dated back to before she even entered my life.

Ignoring my dictum, she reached over her shoulder, pulled and buckled her seat belt. "I can sit in the car while you meet, or go sketch somewhere. Just, I want to be there to make sure you're all right."

"Meet with whom?"

"Slader, Atticus, Tamerlane the Turk, it doesn't matter. You're my father, and I know you're in trouble, and I'm doing exactly what I imagine you would do for me if the roles were reversed," she said.

"Maybe my troubles should stay *my* troubles, not yours."

"Listen, I have a good idea what you're up to. You're making existential amends of some kind, and you're in danger if you don't follow through. How am I doing so far?"

"You've always been very perceptive, but—"

"Thank you," she interrupted. "Now, I may not understand why you're doing it, but I want to help you. Way I look at it, you invited me into this, I joined you without hesitation, and we're in it together."

"I wish I could simply agree, but it's more complicated than you think," was my airy response to her heartfelt words.

Ignoring me, she asked in a different voice altogether, "Have you ever read 'The Masque of the Red Death'?

It's not one of his best, I don't think, but his understanding of color—the 'barbaric lustre,' the ruddy light
through blood-colored panes, the ebony this and scarlet that—well, it's something else. Like a kaleidoscope
from hell."

As I listened, a radical idea came over me, perhaps so
fantastic as to be absurd. Not that it formed in words,
as such, not yet. Maybe its genesis was in that glimpse
of hope in her mother's eyes just a short time before,
a glimpse that suddenly stirred in me a similar hope
that there might be a way out of the quagmire I was
in. Who knew where some of our best, and worst, ideas
finally come from? Much of what I began to ponder as
a possibility came down to the character or caliber—I
was hard-pressed to find the right terms for it, now that
the idea began to frame itself—of Nicole's loyalty. The
affinity she and I had developed from her earliest years
was still profound. And while she wasn't in any way a
so-called daddy's girl—she'd been her own old-souled
woman since grade school—she was, after Meghan, the
person I most counted on in an unreliable world. How
much of the truth about my past I could entrust her
with, without her losing respect for me, indeed, without
her coming to despise, revile, even repudiate me, I would
never know without giving her fidelity a trial test.

"You going to start the car, or do you prefer to spend
the afternoon in the garage?"

I shrugged and backed into the lane, drove to the
rural intersection not far from Maisie's friends' place,
then headed along a series of roads that would eventually
lead us to Rhinecliff, a hamlet set, as its name implies,
on a rampart overlooking the wide Hudson. We parked
at the bottom of a fairly steep hill, and while Nicole

crossed the overpass that bridged the railroad tracks out toward the boat launch, where she planned on sketching the ragtag holiday regatta, I entered another historic clapboard hotel to meet another figure from my past.

"Don't tell me I haven't aged a day, because I won't believe another thing you say," were Atticus's words of greeting. When he took my outstretched left hand in both of his, the wide smile on his face would discredit any onlooker who might suggest we were here for anything other than the most collegial purposes. "Come, I've got us a table outside."

As promised, he was seated by himself on a stone veranda overlooking the tracks and grand river beyond. We sat at a wobbly table on which waited a bottle of white wine in a cooler, and two glasses. Overhead, a canopy blocking the filtered afternoon sun flapped pleasantly in the breezes off the water.

"Here's to fresh beginnings," he said, raising his glass in a toast.

"Or at least clean endings," was my response as I touched mine to his.

Atticus had always been a little larger than life, I recalled, and now, years on, he had become distinguished. He wore a beige panama hat even in the semishade, and his glasses were tinted and thick and gave him an aristocratic air. His cleft chin and strong cheekbones further lent him an aura of casual nobility. The cream-colored trousers and blue blazer he'd worn in Rhinebeck were again on display. Nothing about the man insinuated anything other than success, the outward contentment of a life fulfilled.

Ignoring my toast, he said, "I'd love to do some catching up, but I know we are both on a schedule."

"You, I think, more than I am," I said.

"How's that?" he asked, with a light cough.

Taking another sip of the wine, whose buttery taste I was sure Nicole would be able to identify down to the vineyard and year, I recounted what Slader had told me about Mrs. Fletcher—not mentioning her name—returning from a trip overseas, and *Tamerlane*—not mentioning its title—needing to be replaced, along with a new-old letter, in its solander box.

"No, that's nothing for you to be concerned about. Indeed, it's something I'd rather you make an effort to forget, if that's all right."

"Fine by me," I said.

"I will tell you this, though. Your recent craftsmanship was every bit as sophisticated as what you used to do in the days when we were more in commerce. I might add that your transition from calligraphic to letterpress makes you something of a virtuoso."

Rather than thank him for a compliment I'd as soon not be paid, I nodded, peering out at a catamaran running with other sailboats on the river.

"And while we're speaking of this and that, I'm sorry to see your hand. Of course, I knew about the accident—"

He saw me recoil at that characterization.

"Assault, I should say—but watching you, I'm pleased to see that you've made a full recovery."

"Tell that to my phantom fingers. I think they'd disagree," I said, without hostility. "But, yes, many days go by without my even noticing. For instance, it wasn't on my mind until you brought it up."

"My apologies," Atticus said, his tone of voice sincere. "And I am sorry about it all. I know you probably think I was somehow behind it, but no way was I involved. It was pure barbarism on Slader's part, and he himself paid a steep price for his loss of sanity."

Though I didn't respond to this, it did occur to me that sanity had never been one of Henry Slader's traits.

"You understood that my substantial payment was meant to reimburse you for books I'd sold from your father's library and your own, as well as help with medical debts, as a gesture of friendship, and for your family." As he told me this, he removed his glasses and I could see, for the first time, that both of Atticus's eyes appeared frosted, had a filmy dimness to them, were far more aged than in years past when they fairly danced with vigor. "I never expected you to thank me then, and I don't want you to thank me now."

"You and I are even, Atticus, at least in that regard," I assured him. "I can't really see why you elected to send Henry Slader to deliver the *Tamerlane* to me, though. Maybe it's not finally worth getting into the hows and whys, but he's the polar opposite of you."

"Mostly true, except he's deeply versed in the craft you know so much about, and is my sole connection to that world. A world which, by the way, after *Tamerlane* is brought out into the light, is one I plan on quitting forever."

I crossed my arms lightly, breathed in the soft tang of river air. "You know, you could quit it forever right now. Just give Abigail Fletcher her book back and destroy mine."

Atticus glanced around, a little ruffled by my comment, checking to see if anyone had wandered onto the veranda and was listening. "Don't think it wasn't something that occurred to me as I was driving down here. But I'm afraid the die is cast. By this time your beautiful production is in its new home near Boston. And the original is out in the world waiting to be discovered."

He didn't look well, now that I'd been sitting with him for a time. Given that he had been so out-front about my disability, I considered asking him if he was all right. Instead, I said, "Could you tell me what you mean by 'out in the world waiting to be discovered'?"

With that, he smiled again, put his glasses back on, and the dim nimbus of illness that I thought I'd seen dissipated. "May I ask you a question?"

"Shoot," I said, taking another sip.

"I believe Meghan will act with discretion going forward, but how much can the girls be counted on to keep your work with the Poe book a secret?"

"That's a question you might have asked yourself before you sent Slader on his errand here."

Atticus leaned back in his chair, gazed out at the gray-blue sky. "Henry Slader's admittedly a problem that will need to be solved. But please do answer, and rest assured there's no threat implied in what I'm asking."

"To be honest, I feel confident that my daughters won't break their promises to keep this a secret. I don't think my younger fully appreciates what this *Tamerlane* business is all about, and anyway she tends to keep her own counsel. And regarding Nicole, she helped me with the whole thing, so she's as bound to silence as I am myself." I withdrew the bottle from its cooler and poured more wine for each of us.

"You like the Meursault, I see. Domaine Antoine Jobard," he said. "I brought another bottle down with me if you'd like to take it home."

"Nicole seems to be an oenophile in the making."

"It's all hers then. She'd probably prefer a Montra-
chet, but this is a particularly fine vintage of white Burgundy," he said. "I'll give it to you for her before you go."

"No need, but thanks."

Atticus smiled, shook his head. "I insist, if only on
her behalf."

"On her behalf, thank you. But you should know
that I don't feel as confident about Meg's willingness
to go along with all this as you seem to be," I told him,
and drummed my left-hand fingers before spreading
my hand, palm down, on the table. "You know how
much she hated my involvement with forgery all those
years ago, and she's been a stalwart supporter of my
reformation. It's been a long road to come back from
those troubled times, and seductive as it's been now
and then to want to backslide, until this past week, I
haven't forged anything."

"Aside from forging ahead?"

I didn't laugh. He meant to leaven our conversation,
I knew, but I wanted him to comprehend how difficult
this project was for me, how much it involved waking
old demons.

"So you really and truly gave it up?"

"You don't believe me."

"I just find it hard to comprehend how someone as
gifted as you could walk away."

Looking Atticus hard in the eye, I said, "Meghan may
be a problem."

Unexpectedly, abruptly, he offered me an ardent
close-lipped smile that was the very definition of self-
possession. "I'm glad you've been forthright with me
about this, Will, and I hope you'll trust me when I tell

you that she will not present a problem. I'm feeling good
about things now and am so happy we've been having
this chat. Maybe it's mawkish to say so, but that old
chestnut about true friendships not dying, despite many
years of absence, never seemed truer to me."

"Don't forget that even chestnuts can go bad," I said,
wishing I hadn't.

He rapped his knuckle twice on the table, rose from
his chair, and whispered, "Stay right here while I run
upstairs and get that Meursault for Nicole."

While he was away, I rose and walked to the railing at the edge of the veranda and, shading my eyes
against the sun lowering itself in the west, looked
for Nicole down by the water's edge. A southbound
train, perhaps the Lake Shore Limited out of Chicago, given its sequence of sleeper cars, temporarily
blocked my view as it shot through the station, air
horn blaring. After a minute, I located her sitting on a
riverside bench with her book, and a surge of love for
my daughter swept up through my chest—love, and
an urgent, almost aching imperative that I protect her
at all costs. She was gifted beyond her years, always
had been, but stood at the precipice of adulthood in
a much more precarious situation than I think she understood. I couldn't retrofit the architecture of my life,
so to speak, couldn't replace some of the rotten building materials I'd used to construct who I was. But I
could make sure that my every decision going forward
was in the interest of keeping her, Maisie, and their
mother as free from strife as I possibly could. With
Nicky's invaluable help, unwitting or not, this Poe
conspiracy, this high-stakes confidence game, had to be

seen through to its inevitable end. It was the only way
for everyone involved—or, rather, most everyone—to
slip away unscathed. I had only two paths. Either to
turn myself in or to trust Atticus. And I wasn't about
to turn myself in.

"Lovely view, isn't it?" he said, standing behind me
with a canvas bag dangling from his fingers. "Here's your
daughter's Meursault. It's even better than the bottle
we're sharing. Comtes Lafon Meursault-Genevrières. Tell
her it doesn't want to be overchilled."

"I'll tell her, and thanks, really," I said. "Meantime, if
you don't mind, I do have one more question for you."

"We have another glass apiece left," he said, waving his hand back toward the table. "Let's not let good
wine go to waste. I too wanted to ask a question, but
you first."

"When you said earlier that Meghan would not present a problem, was that intended to sound menacing?
If so, it's more Slader's style than what I'd expect from
you."

"Another reason his usefulness here may have reached
its end," Atticus said, almost as if making a note to himself. "But no, not menacing. Encouraging, rather."

"I don't see how."

"You can't see how just yet," he responded. "I don't
mean to be cryptic, but you'll understand in retrospect
how this all needed to unfold."

Seeing he had no intention of revealing what was
set in motion, I told him, "You know we're leaving for
the city sometime tomorrow. Any further unfolding, by
which I assume you don't mean *unraveling*, will need to
take place down there."

"So I figured," he said, carefully pouring the rest of the wine. "Now a question for you, Will. How well situated are you at your auction house? I mean to say, I know you're not the head of the house or the auctioneer, but as their specialist in literature—"

"Autographs."

"You do both, from what I understand. Either way, how deep does their trust run for you? How would you characterize your level of sway at the house?"

Trust—that vexatious word again. "So far as I know, my status there is solid. Over the years I've proven myself, made few mistakes, and of course everyone there loves Meg."

"Who doesn't? She's consigned them some pretty stellar lots over the years from what I've heard," he said, offering no reason why he'd have such information. "What I'm getting at is, I know you conversed with Henry about the probability of your handling the *Tamerlane* when it manages to surface. That still good by you?"

Another train came in, this one northbound, judging from the direction of the horn sounding around the bend below Rhinecliff station, and, after an exchange of passengers, set off toward Albany. The clamor temporarily brought our dialogue to a halt, during which I studied Atticus as he watched an oil tanker ply the shimmering Hudson, leaving behind a burnt-gold wake the sailboats were forced to negotiate. Again I was struck by an intuition that he wasn't well. The persistent cough. The wan paleness of his skin that I didn't recall from years past. The cane—I now saw it wasn't for show—and milky eyes. Maybe it was a matter of simply having aged, since his personality and movements were as vigorous as ever.

Once the train had pulled out, I told him, "I'm still willing. You haven't filled me in about how you're going to go about consigning it, since your Abigail Fletcher might well catch wind and reasonably wonder how two copies of *Tamerlane* could possibly be handled by a single dealer—"

"Oh, there's an historical precedent. If I'm not mistaken, the late great New York barrister and collector Frederic Robert Halsey owned two copies at one point," he said. "But the pamphlet won't be coming directly from me, so don't concern yourself about that." In the soft pinkening light he glanced at his watch, a vintage Patek Philippe not unlike one Meg had inherited from her brother.

Interpreting the gesture, I said, "I need to be getting back home myself."

We stood, and Atticus extended his hands, which I took in both of mine. "It's been good to see you again after so long," he said. "For what it may be worth, I think your earlier path on the straight and narrow seemed to be serving you well. I'm sorry to be a part of temporarily dislodging you from it."

"Let's hope we both survive the detour."

"My best to Meg and Nicole," he finished, before turning away. "And please promise to give Maisie a special hug and kiss for me. She has no clue who I am, but I was furious to hear how the *Tamerlane* was transferred. Henry may have made a fatal mistake there."

Hearing this, I wanted to ask Atticus more questions. Such as, how deep did his relationship with Slader continue to go after all these years? And speaking of fatal mistakes, what misstep had Ginger-head made to meet the end he had met? How did Atticus plan on secretly recompensing me for my illicit efforts and, indeed, my daughter's? And why the special hug and kiss for Maisie? But before I could summon any words, he was gone.

L eaving the country for the city at summer's end was usually a bittersweet exercise. In years past, my husband and I always found it hard to give up the pastoral simplicity of life at the farmhouse, even as we felt refreshed and ready to return to the swing of all things urban. In years past, trading our neighborhood hoot owl and songbirds for the sirens and shouts of city life was made easier with the knowledge that we would be back upstate as apple-picking season rolled around, and afterward when the leaves changed color and came fluttering down. But this year, our haven had been tainted. Rather than return on autumn weekends, I thought, maybe Will and I should consider the once unthinkable idea of selling the house and resettling elsewhere.

Neither Moran nor any other detectives had come by to question me further. I found myself listening more

closely to news segments between music broadcasts on
my ever-present radio, and also picking up the local
paper from the market, but didn't hear or read anything
more about the murder. Had it been solved, the killer
taken into custody, and the authorities moved on to
fresher crimes without my having known? Of course it
was possible. Had I hallucinated the pale-blue car and
discarded body left like a sack of litter on the deserted
road? Not as likely, but it was beginning to feel that
way, and I knew that I had the capacity to blur painful
memories. How else could I have weathered Adam's
unsolved murder all these years? It wasn't impossible
that I'd begun doing the same with this apparent murder
of a man I never met.

Maisie's friends were with her upstairs, purportedly
helping her pack but no doubt using her coming depar-
ture as an excuse to hang out. To my knowledge, Maisie
hadn't confided anything to them about what had been
going on here. And telling from the peals of laughter that
now and then erupted from her bedroom, such troubles
were far from their minds. It was as much music to
my ears as the Aaron Copland symphony playing in the
background—his third, I think the honey-voiced radio
host had said.

Though conflicted about so many matters, I looked
forward to cataloging the latest collection of books we'd
procured. For a bookseller, or at least for this bookseller,
shelving new stock, emailing or phoning clients to quote
them items on their desiderata lists, finding new homes
for orphaned volumes was a rich satisfaction. While I had
devoted hours to re-sorting the new books into catego-
ries, separating nineteenth-century lit from twentieth-
century fantastika, and pulling volumes I considered the

most valuable for careful boxing, there was no way I'd have time to finish going through them all before we left. With that in mind, I began packing them in tissue and bubble wrap for the drive down.

When Will returned from Rhinecliff, Nicole with him, I enlisted their help in sealing and stacking the boxes by the door so we could load them into the minivan the following morning. Because of the extra weight, we'd decided the girls and I would take the train while Will drove the Taconic to the city. If he arrived before we did, Cal and Eliot, the same bookshop colleagues who'd driven upstate to pack the rest of the collection, would help haul the boxes inside and get them into our back room for processing. Old penciled prices would next be carefully erased unless they had intrinsic bibliographic interest. Protective Mylar jackets would be cut and folded onto books that required them. Some that came to us damaged would be set aside for our freelance binder to inspect for possible repair. It was a process more laborious than our customers might imagine. One, also, that was in my blood.

Alone with Will later in our bedroom, after the girls had retired, I asked him how his meeting with Atticus had gone.

"The truth? It felt as if I were seeing a favorite relative, a brother even, after many years of being separated."

Surprised by the warmth of his words, I asked, "But if he's somehow behind all this madness—"

"He made it clear that the madness was Slader's contribution, and not something he himself condones. In fact, I think Slader's treading on dangerous ground."

"Nothing new for him," I said. "He belongs back in prison as far as I'm concerned."

"He might be safer there," were Will's cryptic words. "Be that as it may, I did notice Atticus seemed unhealthy. He's elegant as ever, eloquent as ever. Just something in his eyes made me think he was staring down mortality while tidying up some loose ends of his life."

"He told you that?"

"I have a question, Meg," Will said, any sentimentality now vanished. "He seemed to have followed your book-selling career over the years with a lot of admiration."

"Nice to hear."

"Was he ever directly in touch with you, maybe about buying or handling inventory?"

That took me aback. "No, I would have let you know. Why?"

"When we were saying our goodbyes, he asked me to give Maisie a special hug and kiss for him, then made a pretty unveiled threat toward Slader over the way he'd gone about getting the *Tamerlane* to me."

"Slader was an absolute ape, and Maisie deserves all the hugs and kisses that come her way."

"The look on his face when we talked about her was, I don't know, complicated," he continued, sitting on the side of the bed. "I'm not clear on how he even knew her name. I never mentioned it to him."

I thought about that for a moment. "Slader must have told him."

"You're probably right," he said with a shrug. "But there was real tenderness in his voice when Maisie came up."

"He's a father of daughters too, remember." Then, "You know, Mary Chandler used to do quite a bit of busi-ness with Atticus after I left the shop, but they drifted apart not long after I bought back in."

"Then she certainly would have mentioned Maisie to Atticus back in the day, wouldn't she?"

"Not to forget the bookseller grapevine. When Mary had Maisie without there being a father in the picture, there was plenty of chatter and buzz. It's not impossible he just heard her name along with the gossip."

"Makes sense," Will agreed. "Do you remember whether he ever met her, Maisie I mean, before Mary died?"

"Mary and I may have been close as sisters, but, like sisters, there were some things we rarely talked about, and Atticus was one," I told him, climbing into bed. "She was sensitive to your falling-out, I guess, and didn't want to ruffle feathers."

After our traditional Labor Day family brunch, a mélange of French toast from the last of the bread and a patchwork omelet made with leftovers from the fridge, we closed the house and double-locked its doors. As we did, I couldn't help but feel we were leaving it vulnerable to intruders. Or, that is, one intruder who seemed able to pass, like a ghost might, through the doors, windows, walls. The girls and I headed for the train station in a taxi, Will already having hit the road with my precious cargo of books. As we pulled away, I glanced back to see the farmhouse with its classic white clapboards, eyebrow windows, and shake roof receding, and felt a twinge of melancholy. Would our upstate sanctuary ever feel safe again?

We saw no bald eagles along the riverside on the trip down to Penn Station, but I did notice how pensive Nicole seemed, watching through the scratched windows of the train as the landscape shot past us.

"Penny for your thoughts?" I said.

She turned, smiled. "My thoughts aren't worth a penny," shifting in her window seat to face me. "I just hope everything will work out for Dad."

Not knowing how much of his forger past her father had shared with her, nor if she'd surmised Atticus's and Slader's different roles in his life long ago, I said, "Your father may have his shortcomings. Who doesn't? But he always seems to land on his feet."

"Like a falling cat," she said.

"It's true he's got a bit of the nine-lived cat in him, I've always thought. Maybe that's why he and Ripley get along so well."

"They both know how to negotiate their terrain."

"Is Ripley going to be all right?" Maisie interjected.

"She's a nine-lived cat too," answered Nicole. "She's probably got another softhearted family down the road somewhere, looking out for her. Ripley's a survivor, worthy of emulation."

"And, not to forget, your father has us," I said, as the gray stone citadel of West Point ranged into view across the river. Though we had both passed it a hundred times before over the years, it occurred to me to ask, because of Edgar Allan Poe's recent presence in our lives, "Maybe you know, but isn't it true that Poe attended there for a time as a cadet?"

She turned again to admire the neo-Gothic architecture of the academy towering over the Hudson like some fortress out of Tolkien's Middle-earth. "You're right. I think he was enrolled at West Point a few years after he published *Tamerlane*."

"Am I also right in thinking he either resigned before they kicked him out, or they kicked him out before he could resign?"

"Actually, he deliberately had himself court-martialed. Troublemaking seemed like second nature to him."

"Wonder if living there among all those granite towers and fortifications inspired his gothic sensibility."

Nicole nodded. "Makes sense. I read somewhere that he liked the Hudson Valley at least enough to spend time hiking one summer around Saratoga Springs. Visited the farm that eventually became Yaddo, and revised 'The Raven' there. For all of his bad-boy brilliance, I think he was a nature lover."

"More into ravens and rats than chickadees and chipmunks, though."

I was grateful that Nicole, her summer job as a studio assistant over, was going to be able to spend a little time more with me and Will processing the new books before her final semesters at school swept her away. Quietly, without making a display of it, she'd amassed quite a store of knowledge. Talking with her, I increasingly discovered, was a learning experience. And Maisie, rather than pressing her face to the screen of some mobile device, lost in a galaxy of scintillant pixels, liked being near her sister for much the same reason.

As it happened, our train was delayed around Spuyten Duyvil, so Will did reach the bookshop and unload the car without me. The girls and I, when we finally arrived, spent much of the day at our apartment, unpacking and reacquainting ourselves with the same familiar rooms we'd known for years. Nicole had done a nice job with upkeep, watering plants, sorting mail, the like. We strolled outside to run errands, restock the fridge, replenish the wine rack, and afterward the four of us went to dinner at a favorite local Vietnamese restaurant, joined by one of Nicole's friends.

The very low-keyedness of our East Village home-coming put my nerves at ease, and knowing that in the morning I would be joined by my family at the book-shop made me happier than I'd been since pre-Slader days. The memory of the man ditched on the road had by now nearly reached a vanishing point. And with it, I suppose, went some ethical part of myself, which, at this moment, I wasn't clear how to retrieve from the edge of the horizon. As I fell asleep that night to the percussion of downtown sounds, I made myself a promise that I would start by finally telling Will what had happened, no more putting it off, no more obfuscating. I had always stood by my husband in good times and bad, and had to believe he would understand how I'd been shocked into paralysis. He was, I knew, the one person I could rely on for insights into what if anything I should do, having lied to those detectives.

On the walk with him across Tompkins Square the next morning, I said, "When we're done for the day, I'd like to take you out for a drink, my treat."

"Good news?"

"No, not really."

"Would you rather just sit in the park and tell me now?"

I wanted to get my hands dirty with the new books first. Nicole and her friend were taking Maisie out to a film later, I told him, and so we'd have plenty of time to talk then.

"Fine by me," he said. "I'm keen on going through the rest of his Wells holdings. That copy of *The Invisible Man* was the best I ever laid eyes on."

"I appreciate your help, you know," hooking my arm around his, bidding my mood to lighten. We were,

I reminded myself, back in our downtown stomping grounds, back on crowded sidewalks and squares. Since all the encounters I'd had with Henry Slader had been in the natural settings of rural life—our isolated Irish cottage outside Kenmare, our solitary Dutchess County farmhouse—his power to threaten me here in the city seemed diminished.

In hindsight, I should have known. Should have foreseen. Had I been more prescient, I might even have been keeping an eye out for it. Though I would never ask him—honor among thieves, and such—I believe the discovery happened exactly as my old Providence colleague intended.

Cal and Eliot, along with Sophie, the senior member of Meghan's small staff, had come in an hour before we got there and were already at work on the collection. They had laid out the better science-fiction titles on one of our long oak library tables in back, and the nineteenth-century American fiction and poetry on another. While Meg worked with Cal to price less expensive stock, Maisie hung out with them and helped to shelve. Sophie, who was most knowledgeable when it came to American literature, searched out comparable offerings online and, with Nicole's assistance, entered catalog descriptions of books by Hawthorne, Irving, Dickinson, Twain, James, and other authors in the trove. As ever, music played on the sound system, some opera or another.

Myself, I went through the science-fiction titles and occasionally consulted with Sophie when she had a question about an issue point or inscription. Many of the works were familiar. A decent jacketed first of Bradbury's *Martian Chronicles* was here, as were Frank Herbert's *Dune* and several, not all, of its sequels. Jules Verne's *Twenty Thousand Leagues Under the Sea* from 1870 was the earliest representative of the genre, and while it was clear from annotations made by the bookseller who originally sold it to the collector that it had been purchased as an autographed copy, Verne's signature was all wrong. His *V*—which typically looked like a drawing of a seagull in flight—was stunted, stubby, a real botch, and the terminal *e* in *Verne*, rather than dramatically descending into a stylized underscore, not unlike that of Oscar Wilde, curled upward, as if raising its hand to bring attention to itself: *Behold Me, a Sorry Forgery!* Meghan wouldn't recoup the steep price the collector had paid, but at least the book wouldn't reenter the market on my watch as a first edition of Verne's classic signed by the author. Indeed, I noted in the volume that the signature was incorrect, and advised Eliot to be sure not to shelve it in the section of autographed books upstairs. The irony of this was not lost on me.

Whether it was *Rigoletto* or *La Traviata* or some other Verdi confection playing on the radio, I couldn't say, but the note, a kind of scream really, that came from Sophie's corner of the room was no less dramatic. Had she, or maybe Nicole, cut herself with one of the knives we used to trim Mylar? But no, when I reached the table, Sophie was standing there, staring at me, mouth open, holding out the pamphlet as if it had just burst into flames. A copy of Mark Twain's *Adventures of Huckleberry Finn* in the original publisher's sheepskin binding, a bit the worse for wear, lay on the table in front of her. Nicole hovered at her side, betraying nothing beyond a convincing imitation of Sophie's shock.

"This can't possibly be right," Sophie exclaimed, shaking her head. "No way can it be right."

"What have you got?" I asked, more nervous than I might have imagined I'd be when this inevitable moment came to pass. While I knew it eventually would resurface into my life, Atticus hadn't let me in on when or how. Then I remembered. The night after we'd watched that Hitchcock movie and gone to bed, when Meg thought she had heard noises downstairs, noises I dismissed as not being Slader because he'd gotten everything he wanted from me—well, he hadn't. Clearly, he'd broken into the house not to burglarize us but to plant the original among Meghan's new acquisitions before leaving for Boston to install my forgery in the Fletcher library.

Feigning naïveté, I took the *Tamerlane* from her with all the clandestine terror and reluctance that only the deeply conflicted, the very guilty, can possibly know. My heart was racing so quickly that there was probably no difference between this physiological sensation, knowing what I knew, and what I would've felt if I were in the midst of *actually* discovering Poe's first book.

"What is it?" asked Meghan, who rushed in from the adjacent room, with Maisie and Cal behind her. "Are you all right, Sophie?"

"It was tucked in the back of a Twain," she said, her voice wavering at the edge of numb elation.

"What Twain? What was tucked?"

"I'm sorry," she said more slowly, catching her breath. "The *Huck Finn* back cover was loose, its hinge was cracked down to the mull, the mesh, and this other book was hidden there between the flyleaf and rear pastedown. It literally just fell out on the table when I was examining the Twain. The collector must've put it there for safekeeping, same way other people hide money in books, or photos, or letters."

Meghan looked at *Tamerlane* in my hands, then hard at me. I glanced again at Nicole, who, I could swear, was gesturing with her eyes to stay cool. Maisie, keying off her sister, was calm and quiet, watching.

"I thought I recognized the title," Sophie continued, filling a brief awkward silence. "But when I saw Poe's signature on the title page, I knew for sure what it was. Am I right, Will? Meg? Is the signature correct?"

So Slader had gone ahead, against all reason, against my categorical insistence that he should not, and forged an autograph. My thoughts flew, like startled birds, in several directions at once. I felt fury toward Slader for having possibly ruined an otherwise transcendent thirteenth copy of the Black Tulip, the first new example to have surfaced in a generation. Fear that Meghan might confess then and there to the scheme—so far as she half understood it—accusing those who had conspired to deposit this *Tamerlane* in her shop, where she and her staff would now be credited with a bibliographic discovery of the first magnitude. But also wonderment that this unicorn my father spoke of in Philadelphia a lifetime ago, when we marveled together at one displayed in the Free Library, had stepped out from obscurity into the light.

"Given how exceedingly rare an authentic first edition of *Tamerlane* is, I have to tell you I strongly doubt it," I said, gamely as I could manage. "But let me have a look."

Carefully, I lifted the front cover to reveal the title page and saw the signature there, scribed faintly in pencil. For one strange instant, I was seduced into thinking, *This is right, how could it be?* The impression didn't— couldn't—last, but I was damned if it wasn't the most faultless Edgar Allan Poe autograph not made by the man himself that I had ever laid eyes on. Slader'd wisely elected not to use the author's full name, just the initial of his long-suffering foster father's last name, Allan, between his Christian name and surname. *Edgar A Poe*, clean, straightforward, beaming with authenticity, and no unnecessary flourish scudding beneath nor a full stop after the initial. Poe would likely have done the same had he ever in fact autographed this book. But I had a question to answer, and my family and Meg's staff were waiting.

"Well, huh," I said with a genuine frown. "It just doesn't seem like a real possibility. If it were right, it would be the only one in existence. And that's too good to be true."

"If it doesn't seem like a possibility, too good to be true, it probably isn't right. We need to be careful," Meg said, the pulse visibly pounding in her temples.

"Previously unknown things are discovered all the time," Nicole spoke up, turning to her mother. "You yourself told me about that Igor Stravinsky manuscript— I think you said it was a funeral score for his teacher, Rimsky-Korsakov—that everyone thought was lost forever during the Russian Revolution. Didn't that just turn up a few years ago?"

"In Saint Petersburg, right," I added, grateful to see Nicole side with me.

"This is different," said Meg elliptically, without shooting our daughter the petulant look I fully expected, but raising Sophie's eyebrows a little. "I know Will's the expert here, but may I see the signature?"

"It's your book," I said, under my breath, right away wishing I had simply done as she asked.

When Meghan took the *Tamerlane* in her hands and scrutinized the handwriting on the title page, I stood beside her, silent, marveling at its outward legitimacy. Whatever I thought of Slader, it was a masterstroke on his part to have signed with an almost weightless touch, using not ink but the dulled tip of a graphite pencil, maybe a carpenter's pencil. A counterintuitive gesture, one that would surely be noticed by Poe experts. Debated, certainly, but which, if proven to be a forgery, would not ruin the integrity of the pamphlet itself as much as, say, ineradicable ink would have. If the time ever arrived when I could congratulate him on this clever gesture, I would do so. Though I hoped that time might never come.

"In early books like this," Sophie said, "when the author's name isn't printed on the title page, many times an owner will just write it there. We have a fifth edition of *A Tale of a Tub* upstairs, originally published anonymously, in which some owner from the eighteenth century wrote in ink *By Dr Swift*, beneath the title. Happened all the time."

"That's true," I agreed. "Swift's first major book. But I don't think this is that."

As I uttered those words, Meghan leafed through the pamphlet and, withdrawing a small folded letter on thin paper that was laid inside, made the second important discovery of the day. Warily, she unfolded it twice and read aloud Poe's brief missive to Theodore Johnston, while Sophie and her colleagues marveled, Cal whispering an all-purpose expletive.

"Can I have a look?" I asked unnecessarily, given she was already passing it over to me. For a moment I was sure Meg must have misread the addressee. So flawless was the forgery Nicole had produced that I might have been holding her letter to the fictional Thomas Johnson—so unimpeachable was the holograph, so credible the paper. Even the creases from the folds had been faultless, aged by my daughter and me using a bone folder to impress the antique stock first one way, then reversing the fold to press it from the other side. This procedure ensured that the fibers, unseeable by the naked eye, were properly broken. With a lightly moistened Q-tip, we'd barely dampened the crease edges, then placed the paper in the studio nipping press, screwed it tight, and by morning it had been deprived of its natural tendency to spring back open. But this letter in my hands was no forgery. Instead, I was holding the genuine, unrecorded handwritten note to Theodore Johnston from Edgar Allan Poe.

"And?" Sophie nudged.

"Nothing here physically suggests to me, at least at first blush, that this is anything other than Poe's original letter to this critic Johnston, hoping he'd review the book," I said.

Meghan then finally weighed in, her tone of voice more exasperated than exhilarated. "Until we decide what to do, we're going to need to put these in a very safe place. Will, are you absolutely certain the book itself is correct?"

"I'm less sure about the signature than the book. Have you ever come across Joseph Cosey? One of the most notorious and successful forgers of all time, and a specialist in American historical documents. His stuff was so convincing, some of it's still in circulation."

"He did Poe?"

"Ben Franklin, Lincoln, Jefferson, your Twain right there," I said, pointing at the *Huckleberry Finn* on the table. "And, yes, Poe."

"You think this could be a Cosey?" Nicole asked, her forehead knotting.

"In a lesser book, possibly," I said, aware that she was slyly helping me muddy the waters. "Cosey was more into forging letters and documents, and, besides, if he'd somehow had the good fortune to come upon a first edition of *Tamerlane*, he could have retired rather than getting caught and sentenced to prison again and again. The letter would be more in Cosey's wheelhouse." Though Cosey, of course, had died many years before Slader put a pencil to this pamphlet.

"We'll deal with the letter. Right now I'm asking you about the book itself," Meghan prodded.

"Over the years, as you know, there have been a number of facsimile editions printed, usually in limited editions. Columbia University Press did one back in the forties with a detailed introduction by Thomas Ollive Mabbott. There's the 1884 George Redway, which I've never seen. William Andrews Clark Jr. had one printed up by John Henry Nash in the twenties. Couple of others, too. The Ulysses Bookshop in London issued one in 1931 that's a pretty accurate reproduction, right down to the stitching and tea-colored wrappers, though they're a little too gray and light."

"We've handled a copy of that," interjected Sophie. "It's stamped 'Facsimile' in red ink on the last page."

"Yes, and if you'll recall, the ink didn't bleed too much into the paper. It could probably be removed with judicious use of a bleaching agent. I imagine more than one gullible collector's been tricked into buying it as an original."

"But, Will, what about this copy?"

"This looks right to me, Meg," I said, firmly looking directly at her. "Right age, right feel, right heft, right everything." The faintest hint of dismay crossed her face and vanished.

When Sophie asked what it was worth, I realized that if ever there was a time for me to feign ignorance, rather than continuing to pour forth with all the lore about *Tamerlane* I had gathered during the past two weeks, this was that time. I realized I'd gone on too long about Cosey and facsimile editions. True, I already carried around a surfeit of bibliographic arcana in my memory, but these gentlemen with their three-name names, the Mabbotts and Clarks of history, not to mention their literary hero himself, would never have been so readily at my disposal had I not recently been immersed in all things Poe.

"Who knows?" I answered. "Small fortune."

"Six figures?" she asked, the import of her discovery becoming clearer to her.

"At least," I told her. "That said, I think Meg would agree that it needs to be carefully collated, photographed, and examined, not just by us but by outside experts after we've gone over it with a fine-tooth comb. I wouldn't feel comfortable assigning it any value, even for insurance purposes, until we've done our due diligence."

"Also," Sophie continued, "we'll need to think about how to go about properly presenting it to the world."

"Maybe auction might be the best way to go," I said, studying my wife, who looked at both our daughters, then at me with an uninterpretable expression on her face, arms crossed. "I think it's the only real way to let the world decide what it's finally worth. But it's Meg's call."

Sophie pulled her long blue-black hair into an unruly ponytail on the top of her head, like a fountain of ink, adding, "If we price it and it moves too quickly, we'll always be haunted by the fear we undersold it. Price it too high, the excitement of the find sinks into a slow-boil tar pit of grousing and grumbling by other dealers and collectors."

Her point was well taken, though I knew that a private sale to an institution might be the simplest way to proceed, and by far the quietest. Price it strongly, then negotiate down to a figure all can agree on. I could easily think of a dozen candidates, places with means, that would love to have *Tamerlane* in their holdings.

Cal asked, "We have clear ownership of everything in this collection, right, Meg?"

As if startled from slumber, my wife responded, "What? Yes, we do. I don't know whether you noticed when we were there, but the estate attorney insisted I sign a contract stipulating that the books were sold in their entirety and as is. Of course, he never expected one rarity might be hidden inside another."

"Onus was on him, though," said Sophie, snatching the words out of my mouth.

I knew it was the right moment for me to intervene. Accepting how events were supposed to unfold, if everyone involved here was to survive, I said, "Onus was really on both sides. If we'd gotten the books back here and realized the shop had grossly overpaid, it's not like Meg could go running back to Tivoli demanding a refund. A done deal's a done deal. But now, if nobody objects, I'd like to sit down and let's examine this thing"—I remembered Slader's admonishing me for using that word—"together."

And so we did. With Nicole and Maisie and the others looking on, all silent in their different ways, I went page by page through all twenty of *Tamerlane*'s leaves, rectos and versos, gingerly observing the same text Nicole and I had meticulously gone through in our studio upstate, worried that Slader might have further sophisticated the book with more contemporary faux-Poe forging. Who knew but that he might've got it in his head to correct, in Poe's early hand, some of the printer's errors, such as "crash" for "crush" to rhyme with "rush" on page 8. Or later, "lisp" for "list" and "wish" for "mist." Perhaps such a restrained hoax might even have passed muster with certain scholars, speculating that Poe, who never in fact corrected proofs of *Tamerlane*, would possibly have made such edits if given the chance.

Fortunately, this was a conceivable wrinkle that would never need ironing. Slader had left the interior text alone. The pages were as Calvin Thomas had printed them, every error in its rightful place, untampered with. We further compared ours with copies pictured online, and everything checked out.

Meg, who had been unwontedly quiet during this procedure, now spoke up. "I think we all need to keep

this to ourselves until we decide what to do"—an opinion
that oddly echoed my own when I showed the book to
her and Maisie upstate not two weeks earlier. "Let's put
the letter and book in the safe. I can move them to our
bank box later."

Everyone concurred that *Tamerlane* was a shop secret
for the time being, although I couldn't help adding that
Sophie should rightfully be credited as the discoverer,
much as a beat cop is ascribed her collar, to which everyone assented, never suspecting this was one more way
of legitimizing the thirteenth copy's new history in the
world. Speculation as to where the deceased collector
might have come upon it could run rampant, I thought.
It wasn't as though he hadn't scouted every book barn
in the northeast, as I understood it. Or perhaps he never
even realized it was concealed inside the Mark Twain.
Stranger things have happened

Work on the books continued over the course of the
day in an atmosphere charged with dueling emotions. Sophie and her colleagues were electrified by the find, one
which, once the gag order was lifted, would afford them
a lifetime of bookish bragging rights. On the other hand,
it was clear to me that Meghan was anxious, uncertain,
even angry. Nor could I blame her, especially given my
role, inadvertent as much of it was, in essentially entrap-
ping her into buying and now selling the *Tamerlane*. It
briefly occurred to me that she could, by way of getting
the monkey off her back, donate it. The Poe Museum
in Richmond didn't own a copy. Neither did the Morgan. There were many worthy repositories that would
be perfect for such a gift. But the other silent partners
in this scheme hadn't gone to such lengths only to remove the copy from one place and simply give it away

to another. No magnanimous idealists were involved in our troubled confederacy, no book-hugging utopianists. Myself, regrettably, included.

Early that afternoon, Nicole and I went out to pick up sandwiches for everyone at a deli several blocks from the store. The neighborhood was teeming with busy shoppers and shopkeepers, kids skateboarding, dogs being walked. Sun was out, filtered by high cirri that swirled above in long wispy hairlike strands. A mash-up of sounds—laughs, prattle, cries—streamed around us while we passed a vintage record store, a head shop, a butcher. Setting aside concerns about *Tamerlane* for a moment, I was musing about how good it felt to be back in the city when Nicole broke in on my reverie.

"You knew that was going to happen, didn't you," she not quite asked.

I not quite answered, "Yes and no."

"What's the yes part?"

"Atticus insinuated the original would end up back with me, one way or another."

"By original, you mean the stolen one?"

This question I chose not to answer. Instead, I queried her, "Do you think it might be better if your mother sold it privately, skipped the fanfare, just got it out of our lives?"

"What does Atticus say?" she asked, without affect, without an accusatory note.

Nicole, I then realized, knew exactly who I was. She had read me like a child's primer, a transparent ABC. All these days, weeks together, our entire lifetime as loving father and daughter, as mentor and mentee, she had known me down to my marrow, had deciphered all my soft-clay truths.

"Atticus gave no clues about it one way or the other. Slader insisted on auctioning it."

"Since when do you listen to what he says?" We'd stopped together on the street. "Slader, I mean."

"I don't, any more than he listened to what I said."

"His Poe signature's pretty impressive, is it not?"

"Impressive is one word for it. Harebrained is another."

Nicole laughed, then stopped me with a gentle hand on my forearm. "I need to make a small confession—"

Those few words made my heart sink. Though I badly wanted to interrupt her, tell her to stop right there, I knew I couldn't.

"How he got my cell number, I'm not sure, but I spoke with him before we went to Rhinecliff that day. I don't know where he was calling from; it was noisy in the background."

I hesitated. "And?"

"And he asked if I'd be willing to make the signature. Told me he knew I was the one who'd written the letter, and that he was impressed."

"Does the bastard have no shame?" I queried no one in particular, seething in silence, feeling at once furious and helpless that he dared intervene, come between me and my daughter.

"You know he claims to have dirt on you, evidence you committed a crime that would send you to prison for the rest of your life."

"He doesn't, though," I countered, scarcely believing I was having this conversation with my daughter.

"Well, he was insistent on the point."

"But was he persuasive?" I asked, holding my breath as I awaited her response.

"I'm afraid he was," she said, looking away in the direction of a small child, who had, whether intentionally or by mistake, released a cluster of silver balloons into the air. Watching them rise above the treetops and brownstones, she added, "And that's my confession."

Was there no end to Slader's intrusiveness, his reckless encroachments into my life and that of my family? In the wake of her revelation, no possible logical response came to mind, so I changed the subject, hoping she'd forgive my reluctance to make any outright confession of my own. "I wonder," I said, "if we could carefully remove the Poe signature without abrading the paper?"

"Maybe use a Staedtler or Hi-Polymer eraser," she proposed, following my blatant deflection away from Slader while no doubt fully aware I was still speaking about expunging the truth, blotting out the past, rubbing out misjudgments. "But I don't think erasing it, no matter what's used, would pass muster with the others."

"The signature's damned convincing, I'll admit," I told her, glancing over to see that one of the balloons had strayed from the others and gotten tangled in a tall spindly ginkgo. "But can we agree that's the last time you'll do any such thing? I don't care how compelling your reasons were."

"I'm my father's daughter, lest we forget," she said, with a frown more magnetic than most people's smiles. "What's good for the pater is good for the filia."

A heartwarming concept, under other circumstances. To hear her say it in so many words, though, made my

heart ache. I forced a smile, surely not magnetic because laden with regret, however fleeting. "Then we're
done with this business after getting out from under
Tamerlane."

"Done," she said, extending her hand, which I took in
both of mine, never feeling more fortunate for being her
father than at that moment, deeply unworthy as I was.

When Maisie and I were driving home with books from the handsome Victorian near Tivoli, she had asked out of the blue if I might ever discover a copy of *Tamerlane* in one of the collections we bought for the shop. This was the afternoon before she was to go sailing with her friends. Smiling, I assured her, "You and the Bancroft twins would have a far better chance of walking on water from the boat launch in Rhinecliff across the river to Kingston."

That made her laugh.

"Not, mind you, that you better try," I'd added.

Less than a week later, the answer to her guileless if prophetic question would be a simple "Yes." Now it was I who seemed to be expected to walk on water, uncharted and dangerous water. Not to mention contaminated. How Slader had orchestrated everything from the opening note of Maisie's scream to Sophie's reprise in the shop, a kind of leitmotif of shock, I wasn't sure. But having tried at every step to avoid involvement with his Poe machinations, indeed to resist them, I still ended up at the center of it all.

"Why didn't you tell me before?" was Will's initial response to my confession about having witnessed the body being dumped out of a powder-blue Chevy that was similar to, or more likely the same as, the one Henry Slader had been conveyed in when visiting—make that plaguing—us at the farmhouse. Before I could answer, he said, "What possessed you to lie to those cops about it?"

"Detectives," I corrected him, just as I myself had been chastened by one of them for the same mistake.

"Cops, officers, detectives, the fuzz—who cares? They weren't accusing you of anything, is my point. You could have leveled with them about what you saw," he insisted.

We were ensconced in our favorite corner of our favorite Irish pub, drinking dark stout at the end of our long and wearying day. In times past, this would've been a celebratory occasion. Beginning of the fall at the shop after a serene, restful August upstate. Back in the swim of things, with fresh inventory of desirable books that hadn't seen the light for years. Will headed into a busy auction season. Both girls in school, one in the middle of her education, the other deciding whether to continue to grad school or take a gap year after finishing college. Instead, this.

"There's more," I said. "I never told you that the night Slader terrified Maisie, he pulled a similar sick trick on me." When Will started to respond, I briefly raised my hand. "Hear me out. He was skulking around in the dark just across the road, wearing a homemade mask with Adam's face on it, smiling and happy and rigid as death. The psycho was taunting me, as if I hadn't suffered enough over my brother's murder and with a photo I'd never seen before. On top of that, he got it into his head to steal that family photo, the one in the hallway, of me and Adam on the beach, only to return it to me in person, apologizing. When I asked him if he knew my brother, he said you knew the answer."

"Meg, I—"

"So, is he gaslighting me or did he know Adam?"

Will averted his gaze momentarily before looking me square in the eyes. "Whether he's gaslighting you is a matter of speculation. But he knew Adam well. To be frank, I even wonder if he and Adam weren't involved."

Now I was thoroughly confounded. "Involved in that he bought books and archival materials from Slader? That's why the investigators questioned him when they were working on the case. Much as I don't like the man, they never found a shred of evidence Slader had anything to do with Adam's murder."

"Any more than they found evidence against me," he said, a declaration so off the point that it made me wonder why he would utter such a thing.

Ignoring him, I asked, "So what you're telling me is that Adam and Slader were lovers? I find that hard to believe."

"It might help explain how he had a photo you'd never seen. Slader does claim to be a photographer. Sociopath of many talents."

I mulled that over. "Adam was private to the point of hermetic, so I suppose there would've been no reason for him to tell me, if what you're saying is true."

"There's more, though, Meg," said Will, his voice lowered. "You need to understand that besides trying his luck at fabricating documents himself—you'll remember asking me to verify signatures in his library after he died—your brother was up to his ears fencing seriously sophisticated forgeries. Was he the amateur apprentice to masterful Slader? We'll never know. One thing is certain—he didn't die a lily-white innocent. My best guess is that whoever did him in was somebody he swindled out of a lot of money."

Numbness spread through my limbs as I listened to Will bare these sordid details. "Or maybe an angry rival," I conjectured, feeling a little nauseated.

"Or," he said, "maybe a jealous lover, someone he might have threatened to expose?"

Every thread of Adam's narrative seemed to lead back to Henry Slader, as if he were the Minotaur lurking at the center of my brother's labyrinth.

"Meg, so why didn't you tell me about his stealing a picture and coming to the house? Why did you stay mum about what you saw?"

I didn't want to cry, especially not in public, here in one of our longtime haunts, but my eyes welled. "I don't have a good answer for those questions, I'm ashamed to say. I guess because you became a black hole after Maisie delivered the *Tamerlane*. You were preoccupied, so anxious, evasive. I didn't want to say anything that might implicate you, make bad things worse."

"Meghan," he said, and reached over to comfort me.

"No, let me finish," pressing his hand. "One afternoon you were on the cell with somebody, Atticus maybe, walking down past the garden into the field. You weren't aware of it, but I watched you from the kitchen, and you looked so alone in the meadow. My heart went out to you, despite my being really angry about what was happening. I guess those secrets I was keeping didn't seem worth burdening you with."

"None of this is on you," Will half whispered. "It's all my fault. I'm sorry about everything."

"Can you tell me why Slader hates you so much?"

"The usual rubbish."

"But why force you into forging again, and don't tell me that's not what it is. Even Nicole seems caught up in this chaos," and with that I did finally begin to weep, pulling my hand from his and cupping both palms against my eyes.

"Shall we leave?" he proposed, and accompanied me from the relative darkness of the pub into the evening, whose ravishing sunset lights of citron and cinnamon lit the high clouds overhead. The bustle of pedestrians, blessedly indifferent to my worries, brought things back into scale. I knew what needed to be done. And it had nothing to do with admissions or accusations. Sophie had made the book discovery of her lifetime earlier today, regardless of how it came into her hands, and I grasped, my heart sinking, the sole path out of the quagmires surrounding that discovery. I felt like a thrown rock.

Having gotten Maisie off for her first day of school next morning, we returned to the shop, where Cal and Eliot were combing through the collection on the off chance more treasures, author letters or postcards, rare ephemera perhaps, had been hidden away in other books. A handwritten grocery list dating back to the turn of the last century was ferreted out of an anthology of Emerson essays—parsnips and coffee were on the tally, along with

"beef meat"—but no further *Tamerlane*, or *Al Aaraaf*, or
other Poe gems surfaced. Which in many ways was for
the best. *Tamerlane* was headache enough.

In consultation with Will and Sophie, I decided to
show it to the powers that be at the auction house
where my husband worked. We had a long-established
relationship with them, and while my assistants wondered if we should solicit proposals from other venues,
it made sense not to break with tradition, at least until
we'd listened to their experts' thoughts. Nor did it particularly surprise me that when specialists from both
their literature and autograph departments, along with
the genial president of the firm, came to examine the
book and letter—again under the express agreement
that the discovery remain under wraps—they were ap-
propriately impressed.

As fate would have it, or maybe as canny Slader had
long since foreseen, they'd scheduled an Americana sale
right around the anniversary of Edgar Allan Poe's death.
While it was mostly devoted to historical documents and
rare tomes by political figures rather than literature, it
was agreed that the *Tamerlane*, once vetted and verified,
would make enough of a fit to work in the context. Along
with the Poe letter, it would, in fact, be the auction's
crowning lot, and could be a separate special addition
to the catalog. As a preemptive measure to quash our
going elsewhere, they waived charging us any commission and instead would make all of their money on the
buyer's premium. Papers were to be drawn up within
the week. I was both dazzled and dazed by how swiftly
all this happened. Nothing about the process comforted
me other than the hope that it meant everything would
soon be over and done with.

Regarding the issue of authenticity, we agreed it was best that they invite outside Poe experts to view the items before the sale was even announced. As this would be the only surviving *Tamerlane* with Poe's signature as well as the only known accompanying letter, corroboration was essential. Indeed, if the consensus was that the title-page autograph had been penciled at a later date by someone other than Poe, that would be important to establish too. Will and his colleagues recalled the brouhaha at Sotheby's in London two years earlier when, not long before the sale was to go off, a Beethoven manuscript purported to have been penned by the composer himself was questioned by one of the composer's most prominent contemporary biographers. Estimated to bring £200,000, it had been personally examined by world-renowned experts, who'd verified it, but after a cloud of doubt had been publicly cast over the score—not as a forgery, but an early copy in a hand not Beethoven's own—the lot failed to sell. Even I remembered hearing about the matter on one of my radio broadcasts, though as for the music itself I remained an unwavering fan of the Allegretto in B minor for String Quartet. It was imperative *Tamerlane* not meet that fate.

Much as I hated admitting it to myself, an odd relief passed over me, like an eerie breeze on an otherwise airless day, when Will's associates left my office. Maybe I was feeling a false sense of safety in numbers. Or maybe I was assuaged by the simple act of opening the Pandora's box that *Tamerlane* represented, guardedly optimistic that, as in the fable itself, an ending that included hope lay ahead. Or maybe I had simply lost my moral compass, and what passed for relief was just so much wishful thinking. No matter, it couldn't and didn't last.

Unable to fall asleep that night, and hearing Will tossing in bed, I softly asked if he was awake enough to answer a question that had been keeping me up.

"What's on your mind?" he said with a yawn, turning toward me in the ambient light that filtered in from the streetlamp below.

"Do you think there's a chance Slader has set all of us up for a fall here?"

Now awake, he said, "Talking with Atticus, it seems more likely he's set himself up. But no. He's not that noble."

"Noble?" I almost laughed.

"Yeah, noble. That level of revenge, going through all this just in order to destroy us, would involve a kind of purity, of nobility, that's not in his character. Vengeance of the kind you're talking about, horrible and destructive as it may be, isn't consistent with such an unprincipled person as Slader."

A dog started barking down in the street, a small one, judging by the high pitch of its yaps. Who, I wondered, would walk their dog at this hour?

"Slader's motivated by a simpler reward," Will said. "Think green. The last thing he wants is to see you or any of us take a fall. He wants us to succeed because it helps him."

He leaned over, kissed me, turned on his side again, and soon enough his breathing slowed and he was asleep. Myself, I continued to lie on my back, watching lights flit across our bedroom ceiling whenever a car passed by outside. That dog stopped barking, which had the odd effect of bringing Ripley to mind. I decided that next time we were upstate I was going to be more attentive to her than I'd been in the past. Try to brush her maybe, or get her to play with a length of yarn. She was, in her feral way, family. And I needed all the family I could surround myself with, one with matted marmalade fur and a life shrouded in natural mystery included.

Once the discovery had become public knowledge, *Tamerlane* and its companion letter were moved to a locked vitrine at my auction house, where they could be examined in a secure environment with staff assistance. Because of the relatively short time between the official announcement of the find and its upcoming appearance on the block, there was a constant stream of interested scholars, librarians, and bona fide collectors, not to mention high-powered booksellers who came to examine the book and letter for well-heeled clients. Without breathing so much as a syllable, Nicole and I read each other's mind, both fully aware that this vetting process could produce a catastrophe at any juncture. All it would take was enough skeptical Poe experts to discredit the lot, and matters would get dicey. It was easy to imagine questions stacking up like so many poker chips in an adversary's pile. Why would Poe sign a book he'd published anonymously? Why were there no other examples of a cover letter for *Tamerlane*? Why was there no record of the recipient working at any prominent review during that era? Where was the envelope that would provide evidence as to what journal the author had submitted his pamphlet? To my mind, these queries were answerable. Yet much as I wished otherwise, I wasn't the final arbiter.

Before the deluge, I did have some control over who was invited to the bookshop to examine the items and offer private assessments. Being prudent, I proposed that Meghan bring in three respected authorities with whom we'd had friendly dealings in the past. Not shills. But not antagonistic either. Each was paid a modest honorarium, though not so much that they could fairly be accused of having been bought off.

Tamerlane itself was unanimously declared the real deal. A personal adage that I'd always adored—*It takes a lot of truth to tell a lie*—was in full play, with the Black Tulip serving admirably as the underlying truth in the equation. All were also persuaded by the physical letter, although Theodore Johnston was unknown to them. Naturally, I couldn't share that I myself had tried researching Thomas Johnson's prototype and, having come up with exactly nothing, had taken a chance that my Thomas was every bit as viable as Poe's Theodore. I nodded, sympathetically frowning, and said nothing, while wondering, was there really any difference between an unrecorded critic and an imaginary one? Any forger worth his or her salt could answer that without a moment's thought. History is mercurial, subjective, arbitrary, even amnesiac half the time. Hell, most of the time. It wasn't that my

Thomas Johnson was any less real than Theodore Johnston. He was equally elusive. I was relieved that this trio
of pundits essentially agreed.

Only one of our appraisers harbored any serious concerns, though he did sign off on the discovery with what
might be described as dour excitement, stating that it
might even lead to the unearthing of further specimens.

"In other words, publicity could prod another out of
the woodwork," Sophie commented.

He nodded, telling a story about how, after an article by the popular columnist and bibliophile Vincent
Starrett, "Have You a Tamerlane in Your Attic?," was
published in the *Saturday Evening Post* back in 1925—
rhapsodizing about the book's rarity and value even
as it denigrated the poem as "a stupid tale of a stupid
monarch"—people all over the country scoured their
attics in search of literary gold.

"A woman named Ada Dodd," the appraiser went
on, "was spurred to action by Starrett's piece and actually found a copy in her house in Worcester, Mass. After
circulating through a couple of other owners, it's now in
the Berg Collection at New York Public Library."

Sophie quipped, "If another surfaces, let's hope it
comes to us."

"Hear, hear," I seconded.

What this expert didn't like was the pencil signature
on the pamphlet's title page.

"It's not Poe for half a dozen reasons from Sunday,"
he warranted, his nose all but pressed to the page. "Why
pencil, not pen? Poe's manuscripts from the period are
mostly in ink, if I'm not mistaken. Why just the autograph, without an inscription to this Johnston fellow?
Why legitimize a book that Poe himself claimed, just two

years later, had been 'suppressed through circumstances of a private nature'? I'm sorry, but for me it's whys and more whys."

"Does it hurt the value?" Meg asked him.

He shrugged, crossed his arms. "Look, I'll be the first to admit that, finally, it's impossible to truly authenticate anything. All one can do is *fail to disprove* its authenticity, and I'm afraid that's all I've accomplished. With respect to this autograph, just consider me a doubting Thomas."

In many ways, I was grateful for his skepticism. Were all three authenticators fully on board, without hesitations, the whole exercise would look like an inside job, a snow job. As it was, Meghan and I were able to take their reports to the auction house and from there arrange the next steps.

During the interim between discovery and sale, Meg seemed to have steeled herself to soldiering forward, though her doubts—her whys—about the whole enterprise ran far deeper than those of any expert. When she privately confronted me about which *Tamerlane* was which, asking, "If this one's authentic, where is the other that you and Nicky worked on last month?" I told her the facsimile copy had been returned to the owner, blurring as best I could the illicitness of the switch. Tucking her hair behind her ear, she said, "I hope you know what you're doing, for the sake of our daughter if no one else," then turned away.

I took, or willfully mistook, her warning as a reprieve and moved on to other parental responsibilities. Maisie's fall term was in full swing and, Poe aside, Meg and I needed to be present and supportive. Nicole's semester was upon her, though I noticed she was spending more time with me than she had since her childhood. She got

it in her head to design a new logo for our letterpress
outfit and made a lovely pen-and-ink drawing of the
Shrubberies stone circle in Kenmare, with its ellipse of
boulders around an egg-shaped dolmen. We decided to
get dies fabricated in several sizes to use on the title pages
of future projects. Life needed to press ahead despite
the upcoming auction, we all seemed tacitly to agree,
knowing from our different vantages just how rarely it
did so in predictable, untroubled ways. Young as she was,
even Maisie understood that the most polished coin must
soon enough tarnish.

Third week of September. We'd been back to the
house upstate once already and found nothing awry. On
arriving for a second weekend, we saw that some maples
were already displaying autumn's blush, and the planted
row of burning bushes along the side of the garage was
beginning to redden. Faithful Ripley arrived at the back
porch on cue to greet us, and Meg's Swiss chard still
thrived in the garden. For a few blessed hours, it was as
if we hadn't a problem in the world. Saturday afternoon,
when Meg and Maisie had driven out to visit local farm
stands to check on the status of early apples, I spent time
with Nicky in the print studio, where we were mortified
to discover that the *Tamerlane* plates were still where
we'd left them, in two boxes beside the Vandercook.
How could we have forgotten? How could Slader, who'd
otherwise been so diabolically meticulous? Unhinged,
for sure, but detail oriented.

Taking shovels down into the woods at the bottom
of the field, we were driven by shared guilt, or so I supposed, to dig a far deeper hole than necessary—not easy,
given the array of roots and jagged rocks in the ground.
After we finished, we tossed in the printing plates and

buried them. Not knowing what to say to each other during this unsavory exercise, we worked in uneasy silence. After masking the hole with leaves, fallen sticks, lichened stones, whatever lay on the surrounding forest floor, I finally spoke.

"Listen to me, Nicole. If things go wrong with this, any of it, you have to promise me you'll let me accept responsibility. No one can know you had anything to do with it."

"That's not—," she began, but I cut her short.

"That's how it has to be. No further discussion. It's settled law between us. Now let's get these shovels back to the house before the others come home."

Never before had I spoken to my daughter about anything with such finality, in such a demanding, conspicuously clipped, even unfriendly tone of voice. It needed to be laid out in so many words, though, and my sense was she'd heard me and would accede to my wishes.

If, as it's said, everything that rises must converge, then by the same token do all things that fall converge as well? News of Henry Slader's disappearance came as a surprise, but not a shock. Back in the city, I hadn't expected to hear from Atticus until after the auction, nor was I sure how safe it was for him to reach out to me by phone—paranoia strikes deep?—although we ourselves weren't under a scintilla of suspicion.

"Seems he'd been taken in for questioning," Atticus continued, "and released for lack of evidence. As you know, he's a seasoned obfuscator."

"What did they pick him up for?" I asked, pausing at a corner to wait for the light to change as I walked home from the auction house—Atticus wisely had waited for my workday to end before calling.

"Avarice and stupidity."

Despite myself, I laughed. "When those become crimes, the whole world will end up behind bars."

"And suspicion of murder."

All laughter ceased. My first worry, assuming Ginger-head was the victim, was what kind of legal jeopardy Meghan could be in for falsely reporting she'd seen nothing on that abandoned road, although who could contradict her, unless there was another witness, say, the highly unreliable Slader himself. My second was whether Atticus could manage, if and when Slader surfaced, to ensure his silence about the Poe business, prevent him from ratting me out along with everyone else. Shadows of uncertainty that had cast their ugly pall over my world now thickened and darkened.

"Cricket?" I asked.

"Guy named John Mallory, if that's who you mean."

"I don't know Mallory any more than you seem to know Cricket. Who is—was he?"

"Seems to have been a fourth- or even fifth-generation plate- and papermaker out of Fall River, up in Massachussetts," Atticus said.

My pulse skipped. That would explain the very high quality of the paper, possibly even vintage, dating back to the nineteenth century, as well as the superior plates themselves, expertly crafted. Idiot, I thought. Why do such an obviously self-defeating thing? Why take out such an invaluable resource? It quickly became clear to me how Slader had managed to produce such superlative forgeries over the years, with odd-lot and leftover papers that might well have been sitting in warehouse drawers for a century or more. I asked Atticus if he had any idea about motive, assuming Slader was behind the murder.

"As I said, greed and lunacy. He'd told me that Mallory, who must be this Cricket, redheaded fellow—"

"Right, ginger."

"—followed him down to New York state. He had a piece of the action and, who knows, wanted to check on his investment. I assume a certain somebody lied to him about the value of his contribution, the papers and plates—real picnic—and he demanded a heftier cut, or else he would blow the whistle on Slader. Simple and banal as that."

"Simple, maybe," I said, as I found an empty bench in Union Square and sat. "Not sure about banal, since how do we know Slader hasn't been swindling Mallory for years?"

"I've tried never to delve too deeply into Henry's history," Atticus told me. "Call it a rational instinct for self-preservation, plus an aversion to picking up rocks to see what's squirming underneath. Bottom line is, I don't know and don't care. What I do care about is that our sale goes off without a certain party gumming up the works."

I couldn't help but recall Henry Slader criticizing me during our first meeting in the Beekman Arms tavern, scornfully asking if he was wrong in remembering me as a cooler cucumber back when I was younger. It stung, although now I had no recollection of what prompted his snide taunt. Whatever its genesis, going into hiding after being questioned by the police was the opposite of a cucumber-cool move. We both had been trawled, netted, and grilled, so to say, before being tossed back into the stream of life in the wake of the Adam Diehl murder. Neither of us was fool enough to vanish from sight afterward. Running gave every appearance of guilt.

To run was to confess. That he knew Nicole's cell number only made me more unnerved.

Agreeing there was nothing either of us could do about our mutual not-friend just then, Atticus asked about *Tamerlane*, and if I had any insight into how much it might bring when the day finally came. I told him that thanks to widespread media publicity following the release of our online announcement and catalog supplement, interest was higher than the house's highest expectations, absentee bids were stronger than was typical, and agents of potential buyers both private and institutional continued to pass through our doors, making discreet notes, trying and failing to mask their zeal. Interest was not limited to American buyers, either, given Poe's international popularity. France, Japan, Abu Dhabi, England—the cosmos of Poe devotees was far-flung. I shared with Atticus that the auction estimate had been set at half a million to six hundred thousand, conservative numbers by my lights.

"I plan to take the train down there to preview it myself."

"I would have thought you'd already seen it when you were working on the Fletcher library."

"To be sure. Just not in its new extra-illustrated incarnation."

"No offense, but if you're coming, let me know so I can be elsewhere."

"Understood, and done," Atticus agreed. "And if you hear from the fugitive, please get in touch. He may be a fool, but he's not a moron. My guess is he'll keep a low profile until after the sale, rightfully demand his rake-off, then spirit himself away to blend into the wallpaper somewhere overseas."

"Tomorrow is today's dream, as they say."

Ignoring my platitude, Atticus asked after Maisie. I told him that she was doing well, back in school, then we got off the phone. If still perplexed by his solicitude about Maisie, I was far more concerned about Slader, who appeared to have plummeted into darker precincts of craziness than before. My mind roiled with other worries as well. Such as whether Abigail Fletcher would hear about her—rather, our—*Tamerlane* and proclaim to the world, finally, that she had a copy too, albeit a respectable fake. Such as whether the Tivoli lawyer, contract or not, might attempt to declare our ownership of *Tamerlane* null and void, reclaiming it for his client's estate even though said client likely never laid eyes on Poe's first book, and certainly never possessed a copy. Such as whether Meghan, jittery and guilt-ridden beneath her forced facade of appeasement, might drop the plot and, in an attempt to clear her conscience, end up sparking the fires of virtue to scorch and finally cinderize us all.

On the first of these counts, I didn't have to wait long for my concern to rise, like a malign flower born of toxic soil, and challenge me. Delivered to the apartment the day after my call with Atticus, it came in the form of a letter from my longtime icon and sometime benefactor, Sir Arthur Conan Doyle. The missive was brief; its phrasing pure Slader.

William the Tell, it read. *My time has run out, & thus so has yours. We must meet at once if your secret is to remain safe with me. You know that figure of speech, A murder of crows? Ours will be, if you'll indulge me in a little joke, A crow of murderers.*

Slader's sense of humor was never his strong point, I reflected, then read further to find the general date and place of his proposed meeting. Fully within character, if character it could be called, he demanded I come with money, an advance on his projected take, though of course none of us possibly knew what that might amount to until the hammer fell. And that presumed the lot wouldn't be withdrawn at the behest of a controversy of critics. However much I might want to debate the panic-stricken logic behind Slader's demands—a crow of murderers, really?—I wasn't feeling a shred of confidence. The reason was simple. If he had managed to convince Nicole of my guilt in Adam's death—to prevail upon my daughter who believed in me, iniquities and all, more than anyone outside of Meghan and Maisie—then little more than a snap of the fingers and a couple of photographs would be required to bring my world down.

That night at the dinner table, I told Meg that I needed to run upstate in the morning for the day, maybe even a quick overnight.

"Can't it wait until the weekend, when we're all going up?"

"It can't, actually," and went on to explain that a man was coming to do refurbishment and repair work on the proof press. "He's hard to schedule, so I have to be there."

"I'm free tomorrow," Nicole said, no doubt seeing through my story as if it were a clear sheet of acetate. "In case you want company."

"No need," I responded. "You have better things to do."

After so many years of silence, speaking with Atticus again for the second time in as many days felt both curious and comforting. Did he have any notion what amount of money Slader was looking for as a down payment on his percentage? How dangerous would the man be if I refused to front him a red cent? Knowing I was out of my mind to meet with him, I saw no way around it.

I got up next morning not with the early doves and chickadees but with the garbage trucks and street sweepers. At the deli downstairs I grabbed an everything bagel with a schmear and a coffee to go, then walked the few blocks to where our car was garaged. I guess I shouldn't have been surprised to find Nicole waiting for me, and, a thousand small cuts of worry aside, I didn't bother to argue against her decision to come along. Truth was, her company was calming. The eight thousand in cash that I'd removed from my personal safe-deposit box the afternoon before would, Atticus and I had agreed, have to suffice. We reasoned it could give Slader enough to survive comfortably in hiding for the next week and a half before the auction. Because successful bidders are required to pay promptly after a sale ends, part of the Poe balance to be dispersed would end up in Slader's pocket via Atticus. Meghan, although she didn't yet know it, was to wire half the proceeds, after commission, to Providence. All of this might have been much simpler if Slader were possessed of a modicum of the restraint and coolness he so revered in others. He wasn't going to like my eight in cash, but many thousands more awaited, Atticus had advised me to assure him, if he kept himself out of further trouble. After that, the list of countries without an extradition agreement with ours was long and promising. Montenegro, Tunisia, Vietnam, Bhutan, perchance Mongolia—he was free to purchase a one-way ticket to wherever he chose, and good riddance.

"Beautiful day," said Nicole, as we got onto the Saw Mill River Parkway.

"Let's hope it stays beautiful," I said, thinking, such are the clichés of the apprehensive.

We arrived hours before I was to meet with him. A quick search around the rooms of the house, as well as nearby outside, suggested he hadn't intruded in our absence. Nothing was out of place, nothing seemed to be missing. To kill time, we gravitated into the printing studio and set up the press to run off samples of the new Stone Circle logo on different test stocks, see how it looked. Ripley rewarded us for having filled her bowls by putting in a purring appearance at the back door, which was open to let in the rich autumn air redolent of fading hydrangea flowers, Russian sage, and asters drying on their stalks. No music played, just the gentlest breeze soughing in the upper branches of white pines. On any other late September day, here with my much-loved daughter in our studio, I would have felt as free as the birds out back that swooped over the field and garden finally fallen into desuetude, playing under the warm sun in the last days before their migration south.

Oddly—though when were his methods anything but?—Slader had chosen not to stipulate exactly where I was to meet him, but rather wrote that when the time came, it would be self-evident. Annoying as ever, I thought. Hide-and-seek was a children's game rather than the deadly serious one we were engaged in.

Half past three, blue-green afternoon shadows on the grass lengthening, and still no sign of Henry Slader. By five, I began to fret that he might be playing a trick on me, so I phoned Meg to make sure she and Maisie were all right, which they were. Just after six o'clock, I called Atticus to see if maybe the man had been taken into

custody again, but my colleague, for that's what Atticus
was now, had heard nothing of the kind.

"My advice is to hang tight," he said. "He's the one
who wants something, not you."

How I wished that were comprehensively true.

"Did you ever open that bottle of Meursault?" Atticus continued.

"Not yet."

"Well, it's meant for a celebratory moment, which
this decidedly isn't. But maybe crack it open anyway,
especially if Nicole's there with you. Calm the nerves."

"Maybe so, thanks," and signed off.

When I filled my daughter in on our conversation, we
agreed the Meursault would remain corked for a happier
occasion. Moreover, if Slader had graduated from maim-
ing people to murdering them, I needed to be sharp. It
even occurred to me that by forcing me to wait around,
his intention could be to dull my edges and drain my
focus.

In the end, the sign of his presence nearby came not
from sighting or hearing him, but through an inexpli-
cable smell, of all things. Smoke, not thick or pungent,
cut into the scent of ink. We searched around the studio,
but nothing was on fire. Checked the kitchen next, but
neither the oven nor stove was lit. Then I glanced down
the long hillside to the woods and saw it. A thin curl of
gunmetal-bluish smoke was wafting out from the woods,
wending its way vaguely toward the house. Back in the
printing studio, I grabbed my letterpress composing stick
just as I had the night Maisie was accosted, slipped it
under my waistband back along my spine, and told Nicole to remain in the house.

The smoke had grown a little denser, not billowing but like a skein or drawn-out ghost, as I strode down the long field, knee- to midthigh-deep in grasses and waning wildflowers. Halfway to where I was headed, I glanced over my shoulder to make sure Nicole wasn't following. The look on her face, even from this distance, was unusual, a melding of terror and anger, and I raised my arm in her direction to reiterate that I wanted her to stay put. As I neared the curtain of trees, I slowed down, then stopped. Shading my eyes, I squinted into the dappling shadowed woodland from the relative brightness of the bottom of the field.

"Slader?" I called out.

No response, so I lunged forward through a low hedge of barberry laden with bright berries and needle-sharp tiny thorns, then spotted him a hundred feet ahead, crouched over a fire surrounded by a girdle of stones. As I approached, he stood up, still saying nothing.

"What's the big idea?" I asked, standing on the opposite side of the crackling, dingy makeshift firepit. "Poor man's papal conclave? Adding arson to your list of offenses now?"

Slader bared his chipped tooth with a disdainful smile. He hadn't shaved in days, looked as if he hadn't slept, and the crescent-moon smudges under his eyes were sooty and damp. But none of his presumptuousness had abandoned him. "Papal conclave, funny. It got you down here, didn't it? No, in fact I figured we could burn the lovely shots I have of you leaving Adam's that morning in Montauk. I even brought negs," he said, pulling a large mailer from the knapsack at his feet and waving it in my direction. "You've got my money, right?"

"Some of it," I said. "If you spoke with Atticus you'll know I've brought enough to tide you over until the auction."

"Yes, and I told him I didn't like that plan."

"Like it or not, it's what we're able to do," noticing a glint of silver winking in the open mouth of his canvas bag. "Your percentage—and I'm not privy to any arrangements you made with Atticus or that poor dead guy—is based on what the Poe brings. For all I know, it'll be withdrawn from sale for some reason, and the money I'm prepared to give you now will be the only profit anybody makes off this whole goddamn mess."

"Let me ask you a question, Will," said Slader. "Do you think I'm capable of killing another person? You of all people know that when I came after you, I did so without a murderous thought in my head. Sure, I could have finished you, but I only wanted to punish you. Butchered the wrong hand, as it happened. Still, I never had it in mind to kill you like you killed Adam Diehl."

Shifting my weight from one foot to the other, I said, "I'm not here to counsel you or console you, Slader, not here to listen to your excuses. I'm here to make that exchange we discussed back at the Beekman Arms, when I agreed to counterfeit a Poe letter and forge the *Tamerlane*, for supposedly incriminating photos. Whether you killed Cricket or Mallory or whoever the sorry sucker was is of zero interest to me."

Slader looked up through the leaves to the dimming sky above before leveling his eyes at me. "You know, I've just realized something important—"

"Important to you maybe, not me."

"No, no, no," and with that he began to chuckle, however softly, as he dropped into the same crouch as when

I first approached, his knees apart and forearms resting on both thighs with the knuckles of his hands gently touching. He looked limber, apish. "Important to you too. Maybe more important," he said, glancing up at me through the smoke, and winking before returning his gaze to the fire.

Everything had abruptly changed. It occurred to me that he hadn't asked how much money I'd brought, which was, as I understood it, his main interest in this entire unholy exercise. He was staring at the smudgy flames, grinning like a soulless fool, shaking his head from side to side with a look on his face that suggested a kind of existential weight had lifted off the man, replaced by his private realization, whatever it was. We remained like this, an uninterpretable tableau, for a minute, and another minute, until I finally broke the silence, saying, in a low voice, "Slader."

In a single graceful and uninterrupted motion, he conveyed the butcher knife with his left hand from the sack, passed it into his right, and lurched across the pathetic fire itself, swiping the blade through the smoke without uttering a word. I fell backward, landing hard on the sharp-angled composing stick, yanked it out from behind my belt, and, regaining my footing, stood. My eyes were tearing from the ash he'd kicked into the air when he jolted through the shallow firepit. As I turned to face him again, his knife a revenant, a dream of a knife, it seemed, rather than something forged of metal, I heard a wet crack and an exhalation, a sorry moan, and witnessed Slader wheel around, buckle, and fall face-first into his fire. Before I could make sense of what was happening, my daughter was dragging the man by his feet—for all his dishevelment and blood welling now at his crown,

his black shoes seemed to have been recently polished—
pulling him away from the flames. The shovel she'd used
lay in the tumble of brown needles and fallen leaves
next to Slader's knife, one I now recognized as Meghan's,
which I hadn't noticed missing from the kitchen during our earlier cursory search. Nicole was paler than I
remembered ever seeing her. An atmosphere of efficient
savagery, how else to put it, had settled, if briefly, in all
of her next gestures and words.

"First we burn his photographs, assuming he has any,
and ID," she said, as I stood there above my nemesis inert
on the ground, feeling a strange sense of melancholy
rather than relief or triumph or terror about what had
just happened. "Then we put out this fire."

Rifling through his knapsack, she found an apricot, a
candy bar, a wallet stuffed with singles, a bus-ticket stub.
The mailer he had waved at me was empty. A forger, a
fraud to the last. Together my daughter and I excavated
the hole we'd dug to hide the cache of plates and, en-
larging it as twilight enshrouded the forest, the field, the
house, and the rest of my world as I'd known it, we laid
Slader, settled into a fetal position, in his grave, along
with the worthless sundries he'd brought in the expecta-
tion of a different outcome to our final visit.

While we finished our work in the woods, Ripley, ma-
terializing out of nowhere like some mangy deity from
the forest-spirit underworld, looked about and, as if con-
firming that what was done was done, turned to meander
ahead of us, back up the hill to the house. We hosed off
the shovel before putting it away in the garage, put the
composing stick back in the studio, scrubbed the hefty
knife and restored it to its block in the kitchen, changed
and laundered our clothes after washing up. Our nerves

were more jangled than either of us could admit—it was fair to say we were benumbed, in shock even—so though we debated whether to drive back to the city that night, I thought it best to set out early the following morning. That settled, Nicole proposed there was probably never going to be a right time to open Atticus's gift of Comtes Lafon Meursault-Genevrières, so she carefully peeled away its foil wrapper, opened it with a corkscrew, and poured two glasses. We drank, having made no toast, as there was nothing in the world here to toast.

Much as a fast-moving storm can sometimes gather over the mountains, rush across the river, its wind and driving rain overwhelming the meadow and woods surrounding the farmhouse, only to be gone a quarter of an hour later, tears finally overcame Nicole. I hadn't seen her cry, I realized, since she was much younger. Standing up from the table, I walked over to where she was sitting, placed my hands on her shoulders, and said, "I'm so sorry, Nicole."

"So am I," she told me, reaching her hands up, without turning, to cover mine.

With that, her weeping soon enough ceased and I returned to my seat, downed what wine was left in my glass, and poured some more. Curiously, any horror we'd felt began to dissipate, and our mood began to lift. Not lighten, as such, but fade, disperse like storm clouds replaced by a tentative sun.

Still, neither of us had any appetite. The salad we made sat largely untouched in our bowls, as we talked, roundabout, in fits and starts, of what had just happened. We didn't wallow in platitudes like *He deserved what he got* or *We had no choice* or *It was a matter of self-defense.* We did, however, wonder if Slader had stashed his vaunted photographic evidence of my supposed crime somewhere safe, somewhere it might be discovered. Should that be the case, we would never know until it was too late to avert whatever the consequences might be. Worrying about it would be worry wasted, we concurred. I insisted again that if the authorities ever came around with evidence about any of these misdeeds, it was I who must take the fall.

After a pause, she asked, seemingly out of the blue, "When was the last time you read 'The Purloined Letter'?"

"What? Been a while," I admitted, despite having been inundated by Poe for weeks.

"Poe's Sherlock, Dupin, had no patience with the police, as you know."

"I remember well," I said, noticing Ripley had joined us inside and was rubbing her whiskers against the table legs.

"When he solved the case of the missing letter, he said, and I paraphrase, 'The Parisian police are very able in their way. Persevering, ingenious, cunning.'"

Now I saw where she was going with this. "And versed—by which Dupin meant *mired*—in the knowledge their narrow duties required of them," I said, knowing that was essentially what Poe had written, though not his exact words.

Without further comment, I understood why Nicole was channeling Dupin. Our own police are no less persevering and all the rest. But also, like Poe's, ours are capable of blind spots, missed leads, dead ends. All I could hope was that the brilliant Dupin, haloed in smoke from his meerschaum pipe, had it right in his long-ago assessment.

"You remember that at the heart of the story is a forgery?" asked Nicole.

"Yes," I said, "but one that was fabricated not by the villain but our hero."

"By both, actually."

Incessant, the kitchen clock ticked as we sat in silence. Ripley, being Ripley, vanished as unexpectedly as she had appeared. Far off, after some stretch of time, our resident great horned owl called out from the depths of the darkness. He waited in vain, as did my daughter and I, for another owl to hoot in response, somewhere farther away in the thicketed forest that enveloped us all, living and gone.

Waking to the steady crash and murmur of the River Sheen below our rooms at the lodge, on our first morning back in Kenmare, I was overwhelmed by a wave of relief. Not that I was so simple or sanguine as to believe it would last. Yeats, my favorite poet, wrote, "Things fall apart; the centre cannot hold." The sum of my experience tells me he was right, as ever. But he also believed that we can begin to live fully only when we conceive of life as a tragedy, a maxim that would always be far more difficult for me to embrace, although I recognized its fundamental truth. Will had quietly left our room to meet with Maisie and Nicole for an early breakfast before they headed off to hike upriver past the stone-arch bridge above the falls. Outside my window, it looked to be a perfect December day for their exploring, the sky running with low spry clouds beneath a perfect dome of lapis. Myself, I had no ambitions beyond a "cupán tae," as my Gaelic forebears called it, and a long sit with a book beside the peat fire downstairs. Later, we planned on driving over to the cottage where Nicole was conceived and, after that, the two kilometers to Kenmare village proper to see if Brion Eccles, owner of Eccles & Sons, Stationery and Print, where Will learned how to run a Vandercook, was still in business, still hale and hearty. A pub dinner later, maybe lamb stew or Kenmare Bay mussels, at Crowley's or O'Donnabhain's on Henry Street, just doors down from Eccles'.

We were here to fulfill the family promise we'd made to ourselves during the worst of the bad days of summer when Slader besieged us, and to do everything possible to pull our lives back together, to regain the balance we'd taken for granted before *Tamerlane* made its appearance. Yeats and his philosophy aside, I was determined to reclaim all that I loved.

To say the auction, two months and as many weeks ago, had been successful would be a serious understatement. Bidding in the room, as well as by phone and online, had been furious, despite a newspaper article that had called the penciled autograph in *Tamerlane* "possibly spurious" and suggested even the letter was not without its concerns—ironic, since, as I now knew, it was the real thing. But this detractor's criticisms were like stacking a few sandbags in the face of a mountainous tsunami—he did, in fact, hail the unveiling of a genuine thirteenth Black Tulip as a "major literary event"—and had no discernible effect on the sale. Beethoven's doomed string quartet manuscript proved not to be a harbinger of Poe's fate at auction. Once the lot marched decisively into seven figures, the numbered paddles in the gallery rose less frequently, then finally ceased, leaving the last of the bidding to proceed from afar. Vanquished bidders and curious onlookers seated in folding chairs facing the auctioneer's podium whispered and exclaimed as bids jumped by larger increments until there were only two parties left, both on the telephone and thus enshrouded in anonymity. Applause filled the room when Edgar Allan Poe's first book was hammered at well over three times its high estimate, though most could do no more than guess who its new owner was.

If Will knew, he didn't let on. Nor did I ask. Grateful it was out of my house, my shop, my life, I didn't care one whit who owned it now, although an educated guess would be that it went into a private collection, since most institutions would announce their stellar acquisition to the world and plan to exhibit it sometime soon. I recalled my husband saying back in August that two of the twelve prior known copies were in private hands, one of the owners anonymous. Now, for the foreseeable future, another would disappear into the shadows. I couldn't help but believe Poe himself might revel in such concealment and mystery.

To say, further, that the strange dispersal of proceeds from the sale came as a shock to me would be a stone-cold lie, cold as the tumbling waters of the Sheen below the balcony outdoors. Close as my husband had once been to Atticus, he, along with the rest of those in our small world of book people, couldn't know, as I did, that Atticus's allotment from the *Tamerlane* sale was to go into a blind trust for his covert daughter with Mary Chandler. I always figured that as Maisie got older, the resemblance to her biological father would become clear to Will, and maybe even to their not quite shared daughter.

But Atticus had been religious about keeping his distance, and likely would have denied speculation anyway, never wishing to acknowledge Maisie as his progeny because he didn't want to destroy his family, and, even more persuasively, because Mary had sworn Atticus and me both to secrecy. Even when his own diagnosis of a cancer not dissimilar to Mary's intervened, he took the risk of meeting with Will only that once in Rhinecliff. Distracted as he was with other matters, my husband didn't see that he was sitting with Maisie's father.

Atticus took the further step of meeting with me and Maisie, albeit briefly, for a gelato near Washington Square Park, when he'd traveled down from Providence supposedly to view the Poe. Furtive, we signed documents while we sat on a bench as Maze tossed crumbs of her uneaten cone to pirouetting pigeons near the fountain.

"Death's just that way," he said, watching Maisie from behind the dark screen of his sunglasses. "We can know the why, but never precisely the when."

"Speaking of the when of things, when can I tell Will about you and Mary?"

Atticus coughed, cleared his throat. "Mary thought never. Not to protect herself, but to protect me. Me, my family, Will, and, above all, Maisie," he said, slowly, pausing on each. "For myself, I think it's best to leave it up to you, Meghan. I'm putting things in order, including what you insisted on the phone, that I take care of Abigail Fletcher by overpaying for manuscripts and books she seems finally willing to let go of. Restitution, you called it."

"That, and penance," I said, leveling my gaze at him and, disconcertingly, seeing my face mirrored in his tinted glasses, darkened and distorted. "May I ask what will happen with that facsimile Will printed with Nicole?" I ventured, not wholly sure I knew of its real place in the larger picture.

Atticus shook his head. "Honestly? I thought about destroying it, but it was truly a beautiful piece of work, something I sense would give Abigail Fletcher the same satisfaction, whether spurious or not. Besides, when such things are out in the world, they often take on a life of their own, become as indisputable as the originals. So, to answer your question, it's in Abbie's collection," he said, looking away. "As for telling Will about Mary and me, let me finish up my own finishing up. After I'm gone, as I say, you can decide what's best."

I told him he could trust me, shook his hands, kissed his cheek. Afterward, when Maisie and I said our good-byes and walked toward Broadway and the East Village, I could feel his eyes on us, on Maisie in particular, as we receded from view. Before we reached home, I decided she would learn about her parentage on her twenty-first birthday, when her trust was opened. If Atticus wanted to die in peace, taking his secret with him, who was I to interfere?

Downstairs in the tearoom at the lodge, I found myself a wingback chair of floral damask nearer to the fire than the windows, and settled myself in. Soda bread and blackberry jam were delivered on a tray along with my black tea. The sun poked in and out from behind the clouds. Piano music, improvisational and romantic and unknown to me, played softly in the background.

I had half expected to see Slader show up, menacing and proprietary, at the auction, but he didn't. And after *Tamerlane* was sold for a record amount, I was certain he would appear, like an unwelcome specter, an inescapable bane, when we were upstate during the full glory of the Hudson Valley autumn, but he never showed his sallow face. Oddly, his absence was more of a noticeable presence than I might have expected. The paranoiac needs a foe in order to persist. Slader had worthily filled that role for years. I had seen no notice of his, or anyone else's, arrest in the apparent murder of that man on the road. The simplest answer was that Slader had gotten what he was looking for and moved on into another life far beyond these precincts.

One morning in late October, when Will and Nicole were sequestered in their printing studio working on a new Stone Circle project and Maisie had ridden her old Schwinn Black Bomber to the village to visit the Bancroft twins, I remembered something Slader had used to taunt me. For whatever reason, I'd hardly thought about it in the weeks after he assailed Maisie and terrified me with his photo mask of my brother Adam, floating surreally in the woods across from the farmhouse. I closed my laptop in the study, where I had been doing some remote correspondence for the shop, and, after tying the laces of my walking shoes, descended the front porch steps and crossed the road.

Fallen leaves crunched underfoot as I stepped deeper into the tangled woods, searching for the ash tree where, back in August, I had discovered the glossy photograph of Adam, fixed with an elastic string on either side and with my brother's eyes scissored out for Slader to see through. The photo seemed nowhere to be found. After these intervening months, had the paper disintegrated, or been blown away? Or, perhaps, had Slader himself retrieved it? Hands on hips, I paused to look up through the forest canopy. A brisk breeze detached some of the

highest leaves that came floating down, like so many
lost souls, to the woodland floor, a few alighting on my
shoulders and head.

Then there it was, sheltered still among tiny wildflowers now dead, club moss that had yellowed, and
faded orchard grass that had collapsed and fallen over
the image, partially obscuring it from view. I knelt down.
Still hesitant to touch the thing, I brushed away stems
and leaves that partially buried it.

"Who killed you?" I asked, startled by my human
voice here in nature's surround. No answer was forth-
coming, of course, but for the first time since the murder, I felt as if no answer was possibly the only answer I
would ever have. No answer was possibly even for the
best, given the alternatives.

Reaching out, I removed the photo from its makeshift
shrine and carried it back to the house, where, with Nicole's help, I would restore its eyes and frame it to place
among other family mementos on the chestnut side table
in the foyer. While it would never represent full closure,
it would have to constitute, for me, closure enough. Will
once referred to forgery as not a distinction without a
difference, but a difference without a distinction. So it
would have to be with my forged reconciliation with
Adam's death.

"Mom? Meghan?" was followed by nervous laughter,
and when I looked up to see Maisie and Nicole standing over me in the tearoom, I realized I'd fallen asleep
by the fire.

"What's doing?" I asked with a yawn, closing the un-
read book in my lap.

"What's doing is we're ready to go see my birthplace,"
Nicole said, reaching her hand out to me as Maisie

retrieved the book on my lap, a Jane Austen novel I'd read many times before and returned to as a kind of security blanket.

"Not your birthplace," Maisie corrected her.

"The place where my birth began then."

As we drove to our old cottage, crosscurrenting memories flickered in and out of mind, like the rushing sunlight on the windshield, glinting through the tunnel of trees overhead. Yes, this was where Will and I had attempted to escape our troubles long ago, and succeeded but briefly. Happy times, unhappy ones. Nicole's life began here, true, and Will's almost ended.

Because I believed, as most of us tend to do, that I'd retained an unblemished image of the past, of the fairy-tale house and its rustic surroundings, I was surprised by the gap between my remembrance and what was there before me as we pulled into the drive. Smaller than I recalled, it had been repainted and rethatched. Some rhododendrons that Will and I had planted on either side of the front steps had grown into stately sentinels. We knocked on the door, but no one was home, so we furtively peeked through the windows. The rooms looked for the most part to have refurnished, although an antique walnut cupboard elaborately carved with griffins and winged serpents remained where it was before. An oil painting of fishing boats bobbing up and down in Bantry Bay still hung over the fireplace. To think we had lived here filled me with wonder and wistful melancholy. Happy as I was for Nicole to see her place of origin, it was time for us to move on.

Eccles was thriving. He proudly showed Nicole his Vandercook press, warhorse for the ages, telling her it was still used for printing wedding announcements, funeral programs, and everything between. Afterward, down the street in the raucous pub where we had dinner, both girls clapped and sang along as best they could with the live trad music accompanied by guitar, fiddle, tin whistle, and stomping feet. In bed that night, the River Sheen whispering words I could no more understand than the Gaelic I'd once tried and pretty much failed to learn, I slept untroubled by dreams.

Next morning, though it was overcast and promised rain, we were to take the ferry out to the Skellig Islands, where monks—and Jedi—once lived in utter austerity, cut off from the outside world, like the pillar saints of bygone centuries, atop their barren rocks hundreds of feet above the gnawing ocean. When I came downstairs to join the others, I noticed Will was sitting with two men at the far end of the spacious breakfast room. They huddled in serious, private conversation at a table by large windows overlooking the greens where some jackdaws pranced and marched in circles. One of the men wore a uniform of the Garda Síochána, as the Irish police service was called. I waved nervously at Will, who saw me and waved back, offering me a calm smile. Maisie was poring over a brochure about the Skellig monastery while distractedly eating her porridge, but Nicole, I noticed, was as focused on Will as I. A fierce look, much like that of her kingfisher, was set on her face, and though the men were quite a way from where we were seated, she seemed to be trying to read their lips.

Once they finished their discussion, the three stood and, without shaking hands, bade one another farewell. When Will joined us, he said we needed to get on the road, but he was famished and ordered a full breakfast, complete with a black pudding of groats and blood. I asked him what the officers wanted and he replied that a felon we knew from here and home, one whose name needn't be repeated, had gone missing. Aware of Will's horrific encounter with the man in Kenmare before the new millennium, the Garda requested that he alert them should he happen to see his sometime assailant in County Kerry during our stay. He most certainly would do so, Will had assured them.

As my husband unfolded his starched white napkin, the loving, if unsettled, look he gave our elder daughter was one I wouldn't soon, indeed ever, forget, even though I had no idea how to interpret its meaning. "So there it is," he said, as that ragged flock of jawdaws, startled by who knew what down along the river, vaulted crazily from the emerald grass and wheeled together toward the lower reaches of the leaden sky above.

ACKNOWLEDGMENTS

Deepest thanks to the preeminent Edgar Allan Poe collector Susan Jaffe Tane for advising and encouraging me as I researched this book, for generously introducing me to several Poe authorities as the project developed, and for allowing me to examine her copy of *Tamerlane* and other Poe treasures. I'm grateful, too, to her wonderful assistants Gabriel McKee and Julie Carlsen, as well to the book designer and typographer, Jerry Kelly, who introduced me to Susan and advised me on passages related to letterpress printing and calligraphy.

I owe a great debt of gratitude to Chris Semtner, curator of the Edgar Allan Poe Museum in Richmond, Virginia, who answered a wide range of biographical and historical questions during the course of a richly rewarding email exchange that included, no less, postscript updates on the flowers blooming in the Enchanted Garden at the museum. I'm very grateful also to renowned Poe expert Richard Kopley, who read the manuscript and offered invaluable, detailed commentary about Poe's life and *Tamerlane*. Jeffrey A. Savoye of the Edgar Allan Poe Society of Baltimore responded to a variety of questions early in the process, and I thank him for his insights. Carolyn Vega, Director of the Berg Collection at New York Public Library, kindly allowed me peruse the two copies of *Tamerlane* in the collection's remarkable Poe holdings, as well as original Poe letters and manuscripts. Thanks also to Caitlin Goodman, Curator of the Rare Book Department, Free Library of Philadelphia, for helping me identify when Will saw his first copy of *Tamerlane* on exhibit at the library as a boy.

Great gratitude to my longtime friends Tom Congalton of Between the Covers Rare Books, James Jaffe of James S. Jaffe Rare Books, Thomas Johnson, and Pat Sims for their close readings of the manuscript. Sincere thanks as well to the distinguished bibliophile Nicholas Basbanes, who perused and commented on the final draft of the novel. Christine von der Linn, Senior Specialist in the Book Department and head of the Illustration Art Department at Swann Auction Galleries in New York, thoughtfully went through auction references in the book and offered her expert advice. Others who shared important ideas with me during the course of writing the novel include Alexis Hagedorn, head of the Conservation Program at Columbia University Libraries, along with my friends Larry Bank, Sean Condon, Michael Sarinsky, Douglas Moore, and Nicole Nyhan. Many thanks to all.

I am grateful to Deirdre d'Albertis, Dean of Bard College, for allowing me to take a leave of absence that gave me the time necessary to complete *The Forger's Daughter*, and to everyone at Bard for their support.

My intrepid agent, Henry Dunow, offered sage advice from beginning to end and, as always, I can't thank him enough for his steady encouragement. Boundless appreciation to Morgan Entrekin, Sara Vitale, Deb Seager, Kaitlin Astrella, Julia Berner-Tobin, Judy Hottensen, Amy Hundley, Gretchen Mergenthaler, Becca Fox, and all the good people at Grove Atlantic for their continued belief in my work.

Otto Penzler, editor and publisher extraordinaire as well as a cherished friend, originally encouraged me to write *The Forgers*, a bibliomystery drawing on my lifelong passion for books. I'm profoundly thankful to him for urging me to continue the story here.

As for the brilliant Cara Schlesinger, she is ever an inspiration and lodestar, and my gratitude to her is inestimable.